# If Necessary Alone

V. M. Knox

Cover design | Brand House Company

For Peter

Also by V. M. Knox

*In Spite of All Terror*

*"I have, myself, full confidence that if all do their duty, if nothing is neglected, and if the best arrangements are made, as they are being made, we shall prove ourselves once again able to defend our Island home, to ride out the storm of war, and to outlive the menace of tyranny, if necessary for years, if necessary alone."*

Winston S. Churchill
Speech to The House of Commons
4th June, 1940

# Great Britain 1941

# 1

London, Saturday 22nd February

The taxi pulled up at the corner of Whitehall Place. Alighting, Clement pulled up the collar of his overcoat and walked towards the elaborate stone entrance of Number Seven. Taking a deep breath, he reached for the door handle and stepped inside. Five months had passed since he'd last been here; the airless smell of the foyer made it seem like yesterday.

He felt ambivalent about his return. The letter asking him to come to London burned in his top pocket. As he climbed the grey stone stairs he recalled the day he'd received it and how his heart had sunk at the sight of the envelope. He wasn't entirely sure why; he had, after all, expected it. Perhaps it was because it meant he could no longer avoid the world. Or maybe he just hoped they would leave him alone now. If Johnny Winthorpe had anything to do with it - and Clement guessed he did - then Colonel Gubbins's letter was a summons, not a request.

Clement remembered the first time he had set eyes on the charismatic colonel. Then, Clement had been a rural vicar, living in one of England's prettiest East Sussex villages, Fearnley Maughton. But that was before. Before the war. Before his involvement in the covert Auxiliary Units. Before all manner of things. But mostly before Mary died. He cleared his throat. His wife's death was still too raw.

'Reverend Wisdom?'

The sound of someone calling his name made his ghosts vanish, at least for now.

At the top of the stairs stood a smartly-dressed young woman. 'This way, please.'

Clement joined her then followed her along the corridor, the sound of her shoes tapping out an energetic rhythm on the marble tiles. Yet despite her brisk manner, his attention was on the elaborate surroundings of the third floor. 'Has Colonel Gubbins moved office?'

The young woman continued walking. 'Yes, but I am taking you to Captain Winthorpe's office.'

'Not Commander Winthorpe any more then?'

The woman stopped and turned, her face breaking into the sort of grin that reveals neither emotion nor information before continuing her march along the corridor.

Clement felt a sigh rising. Official secrets. Whitehall was full of them. No one chatted any more. His thoughts returned to Johnny Winthorpe, his old colleague from theological college days. Johnny's promotion didn't surprise Clement. His mind went back to the night on Winchelsea Beach and the two men with whom he had expected to die: Johnny Winthorpe and Chief Inspector Arthur Morris of Lewes Police. That had been in the autumn of the previous year and Clement hadn't seen either man since. Gubbins had ordered his removal to the West Country to recuperate. Although, convalescence was not the only reason for Clement leaving Fearnley Maughton, the village he had served for over twenty years.

It had been for his protection. He visualized the villagers - people whose lives he had shared - and imagined their bewilderment at his sudden departure. Every time he thought about Fearnley Maughton he felt guilty. If he lived through the war, Clement resolved to make it up to them. But his greatest sense of regret was for Mary. More than regret, he felt the overwhelming burden of inextinguishable guilt. Just thinking of her made his eyes sting with tears. Not even during the Great War in the trenches of France had he heard such coughing; the exhausting rattle of pneumonia that had convulsed her small frame until death overcame.

Looking up, Clement saw they were standing before a closed door. The young woman knocked twice. Opening the door for him, she beamed her joyless grin then disappeared.

Before him was an office that was vast in comparison to Johnny's former office on the top floor. There, Clement had had to squeeze past the door in order to sit down. Now he saw the elegant surroundings of establishment; large windows, heavy curtains and expensive furniture.

'Clement! How good to see you.' Johnny came around his desk, hand extended in greeting, the naval captain's uniform immaculate. 'May I offer my sincere condolences on Mary's passing.'

'Thank you.' Clement cleared his throat. 'So how is the intelligence business?'

'More in need of men like yourself than ever.'

'Church affairs still on the back burner then?'

'People in glass houses, Clement.' Johnny indicated a chair before his desk.

'Colonel Gubbins has moved office, I hear?'

Johnny sat down. 'Yes. But he comes and goes from time to time. Can I get you some tea?'

'No, thank you, Johnny.' Clement was aware that he hadn't learned where Gubbins had gone. It didn't matter. The Colonel was, no doubt, a busy man and the War Office was a large place. Clement's gaze shifted to the portraits on the walls of stern-faced generals and admirals whose identities he didn't know. 'With promotion comes a larger office?'

'Something like that. But it also comes with added responsibility.' Johnny's hand reached for a plain white envelope lying on the desk and passed it to Clement. He tore it open.

Inside was a letter, signed by Gubbins, informing Clement of his promotion to the rank of Major.

'Can't confer upon you a medal for something that didn't happen on Winchelsea Beach, Clement. But Gubbins can arrange promotions.'

In his mind's eye he could see Mary. She would have been proud. He felt his throat tighten. Sometimes it caught him off guard and he blinked several times wiping the evidence of his sorrow from his eyes.

Johnny had stopped speaking. 'Are you fully recovered, Clement?'

He bit into his lip, the emptiness of grief rising from his gut. 'I can't talk about it, Johnny. But if I am totally honest with you, and myself, I am more at war with God right now than I am with the Germans.'

He saw Johnny's head nod, but Johnny had never married. What could the man know of the bond between husband and wife? For Clement, Mary's death was unfathomable and crushing in its intensity. It made him angry and distraught in equal measure. But even though he wrestled with God about her futile death, his faith was not extinguished. It never could be. Despite everything, he had felt the hand of God in the trenches of France and he couldn't deny it. Moreover, he had taken solemn vows at his ordination. They were as important to him as his marriage vows and never to be broken.

Having no mortal enemy to blame for her premature death made it harder and despite all attempts at justification, Clement felt responsible. If he had remained a vicar and never met Colonel Gubbins, she would still be with him. If she hadn't walked from the village of Combe Martin to their cottage on the hilltop, she would not have been caught in the downpour and she would not have succumbed to what the doctors called "the old man's friend". He blinked several times.

Johnny sat waiting, an anxious frown creasing his handsome face.

'I will be alright, Johnny. In time. "We are in God's hand, brother, not in theirs".' Clement quoted his favourite line from Shakespeare's *Henry V*.

'I wish I could say take as much time as you need, Clement but...'

'It would do me no good, Johnny,' Clement interrupted. 'And Mary would be the first to tell me to pull myself together.'

'Well, if you are sure.'

'No. But I think it is the right thing to do. Self-sacrifice. Isn't that what men like you and I are called upon to do?'

A door opened behind him and Clement swivelled in his seat. A man he did not recognise entered the room.

Johnny stood. 'Sir, may I introduce Major Clement Wisdom.'

Clement turned and rose from the chair. Before him stood a man of about his own age. He was of average height with a symmetrical face, wore a neat moustache and a tweed suit and looked the most ordinary of men. The eyes, however, Clement decided, told a different story; neither lugubrious nor maniacal, but eyes that knew from experience both the heroic and the evil capacity of man.

'Ah, yes! The Vicar. Colonel Gubbins speaks highly of you. I am informed you are recently bereaved. My condolences.'

'Thank you.' Despite the man's palpable charisma, Clement considered Mary's death was not a topic for discussion with strangers.

'They call me "C",' the man went on. 'We have a small problem in the north and your name has been put forward. Winthorpe will fill you in.'

"C" turned to leave but stopped, the perspicacious eyes again holding Clement's gaze. 'Thank you, Major.'

Clement stared after the man then turned to his old friend. From Johnny's reaction and the authoritative demeanour of the man called "C", Clement surmised he had just met the Head of The Secret Service. In all the years Clement had known John Winthorpe, he had never seen the man lost for words until now. Clement sat down and waited for Johnny to resume his seat and his wits.

'Well! Quite a compliment! You won't be aware of it, Clement, but "C" rarely makes such appearances.'

'What's going on, Johnny?'

Johnny pursed his lips. 'I didn't move with Colonel Gubbins. I now work exclusively with the Secret Intelligence Service. There are - how shall I put it? - certain rivalries between The Service and some of the more newly created departments. And, in fact, it was I who suggested you for this job.'

Clement wanted to ask why, but he knew Johnny wouldn't, or perhaps couldn't, say. But whether it was a career move for Johnny or simply to dodge interdepartmental feuding, it mattered little to Clement.

Johnny reached for a file on his desk. 'Whilst your recent involvement with the team in East Sussex cannot continue, we would like you to join the Special Duties Section. You won't have heard of them before. Totally secret. You have, however, already met one of the trainers when you went to Coleshill House for your initial training for the Auxiliary Units.'

Clement nodded. He knew to whom Johnny was referring.

'Have you kept physically fit?'

Clement nodded thinking of the long hours of running over the steep hills around Combe Martin since Mary's death. 'I follow the programme I learned at Coleshill.' Although he knew his almost excessive exercise regime had more to do with mitigating grief than desire to remain physically fit.

'Excellent. How are you with cold climes?'

'Where, exactly?'

'Scotland. About as far north as one can get on the mainland.'

Clement had never been to Scotland but the thought of the remote and cold northerly borders of Great Britain, especially in winter, wasn't warming him to the idea.

Johnny opened the file before him. 'We would like you to rendezvous with the Special Duties Branch Operative in the village of Huna, in Caithness. Apparently they are picking up some unusual radio transmissions in the area. Could be nothing, but given its proximity to the North Atlantic, and our fleet in Scapa Flow, it is best to investigate. There is also a Royal Air Force Base in the area at Castletown and a radar station operated by the Royal Navy on Dunnet Head. Caithness may not be the centre of the known world in peace time, but right now it is a tightly restricted area.'

'What are the operative's duties?'

'Local information gathering and wireless operator.'

'Are they at a Y-Station or an out-station?'

'An out-station. There are about ten covering Caithness. Quite a few of the more remote rural areas already had wireless transmitters. Stands to reason in isolated and cold regions. With all that is going on in Caithness, and their proximity to the coast, most were confiscated. And those that weren't are operated in secret. They report on happenings in their own sector and radio in to the Y-Station on Dunnet Head.'

'Could the transmissions be coming from the Y-station?'

'Unlikely. In fact, the information supplied by the operative was passed on to us by the Y-station personnel. Not something I believe they would do, if someone there were sending out illicit transmissions. Besides which, no one working there is ever left alone. At any time.'

'And no one locally can investigate?'

'Not really possible, Clement. The Royal Air Force chaps and Y-station personnel are kept too busy to spend time away from the base investigating such matters. Besides which, they are not trained for what they may encounter. It must be a covert operation. They have been informed that we are sending someone.'

'Why covert, if you don't suspect them?'

'It is possible that the transmissions are innocent. By that I mean a local who has concealed his transmitter and is still secretly chatting to his neighbours, but it could be an enemy plant located somewhere in Caithness.'

'And the Y-station can't get a fix on it?' Clement asked, suspicious that Johnny knew more than he was saying.

Johnny sat back in his chair. 'Can't involve the Y-station at all, Clement. Nor draw even the slightest attention to them for the simple reason that this particular Y-station is one of only a handful that have direct access to Bletchley Park, our most top-secret code and cipher facility. It has to be handled covertly. More importantly, it has to be handled by someone I know I can trust.'

'Do I have that level of clearance?' He felt a rising anxiety. He had never done a solo mission, much less in unfamiliar territory. He chastised himself. Everything seemed straightforward and nothing he couldn't handle. After all, he had a talent for connecting with people that had helped with his parish work at Fearnley Maughton. If it worked in East Sussex, why shouldn't it in Scotland? He gave Johnny a confident smile.

'You will have. Just a few extra papers to sign.' Johnny passed an already typed page across the desk. Clement read the document threatening him with a charge of treason, the punishment for which was death, should he ever become too talkative.

Johnny went on. 'Huna village, where our operative lives, is a few miles to the east of Dunnet Head where the Y-station is located and nearby is an historic church, Canisbay Kirk. Which is another reason I thought of you, Clement. I have spoken with the Moderator of the General Assembly of the Church of Scotland, Reverend James Cockburn. The cover story we have invented for you is that you are to take up the position of minister at St Peter's on South Ronaldsay, one of the Orkney Islands. Reverend Cockburn is writing to the minister of Canisbay Kirk who will put you up. I have always found there to be greater anonymity staying in vicarages over public houses. You should also make contact with a local fisherman to arrange passage to St Margaret's Hope, the main town on South

Ronaldsay. Of course, you may not need to go to Orkney, if you find the source easily, but everything should look genuine.'

Clement signed the papers and handed them back. 'I know nothing about the Church of Scotland. I'm sure the local minister would see straight through me.'

Johnny placed the documents back in the file. 'We had thought of that. But Reverend Cockburn informs me that with so many clergy in the forces now, they are happy to take men from other denominations. The minister in Canisbay is a Reverend Aidan Heath. He will be notified by Reverend Cockburn of your intended visit but not of your real purpose. Once you have ascertained whether there is any reason for concern, you can leave the area. Send the report of your findings to me through official police channels from the station at Thurso. The inspector there is a man by the name of Stratton. He isn't one of us, so he won't know your true purpose in being there either, but he has been made aware that someone from Special Duties will be in the vicinity. Stratton has been told to comply with any request from a man, cover name *Hope*.'

Johnny handed him another sealed envelope. 'If you need information, you can call us here on the direct number in the envelope. Memorize it, Clement. Don't have the number on you. I have to be away myself in the coming weeks, so if I am unavailable, ask for Nora Ballantyne.' Johnny reached forward and pressed a button on a small wooden box on his desk. Within seconds the door opened and the well-dressed young woman reappeared.

'Miss Ballantyne, should Major Wisdom telephone you in the coming weeks, please give him any assistance he requests.'

Nora Ballantyne smiled her cheerless grin and slid from the room. Nothing further was said, but Clement surmised that Miss Ballantyne already knew everything there was to know about him.

'I cannot tell you how important this is, Clement. Every day our ships are prey to the German U-boat packs operating in the Atlantic. Hundreds of lives and thousands of tons of supplies are at stake, not to mention the sheer numbers of ships destroyed. If there is cause for concern in Caithness we must know about it. Churchill is calling it the Battle for the Atlantic. And it is a battle we must win. Our very survival is at stake.' Johnny drew in a long breath then stood, his hands clasped behind his back and turned to look out the window at the grey skies. 'Hopefully, it will turn out to be nothing more than an over-zealous operative picking up birdsong.'

'And if it is not birdsong?'

Johnny turned to face Clement. 'Try to pinpoint where exactly. Then report in. But this must be neat and above all, quiet. In. Out. All the locals need to know is that you are a vicar going to Orkney to take up a parish. No one must even suspect your real purpose. After all, if this person isn't an innocent local, we don't want him getting wind of us and flying the coop. It should be pretty straightforward. You are, however, on your own with this one. The Special Duties Operative is only a contact and cannot blow her cover to assist you, should you get into any difficulties. I have every confidence that you will do admirably.'

'The operative is a woman?'

'Yes. They make better wireless operators than men. Something to do with having a gentler touch.'

Clement nodded. 'And if it isn't an innocent local chatting, what is to happen to this enemy plant once I've located him, if I can?'

Johnny returned to his chair. 'He will be removed. But that is for others to worry about, which is why it is so important for you to be discreet.'

'When do I go?'

'Monday.'

'How?'

'We have booked a seat for you on the Edinburgh train. Change there for Inverness. A Reverend St Clair will meet you and billet you overnight. Cockburn will have told him not to ask questions. Next morning, take the Thurso bus. There is a daily train to Thurso from London but the route we have chosen will give you greater anonymity. The bus stops at Wick and Huna. Alight there. The post mistress is your contact. She will be there to meet the bus to collect the post.'

'Her name?'

'Sarah Crawford.'

'Does she know I'm coming?'

'Not specifically. If the wireless is being intercepted we cannot use names. But she has been notified that an old friend of her mother's is coming.'

'And if I cannot find the source?'

'I have every confidence that you will, Clement. Stay a few days but not longer than one week. Then make your report through Stratton in Thurso. As Caithness is a restricted area for travel, we have issued you with a pass for your entry along with some basic maps of the area. You should keep the pass on you at all times in case you are stopped by any inquisitive military personnel. I have arranged for you to stay tonight at St James's with the Guards.' Johnny handed him an envelope containing the train tickets and entry pass. 'Get some rest tomorrow, but spend some time studying the maps so that you have a general understanding of the facilities and environs of Caithness.'

Clement reached for his small pack and secreted the papers.

'No uniforms from now on, Clement, except the clerical collar. Everything you need and a pack containing a pistol for you is already at St James's.'

'Fairly sure I would go then?'

Johnny smiled. 'You have always done your duty, Clement. And trustworthy men who operate in shadows are hard to find. Just wait on the curb outside, a car will take you to St James's.'

# 2

Monday 24<sup>th</sup> February

Uniforms of every kind choked the forecourt of King's Cross Station as he hurried for the platform.

'Clement!'

He turned. Standing among the throng was the familiar face of Reginald Naylor, a resident of Fearnley Maughton and a man with whom Clement had served already in this war.

Reg walked towards him. 'I heard you were in the West Country, Clement. Have you been in London all this time?'

'Reg!' he grasped the man's hand and shook it warmly. 'It's a long story.'

Clement stared into the familiar face of his former neighbour. There was so much he wanted to ask; about what Reg had been doing since they'd last met, about Reg's wife, Geraldine, and all the other residents of Fearnley Maughton. He held Reg's affable gaze. But despite their shared past, there was, in that second, a perceptible divide. So much had changed in the six months since Clement's departure from the village. It seemed a lifetime ago. No, not a lifetime, Clement reminded himself, another time. Another life. He glanced at his watch. The train was leaving in six minutes. 'What about you, Reg? I don't recognise your uniform.'

'I'm not surprised, Clement. Pioneer Corps. Fancy name for doing thankless and unpleasant tasks. Have you time for a cup of tea?'

'I'm so sorry. I have to catch my train. There is so much...'

'I know.' Reg shrugged his shoulders. 'Time is against us, Clement. It's the war. It was good to see you, though. Where are you headed?'

'North.'

Reg laughed. 'By that remark, I'm guessing you're still working with the Cloak and Dagger Department!'

Clement smiled, Reg's directness refreshing after the riddles of Whitehall.

'We are too, actually,' Reg said, pointing to a small group of men sitting on their packs some twenty feet away. 'Heading north, I mean. But not for another hour. Wick, apparently. Although what for is anyone's guess.'

'You should keep that to yourself, Reg. *Loose lips*, remember. May the Lord bless you and keep you.'

Clement shook his friend's hand firmly in farewell then hurried away.

Two minutes later he opened the door to the train and found his compartment. Placing his pack in the rack above his seat, he sat down and stared through the window. His eyes searched the faces for Reg Naylor, but the man had already disappeared into the swirl of humanity.

He allowed his mind to dwell on Reginald Naylor and his wife Geraldine. They lived in a beautiful house on the outskirts of Fearnley Maughton. Clement remembered the day he had asked Reg to be involved in the Auxiliary Units. The man had proved to be an excellent marksman and Clement wondered what Reg was now doing with the Pioneer Corps. He said a brief prayer for Reg's safety.

The compartment filled with five young men in Royal Air Force pilot's uniform. They stowed their packs, their voices raised with excitement. For the young, Clement acknowledged, war was an adventure, and for an instant he smiled, their ebullience contagious. His mind went back to when he had first joined up in the early days of the last war. He, too, had felt both that thrill and camaraderie. Unlike so many others, he had lived through it and knew first-hand the inglorious legacy of war. Forcing those memories from his mind, he listened to the young men's chatter. One of their number looked up and smiled at him. Their conversation had turned to the latest London trend; American Jazz music - a subject Clement knew nothing about. His gaze returned to the window and the endless ebb and flow of people. Idle chatter was discouraged, especially with pilots.

He stood and reached for his pack and took out his Bible, his thoughts returning to Reg Naylor. Clement wondered if he would see his old neighbour again this side of heaven. Holding the Book, Clement noticed the fourth finger of his left hand, where his wedding band should have been. Johnny had advised him not to wear it. He understood why but its absence was a constant reminder. He closed his pack and sat down. His loss, and the thousands of innocents killed, were what it was all about; for freedom and peace and loved ones, like his beloved Mary and Reg's wife Geraldine. That was why decent men went to war. But with Mary gone? Clement pursed his lips and opened his Bible. He began to read the ninety-first Psalm.

A burst of laughter from the young men beside him made him look up. He returned their smile. Only the Lord knew their fate.

Fate. Such an unknown thing, he thought gazing through the window again. Fate was only borne by hope. He reflected on a Biblical verse from Romans chapter eight, "For we are saved by hope". It applied just as much to him as it did the pilots. Strange that Johnny had chosen the word for his cover identity. But it wasn't only pilots, or himself, whose future was so uncertain. He recalled Johnny's words about the horrific loss of life and essential supplies lost daily from U-boat attacks in the Atlantic. Everyone he knew, and thousands he didn't, were suffering in one way or another. He pondered whether such privation and tragedy would make for a more compassionate world after the war? Or, would it be the reverse? And that was supposing the Allies won. While the invasion had not come in

September the previous year he knew it was foolish to believe they wouldn't try again.

Perhaps now the Germans had given up on actual invasion and hoped to win the war by starving the nation into submission. Closing his Bible, he wriggled his left foot, the strap of the Fairbairn Sykes Commando Knife attached to the inside of his leg rubbing against his flesh. Not that he believed it would be needed for this mission but since his training at Coleshill House in Wiltshire, he never went anywhere without it.

A moment later the guard's whistle blew and the train pulled away from the platform. Clement folded his arms, the long-barrelled Welrod Pistol concealed under his greatcoat pressing into his chest. Leaning his head back, he closed his eyes, Scotland still many hundreds of miles away.

At York, Clement stepped from the train with his fellow passengers to stretch his legs. Evacuees with excited children, labelled like parcels, crowded the platform and he wondered where they were headed. To Clement it seemed that the whole country was perpetually on the move. To his right, a few yards from the train door, the young Royal Air Force Pilots were already huddled together smoking. Although Clement thought their conversation was less jovial, they still chatted and joked the way people do when confronted with impending adversity. Further along the platform, Clement saw two ladies operating a canteen. Feeling hungry, he strode towards them and purchased a sandwich and mug of tea.

Holding the warm cup with both hands, his gaze fell again on the line of small children. Several were crying, their fear for what lay ahead, heart-wrenching.

Whispering a prayer for their safety, he finished his tea, returned the mug to the canteen and walked back to his compartment. The young pilots had already taken their seats.

One of them looked up at him as he slid back the compartment door.

'Would you like a newspaper to read, Vicar?'

'That's very kind of you, thank you.'

'Where are you headed, sir?'

'North. You?'

The young pilot smiled. 'Can't say. No disrespect intended.'

'Of course. I shouldn't have asked.'

Clement took the folded paper and sat down. Opening it, he glanced over the top at the young pilot. Talking about troop movements was not permitted and Clement knew this but his question confirmed that his clerical garb belied any suspicion about his activities. His eyes returned to the newspaper. A Nazi bomb had hit a railway arch in the East End of London causing almost a hundred deaths. Innocent life lost; the indiscriminate killing of defenceless civilians was what made this war so wicked. The exact location of the bomb's carnage had been censored, but it was when he read about such outrages that he wondered whether, in fact, he should have remained a country vicar. He knew it was too late for such recriminations. He had made his decision to join the shadowy world of covert operations the previous September, and he knew then there would be no turning back. Now he had to live with the consequences. Or die with them. But without Mary, he really didn't care if he lived or died.

Through the window he saw a young couple embracing. Separation, whether temporary or permanent, was a cruel aspect of war. The last verse of St Matthew's Gospel came to his mind, "I am with you alway,". In theory, Clement knew the Lord was with him. But lately he didn't feel it. What he felt was his current reality; alone and adrift, disconnected from any other living soul, surrounded by strangers.

The couple on the platform parted, the man, in naval uniform, boarding the train.

Waverley Station was larger than he had expected. The high cliff up to the famous Edinburgh Castle loomed above like a cat on a wall, surveying its prey. Hurrying to change platforms, Clement boarded the Inverness train and settled into another compartment, the daylight slowly failing.

Postal clerks and merchant seamen were his travel companions now, but his fellow passengers appeared more intent on sleep than conversation. He checked his watch; it was just after four.

The trip from Edinburgh to Inverness was slow and became an exercise in patience. Deep snow drifts had to be removed from the tracks at regular intervals and the increasing darkness obscured the view, adding to the growing tedium within the compartment. Closing his eyes, he dozed in his seat and contemplated his billet for the night, hopeful of a congenial host and a warm vicarage.

A bitter night had already descended over Inverness when Clement stepped from the train and cast his eye around the dimly lit platform. Light rain patted his hat.

Drawing his coat around him, he followed the flow of passengers making their way towards the ticket collector and the street beyond. Outside the station entrance was a small square where a stone statue of a Highland Soldier stood facing the High Street. Walking to the edge of the square, he looked along the street in both directions. A small crowd had gathered a little further down the pavement by a bus stop. He put his pack down and looked around at the grey stone buildings, the biting cold seeping into his bones.

'Reverend Wisdom?'

Clement turned. Before him stood an elderly, gaunt man wearing a clerical collar. He grasped the icy hand of Reverend St Clair and within twenty minutes Clement was sitting in an ice-cold manse by a struggling fire. But other than learning St Clair had lived in Inverness all his life and had been a minister for sixty years, the conversation yielded little.

'Nearly seven,' St Clair said, switching on the wireless. 'I like to have my dinner listening to the Home Service.'

'Can I be of any assistance?'

'No, thank you. It's right ready to serve.'

St Clair returned with two plates of stew as the voice of Richard Dimbleby informed the listeners of the Nazi bomb that had landed in the East End of London.

An hour later, St Clair stood and switched off the wireless. 'Not much in the way of real news. But I expect you know all about it anyway.' St Clair reached for the empty dinner plates. 'I retire early, Reverend Wisdom. Not as young as I used to be. And it saves on the coal. I'll boil the water for the *pig'uns*.'

Clement smiled. Whilst he wasn't sure what a *pig'un* was, he could see from St Clair's expression that the man considered it a luxury.

St Clair shuffled towards the door. Standing in the open doorway, grasping the dishes, the elderly man turned and looked directly at Clement. 'I've been told not to ask about what you're doing for us, but I wish you God speed, laddie. I envy you, Reverend Wisdom, for the Lord has surely called you in our time of travail.'

St Clair turned and left the room.

Clement stared after his host, the sound of the elderly man's shuffling feet disappearing along the hallway. The profundity of St Clair's words were like a lightning bolt. In that second, all Clement's confusion and anxiety about his life's direction vanished. The realization hit him. Johnny had once referred to Clement's involvement with The Service as being part of the bigger picture; what he had done with the Auxiliary Units had been important, but what he was doing now affected hundreds of lives, even if few knew about it. He smiled feeling the Divine hand of reassurance about his decision and gratitude for St Clair's stirring words.

Leaving the parlour, he walked along the icy hallway to the kitchen where he could hear the sounds of St Clair washing up dishes. Before him, in the centre of the room, was a table already laid for breakfast, the cups turned upside down in readiness. He watched St Clair pour boiling water into two ceramic cylinders then wrap each in a red flannel cloth.

'Put it against the kidneys and you'll never be ill,' the elderly Scot told him.

Clement took the ancient hot-water bottle. He felt overwhelming gratitude and not just for St Clair's hospitality. The effect of his brother cleric's words had been like an epiphany; something he would never forget. Grasping the warm *pig'un* he followed his host along the corridor and climbed the stairs to the upper floor.

St Clair pushed open a door. 'I trust you'll be comfortable here.'

'Good night, Reverend St Clair. And thank you.'

Clement closed the door. Before him was a single bed. It had a rose-coloured satin quilt on the top and the sheets were turned down in anticipation of his arrival. The sight of the welcoming arrangement juxtaposed with the single bed; the gesture both kind and an instant reminder of his current status. Clement pressed the warm pot against his chest. Like St Clair himself, the hot-water bottle and the turned-down bed were the acts of a decent man's innate kindness. Dropping his pack beside the bed, Clement placed the warm *pig* under the sheets then checked the black-out curtains over the window. Turning up the lamp on the stand by the bed, he surveyed the room. On the wall opposite was a washstand and basin, but there was nothing in the room that could be considered decorative except one picture hanging over the bed-head; a lithograph of a rotunda surrounded by daffodils in an unknown garden. Clement placed his knife and pistol under the mattress, he undressed and climbed into the cold sheets, his feet on the *pig* at the foot of the bed.

# 3

Scotland, Tuesday 25th February

A sharp knock and St Clair's voice at his door told Clement it was six o'clock. It was still dark and he rubbed his eyes feeling more weary than when he had retired. He could hear rain hitting the window pane. It promised a bleak day. Forcing himself to get up, he lit the lamp and dressed quickly in the chill air, placing the knife in its scabbard on his left leg and the pistol in the holster over his vest.

Ten minutes later, Clement buttoned his jacket and, holding his greatcoat, scanned the room. Nothing of his remained. In. Out. That was what Johnny had said. Closing the door, Clement descended to the kitchen and found St Clair sitting at the table, a pot of tea already made.

'I trust you slept well, Reverend Wisdom.'

'I did, thank you.'

St Clair poured the tea. 'I hope you like porridge.'

Clement had never liked porridge but he could see the heat rising off the mixture as St Clair ladled the hot cereal into two bowls. Thanking the Lord for the meagre meal, Clement swallowed a spoonful and felt the warmth radiate, no longer wondering why the Scots reputedly ate so much of it.

Just before seven o'clock, they left the manse and walked to the bus stop at the end of street. 'Thank you again for your hospitality, Reverend St Clair.'

'I'll leave you here. I have correspondence to attend to. There's a waiting room there.' St Clair pointed at a closed door. 'The bus for the north will be along directly. God speed to you.'

The old cleric extended his hand in farewell and again Clement felt the icy touch. *Cold hands, warm heart.* The old saying came to him in the loving tones of his late mother's voice. He felt the instant glow in his heart that always came when he thought of her. Logic told him the saying was nonsense, but he did acknowledge that it was true of St Clair.

Clement huddled into his greatcoat as the first faint light of day struggled to permeate the dour morning. He checked his watch; the bus was due in five minutes. Perhaps it was the hour or the still, colourless morning, but the closed doors and ubiquitous grey stone made the place seem unwelcoming. The distinctive odour of burning coal drifted on the chill air. Inverness was stirring. Grasping his pack, he strode towards the waiting room and hoped for warmth.

Given the earliness of the hour, it surprised him to see two ladies of mature years sitting by the fireside. They looked up at him, their eyes on his clerical collar, their conversation pausing. They smiled at him but immediately recommenced their chatter. By the way they huddled together, he could see that whatever they shared, it was not intended for his ears. A squeal of brakes outside relieved any perceived embarrassment. The ladies stood and wrapped themselves in coats and scarves. Holding the door open, Clement followed them towards the waiting bus.

'Good morning to you, Sean. Cold day we're in for,' one said boarding the bus.

'You got that right, sure enough, Mrs Brewster.'

The bus driver's thick Irish accent surprised Clement, but, he now knew the man's name. Clement guessed the driver to be in his late forties, but he wondered if the man's hardened visage had more to do with weather than actual age. Clement glanced at his watch; he had plenty of time to learn about Sean.

'Good morning.' Clement placed the fare in the driver's cupped hand. Looking along the rows of seats, Clement saw that he and the two ladies were the only passengers. He decided on the first seat on the left-hand side. Rumour had it that Ireland was providing the Nazi U-Boats with safe harbour from storms in the Atlantic. He stowed his pack and taking his seat, glanced again at the Irishman, wondering if the man played with radio transmitters in his spare time. One thing Clement was sure about; few know other people's lives better than the postman and the bus driver.

Wick was bleak in the drizzling rain and it surprised Clement to see that several buildings appeared to have suffered bomb damage. Shop windows had been blown out and were now boarded up. Further along the row of shops, one building had been almost completely destroyed. No doubt the large air field a mile or two distant from the town had been the reason for the raid, but it was a salient reminder that it wasn't just the large cities that were being targeted.

Crossing a low stone bridge over the icy river, the bus headed up the hill and stopped outside a barn-like structure. Clement's eyes scanned the streets in the hope of seeing the familiar face of his old friend. Of the few people in uniform who braved the inclement conditions, most were Royal Air Force. None wore the uniform of the Pioneer Corps. For one moment, Clement wondered why Reg's corps was even in Wick. But he wasn't concerned for Reg. Despite the man being in his late forties, Reg was about the most practical and resourceful man Clement had ever met. In fact, of all the men with whom he had served in the Auxiliary Units, he believed Reg was the most likely to come through the war. The bus door opened and a freezing wind rushed in as the two women who had boarded the bus with him in Inverness alighted. Clement watched them walk away, disappearing between the buildings.

Five new passengers now boarded the bus; three men and two women, all of whom greeted the driver by name. Clement watched each of them pay their fare and smiled as they filed past him, moving to the rear of the bus, no doubt to speculate about the stranger in their midst.

The bus door closed. As the motor roared and the odd syncopated hum of the gears resumed, Clement contemplated his new fellow travellers. The two youngest were evidently a couple. Twisting around, he could see that they had taken a seat towards the rear of the bus. The woman looked delicate, but the husband was a healthy, robust man of approximately thirty years of age. They sat together, their bodies touching, their conversation quiet. The man was not in uniform. Neither did he have the hands of a man who routinely did manual work. Conclusion: the man was in a restricted, perhaps administrative occupation. An older couple sat in the middle of the bus. Although they were not conversing, there was the easy rapport between them formed from many years of marriage and he decided the man was a professional of some kind. The fifth passenger was a very elderly man who sat some rows behind Clement on the left side of the bus. He had seen the man's hands when he'd paid his fare, and Clement had no doubt whatsoever that the man was a farmer.

'What takes you to Huna, Father?' Sean shouted, not taking his eyes from the narrow roadway.

'I'm taking up a parish on South Ronaldsay.'

'Is that right, Father?'

'I prefer, Vicar, actually.'

'Crossing at Gills Bay?'

'Yes.'

'You staying with Reverend Heath, then? In Canisbay?'

'Just a few days. Until I can arrange the crossing.'

What conversation there was at the rear of the bus had ceased. Clement knew they had heard. He surmised that within an hour of them alighting at their destinations most of the neighbourhood would know of his presence and his destination.

'You know the minister there?' Clement asked.

Sean nodded. 'A good man. Loves his fishing and going out on the boats.'

'Has he been the pastor there for a long time?'

'A good few years. Comes from Ayrshire.'

'Really?' he said, but he didn't really know where Ayrshire was. 'Does he have family?'

Sean shook his head. 'Now there is something I never really thought about. All the holy fathers I'm used to certainly didn't have a wife tucked away. The One True Faith, me. Or so the nuns would have had us believe. Not too many of us in these parts.'

Clement smiled.

'I suppose the reverend never got around to it,' Sean continued. 'And he won't find a bride in Canisbay.'

'Have all the young women left?'

Clement saw Sean's eyes in the rear-view mirror, their gaze meeting. 'There are no unattached young women in Huna or Canisbay, Vicar.'

'It must be very isolated and I suppose, like most small villages, they all know each other.'

Sean's gaze remained on him. 'And each other's business.'

'You don't live in either place then?'

'Not me.'

Clement sat back on the seat. Without turning around he knew what the expressions of his fellow passengers would be like. Sean had, Clement believed, touched a raw nerve. He stared through the window at the snow-covered landscape as the bus's strangely syncopated gears droned on. He knew that Sean's remark reflected the man's lack of acceptance in the community. Small places. Was Sean an outsider simply because he was Irish or Roman Catholic or both? Perhaps the locals held something else against him? Clement hadn't witnessed any unfriendliness from the passengers towards the bus driver, but then Sean drove the bus which took them home. Clement remained gazing at the passing scenery and the grey swell of the North Sea.

The road dipped into several small ravines where thick snow still clung to the roofs of dwellings and piles of the stuff remained heaped on the leeward side of the barns. Then up again to the ridge top where the bus swayed in the increasing wind and short, grey, rain squalls traversed the paddocks, hiding the dwellings then passing on. As the hours passed, the country became less and less mountainous and small, low roofed, stone dwellings half submerged into the winter landscape dotted the scene. To Clement's eye it was profoundly unwelcoming for it was not just grey, it was bleak. He had never before seen pure cold, but he saw it now in all its colourless misery. No one was out-of-doors. He surmised that the wind and snow rendered outdoor activity, for everything but an emergency, impractical. In fact, if he had not glimpsed the yellowish smoke issuing from the cottages' chimneys, he would have believed the place to be deserted. He thought of Fearnley Maughton - of the blue-bells in the forest and the sights and fragrances of the East Sussex village in early spring. They were two different worlds really. Yet, despite this, both places held secrets and both places, perhaps like all villages, had unseen eyes, forever watching.

'Is the minister at Canisbay elderly, driver?'

'Sean,' the man said, pointing to himself.

31

'Reverend Wisdom,' Clement replied for all to hear.

'Reverend Heath, do you mean?'

'Yes.'

'I've never really thought about the man's age. He is a man of God, ageless really. He's a good fisherman and he's helpful on a boat. Or so Tom Harris says.'

'Tom Harris?'

'One of the local fishermen. Also a bachelor.'

Clement wanted to ask about Sarah Crawford but with everyone in the bus listening he thought it wisest not to.

'There's only one beauty in Huna,' Sean went on. 'Sarah Crawford. Now she would once have been a real stunner. She is still a handsome woman, although, that husband of hers is a suspicious and sour old bugger who doesn't know how fortunate he is.'

The level of animosity in Sean's remark surprised Clement, but he knew both the comment and the intonation had been intended for other ears.

Clement's gaze remained on the bus driver.

'I've never once seen him lift a finger to help her,' Sean continued, shaking his head the way people do when they cannot believe something to be true. 'In fact, in the ten years the Crawfords have lived in Huna, I have only ever seen Donald Crawford collect the mail bag once. And that was when she was in Edinburgh caring for her sick mother.'

Clement kept his eyes on the Irishman. He sensed Sean's vitriol hadn't finished.

'She does almost all the work. And more else besides.'

# 4

T his is your stop, Vicar,' Sean called.
Clement stood and reached for his pack, the bus slowing. Caught in the faint beam of the bus's headlights, Clement saw a woman standing beside the road. She was alone and wearing a red plaid tam o'shanter, a long overcoat and knee-high boots. The bus door opened and he stepped into the icy chill of the late afternoon. 'Thank you, Sean,' he called back over his shoulder.

The woman boarded the bus, but the door remained open. Clement waited, hoping the woman was his contact - the post mistress, Sarah Crawford. Placing his pack on the road, he buttoned his coat and tied his scarf around his neck as the wind tore at his body, the temperature not much more than freezing.

'Just a small one today, Sarah,' he heard Sean say.

Clement waited, the woman's identity confirmed.

He looked up at the broad expanse of evening sky. Even in the dwindling light, there was little cloud visible. It promised a freezing night. Walking around the bus, his gaze fell on the two buildings in front of him. The one on the right had a wide glass window through which he could see the counters and shelves. Above was a sign, "Crawford's Post Office and General Shop". To the left of the shop was a large double door which he presumed led to a yard of some kind. He turned to the other dwelling. The sign there read "McAllister's Garage and Farm Supplies". It also had large double doors. Adjacent to them were two narrow windows where black-out curtains were drawn. There were no other buildings.

On the opposite side of the road was a red telephone box. Clement glanced along the road in both directions. *Village,* he considered, was too elaborate a word for Huna.

He heard the bus door close. Two seconds later, the engine roared and the bus drove away in the failing light of a Scottish afternoon, the syncopation disappearing on the wind.

Sarah Crawford glanced at him, the Royal Mail bag in her grasp, an enquiring frown forming on her forehead. She was older than he had expected but she was still a very attractive woman, with auburn hair tied in a low roll at her neck. He stepped forward. 'May I assist you with that?'

'Thank you, but I can manage.'

'I am your mother's friend.'

Sarah Crawford paused. 'I was expecting a woman.'

'Sorry to disappoint.'

Sarah's gaze fixed on his clerical collar. 'You're the visiting vicar staying at the manse. It makes sense now. Is it real?'

'Yes.'

'We need to talk. Come to the shop tomorrow at ten o'clock.'

'How do I get to the manse?'

'Walk! It's only about a mile and a half down the road. Walk as far as the kirk, there,' she said pointing to a large building some distance away, silhouetted against the western sky. 'Then take the road directly opposite it to Canisbay village. The manse is a two-storey house on the left about three hundred yards from the intersection. If you keep to the roads you can't get lost.' She turned to face him. 'Ten o'clock tomorrow. Don't forget. And don't be late.'

Sarah Crawford tightened her grip on the canvas bag then marched towards the shop. Clement heard the door being bolted from the inside.

He had expected a more cordial greeting. Sean's words echoed into his mind, "She does almost all the work. And more else besides". Why had Sean added the final words? The statement worried Clement. He stored it away. Retying his scarf around his neck, he tucked the ends into his greatcoat collar and turned a full three hundred and sixty degrees, his eyes scanning the darkening landscape.

Several dwellings dotted the scene. Snow lay in the surrounding meadows and over the undulating hills. On the air he could smell burning coal. To the west, the dying shafts of light were tingeing the evening sky; flashes of pink and orange and gold framed the high, thin cloud and mingled into the translucent blue. He wriggled his toes as he felt the cold rising into his bones. Despite his numbing extremities, he stared at the sight. Although he could not see the cliffs, he knew from the maps he had studied before leaving London that Huna was on the edge of Great Britain. The open sea and Pentland Firth lay just below the adjacent cliffs to his right. Grasping his pack, he started to walk, the twilight diminishing with each step.

Within minutes his body had lost the heat he had gained from the warmth of the bus. A freezing north-west head wind bit hard into his face and chilled his whole body, turning the simple act of breathing and walking into a struggle of endurance, if not survival. Wrapping his scarf over his mouth and nose, and pulling his hat down, he swung the bag onto his shoulders and broke into a run, his chest heaving and his feet breaking the thin layer of ice which had reformed on the roadway since the wheels of Sean's bus had crushed the snow into slush.

Clement knocked at the front door to the manse and a minute later it opened.

'Reverend Heath?'

'Reverend Wisdom, I'm guessing, under all that clothing. Come on in. It's a cool night we're in for.'

Clement stepped inside and grasped the extended hand of his host. Heat radiated from Reverend Heath's handshake and Clement couldn't help but compare the man who stood before him now to the kindly but puritanic Reverend St Clair. Heath closed the door on the wintry evening. 'Let me take your coat and hat?'

Without waiting for a reply, Heath pulled the greatcoat from Clement's shoulders and hung it along with his hat and scarf on a stand in the front hall. Placing his pack on the floor under his coat, Clement followed Heath into the sitting room where two armchairs sat in front of a roaring fire. It was the most welcoming sight he'd had seen since arriving in Scotland and the level of warmth in the house was unexpected. A mixture of masculine and domestic odours assaulted Clement's nostrils; dust, tobacco, coal-fire smoke, a hint of whisky and drying socks.

'Your boots will soon dry here,' Heath was saying. 'Take them off and warm your feet. They must be frozen.'

Clement smiled at his brother cleric, wondering if affability was a pre-requisite for Scottish clergy, but there the similarities between Heath and the elderly St Clair ended. Clement guessed Heath to be in his mid-forties; robust, with a firm handshake, sandy hair, blue-green eyes and a square jaw. He wore an old hand-knitted cream jersey, well-worn brown-plaid slippers and no clerical collar.

Heath caught Clement's gaze. 'I expect you're wondering why I don't wear the collar.' Heath reached for a poker and prodded at the coal in the grate. 'The simple truth is, I don't need one. Everyone knows who I am.'

'Of course. Do forgive me. I meant no disrespect.'

'None taken.'

Clement sat in the chair by the fire and began to remove his boots feeling uneasy about his unspoken and so easily spotted judgement. He made a mental note to be more guarded.

'Are you hungry, Reverend Wisdom?'

'Please don't go to any trouble, Reverend Heath.'

'Aidan, I insist. There is no formality here.'

'Clement,' he said, wriggling his left leg, the scabbard that held his Fairbairn Sykes Commando blade rubbing on his ankle, reminding him why he was in Scotland. He had meant the comment; mealtimes held little pleasure for him now. In fact, if his body didn't need sustenance for survival, Clement believed he would never eat again.

Aidan disappeared into the kitchen and Clement heard the sounds of dinner preparation. Standing, he warmed his back and legs, the heat seeping into his limbs. His eyes roamed the room. Black-out curtains covered a long window which, he surmised, overlooked the side of the manse, while bookshelves lined two of the remaining four walls. On every available surface and table were piles of books, magazines and pipes in a partial state of being smoked. He stared at several items of drying underwear hanging over the arms of a velvet upholstered chair. "Personables", Mary used to call them. Wriggling his ankle, he looked away and wandered towards the bookshelves, the warmth enveloping him. Theological tomes he knew were on one side, but Heath's evident passion was fishing. Numerous books on the subject filled the shelves and magazines were randomly stacked on ledges and tables. He reached for one as his host entered the room carrying a tray.

'Fish breeding. Those magazines.' Aidan nodded in the direction of the periodicals on the shelf as he placed a tray on the table in front of the fire. 'Tiresome really, but they pass the time.'

Clement replaced the magazine, glancing at its cover. A wide-eyed fish stared back. The lead article, so the cover proclaimed in large type, was on the breeding habits of cod. He couldn't imagine anything less interesting. Either Heath's parish was very small or no one much needed his help. Clement chastised himself. Scotland's winter was formidable and it stood to reason that only an emergency would take the minister from the warmth of his hearth. Leaving the magazine on the bookcase Clement turned to see two bowls of porridge on the table. A large dollop of cream sat on the surface of the thick mixture. Beside the bowls were two plates each with a thick slice of bread spread with lard.

'I've been saving the dripping to share with a visitor. I understand you are going to take up St Peter's on South Ronaldsay?'

Clement smiled. 'Have you been to South Ronaldsay?'

'I've been most places hereabouts. You will notice the cold more there.'

'Colder than here?'

Aidan laughed. 'It's only about ten miles away, but we have an unusual climate. You will have driven through thicker snow further south than you'll see here. It's the warm air currents from the Atlantic that keep the deep snow at bay. Although, this year the winter has been more severe than usual, it is the wind, more than the snow in Caithness that will kill you.'

Clement smiled, having experienced first-hand the truth of Heath's remark, but he wanted to steer the conversation onto the people of Canisbay and Huna, not its weather. 'Do you have a large congregation, Aidan?'

'Not as big as it was, of course, what with all the young people going off to do their bit.'

'Are you still doing an Evensong as well as Matins on Sundays?'

'We are Church of Scotland here, but be that as it may, I only conduct one service on Sundays now. It has more to do with winter than wartime. Most people like to be at their fireside by mid-afternoon.'

Aidan picked up a bowl and handed it to him. 'Will you say grace, Clement?'

'For what we are about to receive, may the Lord make us truly thankful.'

'Amen.'

Clement reached for the spoon. Steam was rising off the thick cereal. He decided to persist with his questions while his supper cooled. 'Has the war affected many families in the area?'

'Nothing much perturbs them. They are used to privation. Comes with the territory.'

'And they don't fear invasion?'

'Here?'

Clement nodded.

'Not something I've had to deal with. As I said, they are hardy folk. We have had some air raids, but Wick gets more than we do. I had to assist with quite a few funerals there just before Christmas. Sad business.'

Clement remembered the bomb damage in Wick. 'You haven't had any here?'

'It would appear the Germans are more interested in ports and airfields, neither of which we have in

Canisbay. And I can't see them scaling the cliffs here to invade us.'

Clement took a spoonful of porridge and gazed into the glowing coals. While he had hoped his questions would have yielded more information, he didn't wish to make Heath suspicious. The conversation turned to Heath's favourite subject - fishing - something Clement knew almost nothing about. He was on more familiar ground when Heath introduced the topic of the German cleric, Dietrich Bonhoeffer, and his struggles against Nazi ideologies. For a rural priest, Heath's knowledge of Bonhoeffer's theories was impressive, but as Clement had formerly acknowledged, Scotland's winters were severe and other than tending to one's laundry, reading was the evening entertainment. Gazing at the well-stocked book shelves Clement had no doubt Heath's knowledge was wide ranging. Around nine o'clock and pleading genuine tiredness, Clement retired.

The bedroom on the upper floor was similar to St Clair's with the same utilitarian furniture, but the room was warm. No need for a *pig'un* in Aidan Heath's manse. Clement's gaze fell on the bed-covers. They had not been turned down, but it didn't matter. Where St Clair had exhibited his inherent kindness in the small things of life, Aidan's intellect and engaging conversation had more than compensated.

Clement closed the door and placed his knife and pistol under the mattress and his pack under the bed. Walking to the window, he drew the curtains then turned up the wick on the bedside lamp. He glanced at the bedroom door. No lock. He thought for a moment. He couldn't risk any of the weapons in his pack being discovered. Hanging his jacket and coarse weave, woollen shirt over the chair and his greatcoat on a stand in the corner he withdrew the rounds of ammunition from his pack and placed them into his webbing. From now on, whenever he left the house he would need to wear it all.

# 5

Wednesday 26th February

The air in Clement's room was cold. He guessed the fire must have burnt itself out during the night, yet, despite the firmness of the mattress and his nose feeling like ice, he had slept well. Rising, he walked to the window and lifted the curtain. The view was of the rear garden. Below, he could see the snow-covered roof of a single storey annexe connected to the manse. Beyond the garden, some thirty feet away, was a stone fence with a gate leading into a neighbouring property. The adjacent house was a three storey, stone dwelling of some size with numerous large windows on the lower floors and attic windows set into a high-pitched roof. A large beech tree hugged the southern end of the house.

Clement watched the scene for some minutes but nothing stirred. He let the curtain fall. Pouring some water from the jug under the washstand, he splashed his face with the icy liquid then reached for his webbing. Placing his knife in its scabbard and his pistol in its holster over his vest, he pulled on his thick shirt and jacket and descended to find Aidan in the kitchen, a tray on the bench beside the oven.

'I trust you slept well, Clement. They tell me it's a comfortable mattress. Too soft for me.'

Somehow Aidan's comment didn't surprise him.

'I'll just give my girls their breakfast.' Aidan disappeared outside with a bucket of kitchen scraps. Clement watched him from the kitchen window. His host was still wearing the cream jersey, but Clement could now see the large holes over the elbows; a true sign, in his opinion, of bachelorhood. The brown plaid slippers were leaving long stride marks in some fresh snow. Leaning on the windowsill he watched Aidan open the door to the annexe that Clement had seen from his bedroom window. An excited cackle of hens responded. Minutes later, Aidan returned with the empty bucket and four fresh eggs. Despite their arrival however, breakfast still consisted of porridge. Whilst his dislike for it had not diminished, Clement had to admit, porridge warmed the body and didn't leave one hungry.

'I thought while I was here I would like to take a look around, to see the view from the cliffs. The sky was so beautiful last evening when I arrived. I'm looking forward to seeing the coast in the daylight.'

Aidan smiled. 'It's quite a sight. You forget when you see it on a regular basis. I have to see the lassies, my neighbours, this morning about the rent.' Aidan

44

nodded in the direction of the large house at the rear. 'The Frew spinsters are my landladies and the daughters of a previous minister of Canisbay. But afterwards, if you like, I could arrange your crossing with Tom Harris, a local fisherman. He is due back this morning. He could take you to St Margaret's Hope tomorrow, if the weather is fair.'

Clement thought fast, a crossing tomorrow was too soon. 'That would be most kind, although I was hoping to be here on Sunday, to attend your church. If you have no objections?'

'You'd be most welcome, of course. Would you like to preach?'

'I've no wish to usurp your pulpit, Aidan, and I'm sure the people of South Ronaldsay will not hold it against me if I am a few days delayed.'

'You will learn, Clement to take advantage of good weather. You never know when it will return, but it's your decision, of course.'

Clement closed the door on the manse. He'd felt mildly chastised by Aidan but understood that his host's advice came from years of experiencing Caithness winters. Clement dismissed it from his mind. Lifting his gaze, his eyes took in the view from the front gate. In the daylight the scene was extraordinary. With so few trees and only low stone walls and hedges that substituted for fences, one could see across the snow-covered paddocks for miles. Low undulating hills rolled away to the west, a mixture of white snow, long grey-green tussock grass and grey rock, dotted by the occasional barn and farm house. Up to his left and about two hundred yards distant he could see the few houses that made up the village of Canisbay. A two storey Victorian building sat at the intersection of two roads overlooking the cluster of dwellings. He surmised it to be a public house. A grey car was parked outside and smoke was billowing from the building's twin chimneys.

To his right, starkly isolated from all other dwellings and resolute to the winter gales, was the kirk. The building was painted white and had a green tiled roof. There were no embellishments of any kind to its exterior and it had narrow, perpendicular windows. At the western end was a tall unadorned bell-tower. To the east several tall obelisk-styled headstones were visible above a high stone fence that surrounded the kirk. Standing alone, surrounded by pastures on three sides and the sea to the north, it was a most extraordinary, mesmeric sight and easily the most imposing building of the district. It was also unlike any church Clement had ever seen. Sitting on the very edge of Great Britain with Pentland Firth below it, the kirk would be visible for miles in all directions.

Clement walked away from the manse in the cold, grey morning air and headed down the road he had taken the previous evening towards the impressive kirk. The wind that had slapped his face then had now dropped to a light tap about the cheeks. He buttoned his greatcoat concealing the rounds of ammunition in the webbing around his waist.

At the intersection Clement stared at the imposing edifice. Its white painted walls and bell tower were like a beacon in daylight and would serve the local fishermen just as well as any lighthouse. Slowly he turned a full three hundred and sixty degrees, scrutinizing the low undulating hills that surrounded him to the east, south and west. To the north, just off the coast, lay Stroma Island. There he could see a few crofter's cottages dotted about the hillsides but other than these, the island appeared barren and unremarkable. Feeling his shoulders droop, he pondered the whereabouts of the traitor. In Fearnley Maughton everything and everyone was close by, but here, in this rural setting, he could see it was the reverse. Clement turned and started to walk along the road towards Huna and his meeting with the formidable post mistress.

Just on ten o'clock Clement opened the door to Crawford's Post Office and General Shop. Sarah Crawford looked up as he entered. Other than the proprietress, two ladies were in the shop making purchases. A small girl stood beside one of the women while a lanky boy of adolescent years hung around the doorway. Clement heard Sarah Crawford ring up an amount on the cash-register. He also heard her say good-bye to a woman she addressed as Mrs Wallace, and, he believed for his benefit, to the children Billy and Mary. He closed his eyes for one second then dismissed the memory of his beloved late wife. This Mary was no more than ten years old. She was a pretty child, shy and innocent. Billy, the little girl's older brother, Clement assessed to be neither. Acne had made the young face unattractive, but it wasn't the physical unsightliness that made Billy sullen. The boy sulked. His pale, furtive eyes seemed to scan the place constantly. Clement surmised he was searching for something to taunt. Within minutes the woman and her children had left.

'I'll see you later, Sally,' said the other woman in the shop.

Clement looked up.

'Yes. Thank you, Joyce.'

He waited until he heard the shop door close. 'Sally?'

'If one is on friendly terms.' Sarah turned and put a few tins back on the self behind her.

Clement stared at Sarah Crawford's back. He felt the acerbic comment. While he thought it unnecessary, it was an instant reminder that he was not on any terms with the Special Duties Branch Operative. He felt a smile rising. Small communities and their exclusionist attitudes were the same no matter the county. He cleared his throat. 'Can we talk here, Mrs Crawford?'

Sarah glanced at the clock on the wall. 'In the lorry. It's safer that way. Just a minute.' Sarah pushed aside a curtain and reached for the over-large coat he had seen her wearing the previous evening. He waited while she tied a scarf around her neck and tucked it into her coat. Pulling on her boots and red cap, she said, 'This way.'

He followed her into the rear of the shop.

Behind the curtain was a sitting room. In one corner was a desk covered with more papers than were on Johnny's desk, and in the other corner was a small telephone exchange. A man of advanced years sat on a wooden chair with worn padded arms pulling a telephone cable out of one location and inserting it into another.

'This is my husband. I'll be about an hour, Donald.'

The man grunted, 'Hold the line.'

Clement glanced at Donald Crawford but the man didn't lift his head nor make any attempt at any conversation. Clement followed Sarah through the house and out into a yard.

'Get in the other side,' she said, pointing at the lorry.

Clement did as instructed. For some minutes Sarah fetched milk churns and bread baskets and bags of provisions and bundles of tied letters.

'Can I help you with anything?' he called through the open driver's window.

'Thank you, but no. I'd rather do it myself.'

The rear doors of the lorry slammed shut and Sarah climbed in behind the steering wheel and backed the vehicle out of the yard.

'I could have helped you, Mrs Crawford.'

'Thank you, but I don't need the gossip right now.'

'Is that all it takes?'

'You don't know small places.'

'As it happens, I do. But perhaps not as small as Huna.'

The lorry pulled onto the road.

Clement glanced back at the red telephone box opposite Crawford's shop. 'How many telephones are there in Huna?'

'Other than the one outside our shop, there is one at *The Bell*, the public house in Canisbay. And the Frew sisters have one, but they never use it.'

'No one else?'

Sarah shook her head.

They drove in silence for a few minutes. He saw her glance at a stone barn by the edge of the road as they drove west, but she made no comment.

'Why do you do Special Duties work? I would have thought a married woman who runs a shop would have enough to do.'

The pause lasted several seconds. He had not expected overt friendliness from the Special Duties Operative but he hadn't anticipated hostility either. He was about to say as much when Sarah Crawford spoke.

'My husband was a signals operator in the Merchant Navy during the last war. The ship he was on sank and he was burned. He is a good man but not easy to live with. He likes his whisky. Sometimes I think it is the only thing that makes him happy. We had a son but he died when he was five years old from diphtheria. I had to have something to stop me going insane, so I volunteered. Besides, I already knew Morse Code and how to operate a wireless. Donald had one, but he had to surrender it when the war came.'

Clement felt that he had intruded on Sarah's private life. He changed the subject. 'Why was the kirk built here and not in either village?'

'I don't really know. But there has been a church on this site for over a thousand years.' Sarah looked at her watch. 'Would you like to see it? I don't have many deliveries today and we could talk in there.'

'I would. Thank you.'

Sarah drove the lorry onto the grassy verge and switched off the engine. Leaving the vehicle on the side of the road, they walked towards the great kirk. Opening a large heavy wooden door, they went in, their footsteps echoing on the stone floor. He had been eager to see inside the kirk, but compared to English churches, Clement considered the kirk's interior plain. Austere even, especially in comparison to his old church of *All Saints* in Fearnley Maughton.

'Is that the door to the vestry?'

Sarah nodded. 'I've never been in it, and Reverend Heath almost never uses it. If anyone wants to see Aidan they go to the manse. It's warmer there.'

Clement nodded. He saw that the vestry door was closed. He looked around the nave, making sure they were alone. 'Is the wireless here?'

'No. It's in our barn. We passed it on our way here.'

'When do you make contact?'

'Every day between eleven o'clock and noon.'

'Every day?'

'Yes. We may seem remote to you but there are thousands of military personnel stationed around here. What with the Air Force Base in Castletown and a Y-station on Dunnet Head, not to mention the air fields around Wick and the Royal Navy in Scapa Flow; it is a very busy place. The planes flying overhead are not always ours.'

The latch on the door clicked open. He looked up. A pale-faced woman walked in holding a mop and broom.

Sarah stood, her hands thrust deep into her pockets.

An uneasy silence ensued.

'Morag McCrea, Reverend Wisdom,' Sarah said before the woman could speak.

'Good morning, Mrs McCrea.' Clement nodded to the diminutive woman. Sarah was already heading for the door. 'If you will excuse me? Till Sunday, then?' He said, nodding to the woman. Replacing his hat, he followed Sarah outside.

Sarah was standing off to one side by the head stones but Clement could see her expression. Gossip of any kind was long-lived.

'Do you mind if we walk, Mrs Crawford? I'm still getting used to the cold.'

She didn't answer but started to walk east, between the graves and towards the end of the walled graveyard.

'Will you be back in time to attend to the schedule today?'

'I usually do it after the deliveries, but because you are here, Donald will do it today.'

'What did you say?'

Sarah looked down, her boot nudging the gravel under her feet. 'He was not supposed to know about my work. When I did my training at Whaddon Hall in Buckinghamshire, I told everyone here, including my husband, that I was in Edinburgh looking after my sick mother.' She paused. 'Donald didn't believe me. Huna is a small place, Reverend Wisdom, and what with other rumours about me, I had to tell my husband. I haven't told London that Donald knows about my work and I am hoping you will not inform them.'

He felt his eyes widen. Breaching the Official Secrets Act was a serious matter and one that could get her into substantial trouble. He wondered if she was relying on his priestly status for confidentiality. 'I cannot give you an absolute guarantee. However, they will not learn it from me unless your actions endanger others. But you should inform them. And soon. Tell me about the people here. Who was that woman who came into the church?'

'Morag. Morag McCrea. She cleans the kirk. She thinks it will earn her a better seat in heaven. She has two sons, Malcolm and Stewart. Her husband, Duncan, is unwell. Fought in the last war. They have a farm at Huna Crofts and some land over towards Mey.'

'Are they the only farmers hereabouts?'

'Of course not! This is a farming community. The two biggest farms in this area belong to the McCrea's and the Wallace's. That was Mrs Wallace in the shop just now; the family have the farm by the cliffs.' Sarah pointed towards a group of low buildings about midway between the kirk and Huna.

'Anyone else?'

'Farmers, you mean?'

He nodded. 'And others?'

'The Grants and the Hendersons have big farms but they mostly go to Dunnet or Castletown for their needs. And, of course, there are tenant farmers on the Mey Estates. As for the others, well, there aren't too many left. Our little school closed when the teacher volunteered. Even the unmarried women have left to join up. A lot of them are working in Castletown. And it isn't the time of year for itinerant farm workers. Not that you can find many of those anymore.' Sarah paused. 'You met Joyce McAllister in the shop earlier. She and her husband Ian have the garage next door to us. Ian delivers coal and peat around the district twice a week, so he wasn't called up. He isn't a bad man, but he and my husband don't get on.'

'What sort of distances does he cover?'

'John O'Groats to Castletown.'

'And the reason for the animosity between your husband and Mr McAllister?'

'The barn. Ian thinks he should have the use of it for the coal. But it forms part of the lease for the postal service. Which we have.'

'Who owns this barn?'

'Eileen and Elaine Frew.'

'Reverend Heath's neighbours? How old are these ladies?'

'Over eighty.'

'And the bus driver, Sean?'

'Sean Mead? What about him?'

Clement saw her look down.

'Whatever you can tell me about him.'

'He spends a lot of his spare time at *The Bell*. Other than that, you will have to ask him. Anything else you want to know about us?'

'Possibly. But for now, tell me about the irregular radio transmissions?'

'The signal is strong. Not more than ten miles, but I don't know where. I have a transmitter, not a direction finder. And it's always enciphered and transmitted in Morse Code. No spoken words,' Sarah told him, her voice matter-of-fact. Clement believed she had not liked his questions about her and her neighbours and he was left in little doubt that he would never call her *Sally*.

The sound of a truck approaching from the east halted their conversation. Clement looked up but he could not see the vehicle for the high graveyard wall. The noise of the shifting gears lessened. The truck had not stopped.

'That will be Ian McAllister now, doing his coal deliveries.'

'Which days?'

'Wednesdays and Saturdays.'

Clement stored the information away. 'Don't you need an antenna to be attached to the wireless when you are transmitting?'

'Yes, but look around you. No trees. No mountains of any size. In fact, nothing to interfere with the signal. So the rafters of a barn on a cliff by the edge of the sea would do. I only transmit to the Y-Station, not further away, so I don't really need anything bigger.'

'Do you believe, from what you've overheard, that the signals are intended to be picked up locally or more distant?'

'Germany, you mean?'

He nodded.

'It would be more reliable if he had a fixed aerial.'

'And the signals themselves?'

'As I said, in Morse, enciphered and random in length and time. But always in groups of five letters.'

'Can you decipher anything of them?'

'No. I have neither the skill nor the time for such things. I send the messages on to the Y-station. What they do with them is up to them.'

'Do you send in cipher?'

'Of course!'

'But you can't decipher his?'

She stared at him. 'To encipher a message you have to know three things. The algorithm, that is the method used to encipher the original message. The key, which can be a word or number, and the period of time the key is valid. That could change every day, week or month. Regardless of whenever it changes, the sender and the receiver have to know all those things to encipher and decipher the message. Without them, even a simple cipher could take months to break. I'm sure that somewhere people are sitting at desks all day going mad over such things. But not me. I have work to do.'

Clement didn't respond, but his eyes scanned the scattered dwellings dotted among the undulating meadows and treeless pastures.

'All I know is that there is someone transmitting in this area. How or who, I don't know. But it just seems too coincidental to me.'

'What do you mean, coincidental?' Clement asked.

Sarah stopped walking and turned to face him. 'I thought you would know about it. The lighthouse on Stroma.' She pointed out across Pentland Firth to the nearby island. 'It was attacked last Saturday.'

'What?'

'A German fighter strafed the lighthouse. No one was injured and it caused almost no damage. Why on earth should they do that?'

# 6

Do you have any suspicions, Mrs Crawford as to who could be sending these messages?'

'I've been thinking about that. The McCrea boys are both enlisting age but neither has signed up. Of course, farming is a reserved occupation, but you'd think at least one of them would go.'

'Any other reason to suspect the McCrea's?'

'One of the sons, Malcolm, likes his whisky. He told Jean Buchanan, the publican at *The Bell*, that he thinks there are too many foreigners in Scotland and by that I don't mean Continentals. Malcolm believes this war to be an English war, so why should we Scots support it? I'm not saying he is a traitor and he is probably only voicing what others are thinking, but he is vocal about his views. And he doesn't like Reverend Heath.'

'Why would that be?'

'Petty jealousy. Nothing more.'

'What about?'

'Malcolm used to like helping Tom, one of our local fishermen, with the catch. Malcolm is strong and good with a knife, but Tom prefers to take Reverend Heath, if he is available. Apparently he knows his way around a boat better than Malcolm.'

Clement stared out across the firth to Stroma Island. 'McCrea's dislike of Reverend Heath aside, why would Malcolm McCrea collaborate with the enemy?'

'As I said, Duncan McCrea, Malcolm and Stewart's father, was in the last war. He was gassed. Malcolm has always hated the English for taking his father away and feeding his dad and thousands like him to the trenches. Duncan says that the English can't be trusted.'

'And you think that would be reason enough for Malcolm to collaborate with the Germans?'

'You don't understand much about entrenched hatreds, do you?'

He stared at Sarah, a frown creasing his brow. What she'd implied sounded extreme to him.

'We are a long way from London, Reverend Wisdom. And people have long memories.'

Clement didn't respond. He knew very little Scottish history, but he had heard that between some clans, a feud could last generations. As he hadn't yet met the McCrea brothers, he wasn't in a position to judge.

They had wandered some way among the headstones, towards the stone wall that separated the graveyard from the road and the land adjacent to the cliffs.

Clement stared at the stony ground, the frown still on his forehead. The attack on the lighthouse worried him. Johnny had not mentioned it, but then again it had only taken place on the same day he had seen Johnny in London.

Sarah interrupted his thoughts. 'Why would the Germans attack the lighthouse and cause so little damage? Surely if their intention was to cause havoc with our shipping, they would have destroyed it!'

'I can't answer that. What is on Stroma Island?'

'Nothing much. Only the lighthouse and a few crofters.' Sarah checked her wrist watch. 'I need to get back to my deliveries. There is one other thing. Tom Harris, the local fisherman I mentioned, came into the shop late yesterday with his catch. He has been away for about two weeks. He told me that he has seen the same boat on several occasions in the North Sea.'

'Did anyone else hear this?'

'I think Joyce was in the shop for some of the time.'

'Does Tom or Joyce McAllister know about your Special Duties activities?'

'No one knows. Except Donald.'

'Imprudent chatter is not only a breach of national security, Mrs Crawford, it is also unwise. Mr Harris should know this. Did he say anything else about this boat?'

'Yes. He told me that on both occasions he saw it, it was alone. It's just a trawler. Like his. But unlike his, it has some guns mounted on the bow.'

'Did he note anything else about it?'

She nodded. 'He saw its number. NN04. Given what Tom saw, plus the attack on Stroma, I think something is about to happen. Here or perhaps around Orkney. I cannot be sure. It's just…'

'Go on.'

'Even though I don't know what the transmissions are about, I recognise the person's touch. They call it a signature touch. I know when it's him, I know by the way he presses the keys.'

'How can you be sure it is a man?'

'It's in the touch. If it's a woman, then she is very good at disguising it.'

'If the transmissions are random, wouldn't this person have to live in close proximity to his wireless?'

'It's a fair assumption.' Sarah checked her watch again. 'I must go or I will be late with the deliveries and Donald will be angry.'

'If you can recognise this person by their touch, couldn't this person know you by yours?'

Sarah shrugged. 'If he is a good wireless operator.'

'Would he be able to differentiate between you and your husband?'

'It's possible.'

Clement stared at an old tomb stone so weathered the name had long vanished. 'I could walk from here and take the milk and supplies for the manse for you, if you like.'

'Thank you. That would be helpful.'

'Have you sent on the information about the fisherman's sightings?'

'Donald will have done it this morning. How long are you staying?'

Clement looked up at a winged angel headstone off to his right. 'About a week. I told Reverend Heath that I would like to stay for church on Sunday. It buys me a few extra days to locate the source.' He turned his gaze westward, towards Gills Bay. Off the coast the shaft of sunlight lit up the waters, transforming the dark grey-green to the most intense sapphire. 'It really is beautiful.'

'The scenery maybe.'

Clement watched Sarah Crawford's lorry drive west towards Gills Bay until it disappeared from his view. With the kirk at his back, he set out towards the manse. As he walked he stared at the slush under his boots. Sarah Crawford. The woman was hard to read. At times she had been brusque, but since her confession about breaching the Official Secrets Act, he believed she was endeavouring to win his support, should she ever need it. Was it a simple confession or a very clever ruse? Could Sarah Crawford herself be the collaborator? In which case there was no need for another transmitter. He slowed his pace. What had he learned about the woman? She was forty-something, had lived in Huna managing a shop and post office for about ten years and was married to a difficult man with physical and psychological scars that only alcohol placated. Was Sarah as loyal to her husband as she appeared? What kept an intelligent woman with a surly husband doing clandestine work in a remote place? Not to mention the heavy banal work of running a business almost single-handedly? Clement scratched his head as he walked, his other arm clutching the milk and provisions.

Despite knowing that women almost never leave their husbands, even the abusive ones, Sarah Crawford could have, if she had wanted to, left her husband after her training at Whaddon Hall. So why hadn't she? Did that implicate her further? And what of Malcolm McCrea who apparently was politically antagonistic to the Allied cause? Then there was the fisherman Tom Harris. Clement wanted to speak with the man. He drew in a long breath realising just how much he didn't know. Was Tom Harris really a simple fisherman? A fisherman who spent two weeks at a time away, and was close enough to other shipping to read their identifying numbers? Clement lifted his head and stopping, looked across the snow-covered fields and up towards the manse. Wisps of coal smoke were rising from the chimney. The warmth beckoned. But the fires at the home of the elderly Frew sisters were, evidently, not yet lit. 'Tom Harris', he said aloud, trying to concentrate. Was Tom Harris's information concerning the trawler even accurate...?

Johnny had told Clement he was on his own. He felt it.

He knocked at the front door to the manse.

Aidan's raised voice came to him through the closed door. 'Come in, Clement. It's not locked.'

Clement opened the door and walked into the sitting room. Aidan was sitting by the fire, his slippers pushed to one side and a newspaper sprawled across the carpet in disarray. 'Ah! Clement! You have our meagre weekly rations, I see. And the lassies have sent you a sponge cake.'

'You went to visit them?' He thought the old ladies' house must have been freezing without a fire burning.

Aidan's feet reached for the slippers and putting them on, he stood up. 'Paid the rent for another month. Frankly, I don't know what they do with the money. Unless it is baking day, which yesterday was, the house is as cold inside as it is out. I'll make some tea and we can have that cake. Can you bring those things into the kitchen?'

'Certainly.'

Aidan placed one of his fishing magazines neatly onto a shelf and Clement followed him into the kitchen. Through the window Clement could see footprints in the snow.

Aidan reached for the kettle placed it on the stove and lit the gas. 'So you had a good look about? I saw you and Sarah chatting in the graveyard as I returned from the lassies. How do you like our kirk?'

'It is most impressive. Mrs Crawford kindly offered me a lift to the intersection. And while there she showed me around. Despite the weather, there is something almost hypnotic about this place.'

Aidan laughed. 'It's what got me. "Caithness Fever," they call it. And once caught, it's caught for life. Although, I don't go too close to the cliffs. I know it sounds strange, but I really don't like heights. I won't even climb a ladder. Fortunately, Ian McAllister and Robert Wallace take it in turns to do any maintenance at the kirk. They also ring the bells. But I don't suppose they'll be doing that for a while.'

Clement nodded. He didn't think the end of the war would come any time soon either, but an invasion, the only other reason church bells were to be rung, appeared equally unlikely given what Aidan had said about the coastline and the abundance of military personnel in the area.

Aidan opened the bag of provisions and put the items in various cupboards. They sat in the kitchen drinking tea and eating cake. It was warm and he felt the soporific effect of heat for not only was the sitting room fire ablaze, a charcoal brazier burned in the kitchen.

Half an hour later, he could feel his feet tingling from the warmth in the room as it flowed into his numb toes. The cold uninviting day seemed remote from him now.

'Are you too warm, Clement?'

'Not at all! It's wonderful, thank you, Aidan. I am most grateful for it. It was cold out of doors.'

Aidan nodded in the direction of the heater in the corner. 'I installed it to keep my girls warm.'

Clement's bewilderment must have shown.

'The brazier. I ducted it through to the poultry shed. I keep the birds alive and they keep me and the lassies in eggs.'

'An excellent arrangement in view of egg rationing.'

Clement enjoyed the cake. The old ladies made a good Victoria sponge. He wanted to say that it was not as good as Mary's, but he didn't. He looked out the window at the wintry scene. Grey skies had blotted out any blue and the north-westerly wind promised a bitter afternoon. In a treeless place, it is difficult to see the evidence of wind, but he didn't believe it would be long before they heard it.

'It's almost one. What about some lunch, Clement? I wouldn't mind a nap this afternoon.' Aidan took a parcel containing six sausages from the meat safe. 'We can have the sausages now and the eggs for supper or the other way around. Your decision. What do you say?'

'I would probably go for the eggs, thank you, Aidan.'

'Then that is what it shall be.'

Aidan took a shallow pan from a cupboard and cracked the eggs into the skillet.

Clement breathed in the aroma. Bacon would have been nice. But bacon had been one of the first foods to be rationed and he hadn't tasted the wonderful smoked meat since the war came to Britain's skies.

'I thought we could eat in front of the fire. There is a drop-side table in the corner of the sitting room. Could I ask you to set it up for us? Two old clerics together.'

Clement smiled and returned to the sitting room, as Aidan brought in the two plates.

'Would you like to say grace, Clement?'

'For what we are about to receive, may the Lord make us truly thankful.' He lifted his knife and fork just as the doorbell rang. Experience had taught Clement that doorbells only ring at meal times when something bad has happened.

The clock in the rear hall chimed one. Aidan sighed, stood up and went to the front door.

Within seconds he'd returned with a muscular but pale-faced man. 'Clement, this is Ian McAllister. Ian this is Reverend Wisdom.'

'I know. My wife Joyce told me about you.'

Clement held out his hand in greeting to the man who delivered coal to the district twice a week. Physically strong with broad shoulders, Clement assessed McAllister to be in his mid-forties and accustomed to heavy manual work. Ian McAllister's hands remained deep in his pockets. 'Sorry, coal dust.'

'Please don't apologize for honest work, Mr McAllister,' Clement added.

'Aidan, you have to come back with me. Something terrible has happened.'

'What is it, Ian?'

McAllister's anxiety was palpable. 'It's Donald. He's dead.'

# 7

Clement felt his pulse quicken. He swallowed hard, his thoughts racing.

'Where is he?' Aidan asked.

'In the barn. Mind if I sit down a minute, Aidan? I'm not feeling the best.'

'Of course, Ian. I'll pour you some whisky.' Aidan walked towards a cabinet in the corner of the room and emptied the remaining contents of a bottle into a glass.

'Was Mr Crawford ill?' Clement asked.

McAllister perched on the edge of the velvet chair, his face ashen and his large, coal-blackened hands shaking. Reaching for the glass, McAllister threw back the contents in one gulp.

'What happened, Ian?' Aidan asked.

'Billy found him.'

'That would be Billy Wallace, Clement,' Aidan added.

Clement nodded remembering the sullen boy in Sarah's shop.

McAllister placed the whisky glass on a nearby table, the base of the glass hitting the surface twice. 'Aye. Skulking around, as usual, in places he shouldn't be. I always said that boy would come to no good.'

'You think the boy was involved in some way?' Clement put in.

'Who knows!' McAllister fixed his stare on Clement. 'Billy hasn't opened his mouth since. Shock, I suppose.'

Clement pressed the man. 'Have you seen the deceased, Mr McAllister?' Ordinarily, Clement would not have interfered and while he knew Donald Crawford's death was none of his business, McAllister's reaction worried him.

McAllister squeezed his eyes tight. 'Aye. It's a dreadful sight. There's blood everywhere. Donald must have had too much to drink. He shouldn't have been in the loft. He must have lost his balance and fallen backwards, into the window. Billy's as white as a ghost. Vomited at the sight of it. I don't know how the lad got in because Donald always kept that door locked. Either the old fool, for once, forgot to lock it behind him or the boy climbed up the stonework and got in through the hay loft door.' McAllister paused. 'Come to think of it, he probably does it regularly.' McAllister glanced up at Aidan then at the empty glass on the table. 'Anyway, whatever happened, he saw a dreadful thing and once he'd recovered himself, he ran home to tell his mother.

Kathleen, of course, went to investigate the lad's story then she went looking for Sarah. But Sarah was out and Joyce was minding the shop. I had only just got back from my rounds but we knew from Kathleen's expression that something bad had happened. The woman was almost incoherent. So I told her to stay with Joyce and I went to the barn.'

'When was this?' Clement asked.

McAllister checked his watch. 'About forty minutes ago.'

'When did Billy find him, do you know?' Clement urged.

'It's only a guess but I'd say late morning. By the time I checked the barn and found Donald, Sarah had returned.'

'Where is Mrs Crawford now?' Clement asked.

'She's at home. Kathleen Wallace is with her and my Joyce. Although I'm not sure if Kathleen is of much use to Sarah. The woman hardly spoke before. She's as silent as the grave now.'

'How is Joyce coping?' Aidan asked.

'My girl will have them all under control. It's what she's good at.'

'Aidan, I know I am an outsider, but at times like these, people sometimes feel more comfortable with a stranger. With your approval I'd like to come along?'

'Of course, Clement. Have you had any experience with this sort of thing?'

'I have seen my fill of horrific injuries. I was in the last war in France.' Clement wondered how long it would take for that piece of information to be learned by the people of Canisbay.

'We'll come now, Ian,' Aidan said. 'Are you alright to drive?'

McAllister nodded.

Leaving by the front door, McAllister drove them back to Huna.

Sarah was sitting by the fireplace in her sitting room, staring into the low flames, her fingers idly tugging on a loose button on her coat. Beside her was the woman he had seen in the shop previously, Joyce McAllister. She was pouring tea. She exuded competence and although she didn't look at all like his Mary, there was the same practical efficiency that others are drawn to in times of trouble.

On Sarah's other side was Kathleen Wallace, whose face showed the shock of seeing macabre death. He remembered McAllister's words about Kathleen Wallace's lack of usefulness. Whilst Clement had thought the judgement unkind at the time, he could see the paralysed reality on the face of a timid woman. The child, Mary, was on the floor playing with a basket of pegs while Billy was sitting beside his sister, his young face vacant in fright.

Sarah looked up as they entered. Clement had expected to see a sorrowful widow and although he saw her agitation, he didn't see tears.

'You alright, Billy?' The boy looked up as Aidan patted the top of his head.

'Yes,' Billy whispered, then burst into tears.

Sarah stood suddenly. 'I don't know what to do.'

Everyone looked at her, but Clement, who knew she had meant more than the people present understood, spoke first. 'Perhaps, if I may offer a suggestion. Have you called the police?'

All eyes turned to him, but it was Aidan who spoke. 'Why would we do that, Clement? The man has had a terrible accident, that's all.'

'Well, at least a doctor.'

'It's too late for that!' McAllister said, sitting on the chair with the frayed, padded arms.

Clement glanced around the faces. He was the stranger in their midst and he felt their growing indignation, but it was what he saw that troubled him. While there was a rapport of sorts between them, he didn't see the bonds of real affection he would have expected from such a small community. Had it been any other place, he would have left them with their pastor to grieve together. But with his mission now complicated, he needed to know as much as possible about Crawford's death and the people directly involved. He glanced at Sarah. At least she understood why he was there and he hoped the others would take their cue from the widow.

'Mrs Crawford, have you been to the barn?' Clement asked.

'No.'

'We need to remove Donald,' Aidan said. 'From what Ian tells us, it wouldn't be right leaving him there.'

Clement looked at Aidan. 'It would be best to check the barn first. Just to make sure it was an accident.'

A palpable silence gripped the room. The simmering indignation was rapidly turning to resentment. Perhaps even hostility. Clement knew what he'd said sounded accusatory, but he had to know if Crawford's death had been accidental, or something else entirely. He needed to see the barn.

Aidan held his gaze. 'What are you implying, Clement?'

'Nothing at all. But it should be done as a matter of routine.'

'You encountered this in France, too?'

Clement heard the jibe. He knew he had offended these people. It was not his intent. In fact, it went against everything he, as a vicar, believed was the correct thing to do. He glanced at Sarah; the burden of secrecy almost intolerable. 'Not in France, no, but I have, sadly, had to deal with the body of a murdered man.'

'You cannot be serious! Who would kill Donald? Donald wouldn't have hurt a fly!' Joyce exclaimed.

Despite the protestations, from what Clement had been told in the few short hours he had been in Huna, he calculated at least three who would benefit from Donald Crawford's death. Sean, the bus driver, wouldn't be unhappy about the man's demise. Sarah, herself, could also be implicated, individually if not in conjunction with Sean, and McAllister, if Sarah's comment about a long-established feud was accurate, would finally have the use of the barn.

The room remained uncomfortably quiet.

Sarah stood. 'He's right!'

'I expect you have your barn now, Ian McAllister!'

The voice was that of Kathleen Wallace. Clement glanced around the room. The outburst appeared to surprise everyone. The little woman stood staring at her neighbours before tears fell in rivers down the pale cheeks and she sat down again as though defeated. He watched those around him wondering if it was the first time this woman had ever said anything contentious.

72

He also saw something else in the frail woman. As a minister, he had seen it too many times not to recognise the concealed scars of abuse, the suppressed anger that found release in emotional outbursts of an unpredictable nature. He noted that Kathleen Wallace was here with her neighbours, not her husband. Was it only then she felt brave enough to express an opinion? Small communities. He thought back to East Sussex. In his former village, people lived close by; disputes and sorrows were shared, especially so in times of trouble, like the death of one of their number. Kindness was expressed in practical and compassionate ways. He saw little evidence of that for Sarah Crawford.

'How dare you imply my Ian would do such a thing,' Joyce snapped.

'Now settle it down, the both of you,' Aidan interjected. 'You are not helping Sarah with your accusations. Clement, would you mind stepping outside into the yard for a moment?'

Despite feeling like a reprimanded school boy, Clement didn't believe he had said anything untoward. Calling the police would, surely, be routine, even if only to remove the body, but his presence and his advice appeared to have stirred up long held resentments. Remembering Sarah's comments about generational feuds, he followed Aidan into the yard.

'How could you, Clement? You haven't been in the area for more than a day and now you're saying that Donald was murdered!'

'Not quite what I said, Aidan. If Mr Crawford's death is as horrific as others have indicated, then someone should record the details for the Coroner, if not for the police, before the body is touched and before too much time elapses. As I am the stranger here, I am suggesting it should be me.'

Behind them, Clement heard the kitchen door open.

'I agree.' Sarah walked towards them. She was wearing her long coat and knee-high boots. 'But I want to see him first.'

'You don't have to do anything you don't want to,' Aidan said, his blue-green eyes squarely on Clement. 'It is not a good idea, Sarah. If even half of what Ian said is true, the sight will be shocking for you.'

'I know. But I must see him. He was my husband for twenty years. It's my job.'

She didn't wait for a reply. Walking towards the gate, she opened it and strode out of the yard.

Clement glanced at Aidan. 'She seems determined. While we are out of the house, you should call the police.'

'If you think it is absolutely necessary.'

'I do.'

Clement waited until he heard the kitchen door close before running through the gate. Sarah was already twenty yards ahead of him, her coat flapping in the wind. Hurrying, he caught up to her. 'Thank you, Mrs Crawford. Your actions have made it easier for me to see the barn. Are you alright?'

'I just want to see him.'

'I understand, but you have seen Mrs Wallace's reaction. As Aidan said, if what Mr McAllister said is true, it will be something you'll find impossible to eradicate from your memory for many years, if ever.'

Sarah stopped and turned to face him. 'I have to know. Besides, I also have to know about the wireless. And so do you.'

Clement stared at Sarah Crawford's face; at the clenched jaw. He believed she was endeavouring to be stoic by focusing on the practical and he admired her for it. Yet he also knew she would be unprepared for what lay ahead. No one sane can ever be prepared for the sight of macabre death. He saw the pockets in her coat elongate from the force of her clenched fists and he realised it was her way of summoning courage.

They strode westward in silence, towards the barn, the cold quickening their pace. There was no further conversation, but he hoped that she was pleased to have someone with her. Despite their professional relationship, which he knew was tenuous at best, he knew from his time as Chaplain at St Thomas's Hospital that strangers can, in times of great distress, be less judgemental than a friend or relative and he hoped she would understand that his volunteering to go to the barn with her was not solely professional.

The wind blew into his face making his eyes water and his nose drip. As he reached for his handkerchief, he glanced at the woman beside him; Sarah didn't appear to notice the biting wind. Despite the determination of her stride, he wondered if her pace had more to do with ameliorating guilt than desire to see her deceased husband, if, in fact, Donald's death had even the remotest connection to her covert activities.

Ten minutes later, they stood in front of the barn. It was a large, well-maintained, double-storied, stone building with a high-pitched roof and an added single-story annexe on the eastern side. He had passed it last evening while walking to the manse, but then he had paid it scant attention. Above the double-entry doors was a small, closed hayloft door, and while a short beam still extended out over the front of the building, the davit no longer existed. Glancing up, he studied the small opening. It had the appearance of something that hadn't been used in some time.

Ian McAllister's words about the boy, Billy, gaining entry to the barn echoed in his memory. Perhaps with the removal of the davit, no one had checked the door recently. It was certainly not large enough for an adult to gain ready access into the building, but a nimble boy could squeeze through easily enough. Clement scrutinized the building. Other than the main entry, there was no other access into the barn from the road.

Clement reached for the barn door handle. 'Are you ready?'

Sarah took a deep breath, her hands deep in her pockets. Clement pushed the door wide and they stepped inside.

He heard her gasp.

Clement closed his eyes.

A cold wind blew over them from the shattered window opposite.

Donald Crawford's body hung, framed by the window's sill and wooden lintels. He had fallen backwards against the glass, smashing the pane, but his body had not gone through it. Gravity had impaled Crawford on a long pointed fragment of glass some two to three feet in length, piercing the man's torso and protruding grotesquely upwards. His back was arched, his head extended backwards, the mouth wide. Blood had congealed at the corners of his mouth where it had flowed over his chin and onto the window sill below. The deceased's arms were splayed wide, his blood and entrails smeared over the deadly glass dagger.

'Dear Lord!' Clement whispered.

Sarah dropped onto a hay bale by the door, her head forward. She clutched at her stomach, then a second later bent over the side of the bale and vomited into the straw. Several minutes passed before she spoke. 'What could he have wanted so badly that he couldn't have waited for me to return?'

'Go home, Sarah.'

She looked up at him. 'I know they mean well. But I just couldn't stand it. All the fussing. They never liked Donald. And now all they will say is how wonderful he was. Well he wasn't. He was a drunk and bone lazy.' She paused, her gaze staring out into the unknown, unable to focus on anything tangible. He knew that stare. He understood it. He'd seen it in the trenches in the eyes of those who survived more than one day.

'You're in shock. Completely understandable. But you should go home.'

She seemed stuck in time, too early for tears, too late for regrets.

A strong smell of faecal matter wafted over them.

'I hated him,' she blurted. 'After our son died, I died.'

Clement sat beside her and reached for her hand.

She snatched it away, thrusting it deep into her pocket. 'I don't mean to offend. Thank you for your compassion. I'll be alright. You just do what you came to do.'

'If you're sure. But I am still a vicar and I am here for you, Sarah, should you need me.'

She nodded.

He moved away from her. It was probably for the best. He would only be here for a few days at most and grief, as he well knew, takes a longer time to heal than he had to give.

In the icy silence Clement stared at Donald Crawford. His body, silhouetted by fierce daylight, hung, suspended in the centre of the only window in the entire space. As grotesque as it was, there was something almost theatrical about it; like a picture, the corpse framed for maximum effect. What had happened was beyond horrific, but to Clement, the scene screamed unnatural death.

Looking away, Clement's gaze shifted to his left. Four horse stalls occupied the length of the western wall, but no animals were stabled there, the horses, no doubt, having long been replaced by vehicles for delivery of the post. Boxes of every size filled the stalls now. He looked down. Beneath his feet he could see where tyre tracks had compressed the straw on the barn's floor. 'Do you park the lorry here?'

Sarah lifted her head. 'Sometimes. It depends on the weather and if I have to collect things for the shop.'

Clement understood, at least in part, why McAllister felt angst over the barn's usage. It was a large space, surely more useful for storing coal than crates of provisions. Towards the northern side of the building and only a few feet from Donald Crawford's body, a ladder leaned against the edge of the loft floor. Clement lifted his gaze. Some ten to fifteen feet above the stalls and slightly higher than the window where Donald Crawford hung, the loft ran the full width of the barn. But the distance from the edge of the loft to where Donald

Crawford lay suspended worried Clement. He frowned and turning, focused on the small hayloft door that faced the street. If Billy Wallace had used the hatch, he could have entered the barn crossed the loft and descended the ladder. Looking along the edge of the loft, Clement's gaze settled on the hay that had spilled over the edge.

'Do you think you could answer some questions?'

She nodded.

'What is stored in the loft?'

'Nothing. Just hay. We store it for Robert Wallace during winter for his cattle.'

Clement turned, his eye now on a closed door to the left of the main entry. 'And in there?'

'Not much at the moment. There's a bed as well as a table and chair. We rent it to itinerant farm workers around harvest time. The wireless is also there in the wall, behind a timber panel.'

Clement nodded. 'I'm so sorry about this, but I must ask. Do you know if your husband did the schedule this morning?'

Sarah was staring at him, no doubt thinking him uncaring.

'I'll check the book,' she said, standing. 'They'll probably have some request, given last Saturday's fighter attack and what we told them about the trawler Tom saw.'

Clement watched Sarah walk towards the annexe door and open it. He felt wretched about asking her questions at such a time, but he had to know and she knew that. He turned, his gaze roaming over the barn once more before walking towards the ladder. He placed his foot on the first rung. It surprised him that the ladder was not fixed in its position. Steadying it, he climbed up and stood on the edge of the loft. Mountains of hay lay piled up, increasing in height towards the wall. If Wallace used it for winter fodder storage, it stood to reason that no one except Wallace would go up there. So why had Donald Crawford? Sarah's words resounded in his mind.

What could Crawford have wanted so badly that the man couldn't wait for his wife to return? Clement glanced across at the man, the sight and smell of Crawford's mutilated body making him nauseous. Clement looked away, his focus again on the piles of hay and the floor some ten feet below. A pitch fork lay amongst the straw, the tines facing upwards.

Had Wallace come to the barn while Crawford had been attending to the schedule? Had they fought over something in the loft that had resulted in Crawford falling backwards? Clement looked again at the hay that lay around the loft. It didn't appear to be unduly disturbed. His gaze returned to the implement on the floor below. No one would deliberately leave a pitch fork on the floor in such a manner. Therefore, Donald Crawford had been using the fork when he fell. Clement stared at the tool, a frown forming on his brow. Was that what he was meant to think?

He turned again and looked at the distances. How had Donald Crawford fallen into the window some four feet away from the edge of the loft? Surely if he had been clutching the implement at the time of his fall, his body would be on the floor alongside the fork? Perhaps Crawford had been trying to evade the pitch fork, and after falling, his attacker had thrown it to the floor? Clement heard a door close. Sarah was staring up at him, her face whiter than before.

'What is it?'

'The wireless. It's not there.'

# 8

Sarah stood in the middle of the barn, the pockets of her coat elongated. He hurried down the ladder. A bitter wind blew in through the broken window, the pungent smell of death and something he couldn't name whirling around them. 'You should sit down again.'

She walked over to the hay bale and slumped onto it, her head bent over her knees.

'When you're ready, can I ask another question?'

She nodded.

'Was your husband right handed or left?'

'Right. Why do you ask?'

He spoke calmly and slowly, aware she was still in shock. 'The pitchfork on the floor. It could only land there if he was holding it in his left hand when he fell.'

Sarah looked up, her vacant gaze falling on the pitchfork; her hands were shaking. 'I think I'm going to be sick again.'

'Perfectly understandable.' He sat beside her and placed his hand over hers again and waited while she retched the final contents from her stomach. This time she did not remove her hand.

A few minutes later she reached for her handkerchief and mopped her mouth. 'You don't believe it was an accident, do you?'

'No.' He paused. 'I'm really sorry about this, but I need to know if your husband did the schedule. Did you keep a transmission record?'

She nodded. 'Of course. But the book isn't there either and without it it's impossible to know. The Y-station would, but you need a pass to get in there which I don't have.'

'Where was this book kept?'

'With the wireless, behind the wall panel.'

He turned and stared again at Donald Crawford. Why had the killer displayed Donald Crawford in such a manner? Was the gruesome spectacle solely to disguise the theft of the wireless? But how did the killer even know it existed, and moreover, where to find it? So many questions.

Return to the facts, he told himself studying the scene. Clement wasn't sure what he was looking for, but he knew from experience that the answers lay in the detail. He'd learned that from Chief Inspector Morris of Lewes Police. Somewhere, he hoped, the killer had left a trace of himself. Clement took a note book from his pocket and turned to face Sarah. 'Who had access to the barn?'

'Just us.'

'Was it locked?'

'Always. Donald didn't trust anyone with a key. Not with all the boxes in here. And Robert Wallace had to ask if he wanted access. That always led to an argument.'

'And the wireless?'

'Donald didn't care about it. He complained when I asked him to do the schedules.'

'Why?'

'Because *he* was the Signals Operator. In his opinion, it should always have been his responsibility, not mine. He resented it. And he resented me for it.'

'He was jealous of your work?'

'Yes.' Sarah took a deep breath and sat up straight, her eyes avoiding the man she had known for twenty years. 'But we both knew he couldn't have done it anyway.'

'Sorry?'

'Despite Donald's experience, he's an alcoholic…was an alcoholic. And alcoholics are not reliable, nor do they have steady hands. I told you that this person, whoever they are, could only differentiate between Donald and me if they were good. That isn't true. Our signature touch would be as different as chalk and cheese.'

Clement stared at the woman. 'Sarah, if that is the case, then your position here is no longer safe. Is there anywhere you could go for a few days? Friends? Family?'

Sarah shook her head. 'If I leave now, then whoever killed Donald will know we are onto him. In any case, no one else knows about the wireless, and they will wonder why I have gone. I have to stay; even if only to arrange his funeral. My safety lies in doing everything the same and responding as normally as possible.'

While he acknowledged that there was some truth to what she'd said, he didn't like it. The situation was dangerous, especially for her. He looked at her, wondering if she was capable of making such an important decision, given what had just happened. But time was not on his side. 'Very well. But be ready to leave with little notice. Pack some clothes into a small bag. Not a suitcase and please, wear something different to your most distinctive long coat and red cap. Don't go anywhere on your own or with only one other person.'

'I have work to do here.'

'Sarah, you are in real danger. Do you value your job more than your life? Because that is what it amounts to.'

She stared at him.

'I apologize for sounding harsh but someone in this vicinity is not only a traitor but also a murderer. You and I both know this, even if others do not. Don't be alone for a second, and sleep at the McAllisters' until this man is caught.'

At last she seemed to hear him. He saw her hand go to her head, her fingers grasping the red tam. Hair fell from under the cap. It was the first time he had seen any real emotion, but it wasn't grief.

'Is there anything in the barn, no matter how small, that isn't as it should be?'

'Other than a dead man in the window?'

'Sorry, but I have to ask.'

'I know.' She stood and turned around as if seeing the barn for the first time, her fingers all the while playing with the loose button on her coat. 'Not that I can see.'

'Is there another way into the barn?'

'Only the old hayloft door, but it hasn't been used in years. Besides, it's not big enough for a thief to enter.'

'What about a child?'

'You mean Billy?'

'Yes.'

'Billy may taunt midges but that's all. Besides, Donald could lift Billy with one hand.'

'I didn't mean Billy killed your husband, but he may have witnessed something or someone.'

'We must tell Kathleen.'

'That would be unwise and cause unnecessary alarm.' Clement paused, his mind on the likely sequence of events. 'It is unlikely that Billy saw anything.'

'How can you be so sure?'

'If Billy had witnessed something and the killer knew it...'

'I think I'm going to faint.' Sarah sat heavily onto the hay bale, her head forward over her knees.

'I was going to add, that he would certainly have told his mother who would have told everyone and, no doubt, telephoned for the police while in your sitting room.'

'Of course.'

He could see the relief on her face, and he noticed something else; the ever-present, mildly annoyed countenance that he had seen since his arrival, and which he had assumed was permanent, had vanished. It was as though some barrier between them had been breached. He had felt it before, when one human being connects with another and whilst he couldn't actually name it, he knew without question what it wasn't. No one would ever replace Mary.

She looked up at him. 'Thank you for your understanding, but if you really want to help us...me...just do what you came to do, and find out who did this.'

Clement nodded and wandered over to the large entry doors, allowing the widow time and space. He scrutinized every surface and edge but nothing appeared disturbed. Did the lack of any forced entry mean that Donald Crawford knew his attacker? Clement turned and stared again at the scene. Chilly silence was what he saw and felt. There was something not just macabre about it; it was contrived. A manufactured horror. Why? The question haunted. 'We should go back. You need to be with your friends now.' He paused. 'You asked me to do what I came to do, and I will, but while I know I am here as Major Wisdom, I am still Reverend Wisdom. I cannot, nor would I want to, stand between you and your minister but, I am here for you should you need me.'

'Thank you. I just want to get back to work. Perhaps it would be best if you didn't come back with me. They'll see your presence as an intrusion, especially after what you said.'

'As you wish. Would you tell Aidan, then, that I will see him back at the manse?'

She nodded.

Her glance shifted to her dead husband one last time before she turned and walked through the barn doors.

Clement drew his coat higher about his neck as the wind blew into the barn from the shattered window. He pondered what reception Sarah would receive on her return. He knew he had offended the villagers and their pastor by suggesting that the death may not be straight forward, but it could not be helped. They did not know what he and Sarah knew. Neither could they be informed. Although it appeared likely that the traitor and the murderer were one and the same, there was no proof. Neither was there absolute proof that Donald Crawford had, in fact, been murdered. Clement leaned on the door frame to the little room. As grotesque as the sight was, he stared at Donald Crawford.

Fact; Donald Crawford had died between half past ten and midday. That exonerated Sarah as she had been with him or doing deliveries. He shook his head. That wasn't quite true. She had left him before eleven to finish the deliveries. Could she have doubled back after she had seen him enter the manse? It was possible. He knew one could see the kirk and the graveyard from the manse, Aidan had said as much. So it was also possible for Sarah to have watched him enter it then make her way to the barn. He ran the idea around his head. Whilst it was feasible, he believed it unlikely. Her reaction to her dead husband had been genuine and unrehearsed.

Clement tried to imagine the sequence of events. If Donald Crawford had been attending to the schedule at the time the attacker entered the barn, the killer would have heard it and known that the wireless was in the annexe. That meant the main doors had to be un-locked, something Sarah said never happened. Yet the barn had been unlocked when he and Sarah first en-tered it. Moreover, it had to have been unlocked for Kathleen Wallace to gain entry. So had Crawford just forgotten to lock it behind him as McAllister had spec-ulated at the manse?

Clement walked into the annexe, his gaze scanning the small space as a cold blast blew through the broken window. Unlike the unpleasant odour in the barn, the little room smelt fresh. He sniffed the cold air. Such a small room, unused and closed for most of the time would surely smell of damp? He stared at a single cast iron bed in the corner, the only furniture in the room other than the table and chair in front of the wall panel where the wireless had been secreted. He stared at the bed. The mattress, covered in the familiar ticking fab-ric, was folded back in half and a pillow sat on top of it. A coarse-weave blanket was folded over the metal rail at the foot of the bed. Just as Sarah had said, nothing in the room appeared to have been used for some time.

He turned and stared at the table and chair where he imagined the daily transmissions took place. But other than the missing wireless, everything looked as it should. Neat. Orderly. Unused. Unnatural. He pon-dered again whether Crawford had been accompanied into the barn. But if that was so, he would not have at-tended to the schedule and the wireless would still be secreted in the wall. However, if he had been interrupt-ed during the scheduled broadcast by someone entering the room unexpectedly, surely he would have reacted? There would be some evidence of a struggle. Crawford would, presumably have stood, the chair pushed away from the table. It could even have been overturned and the wireless would be on the table with the headset still attached and the wooden panel open. Clement pressed the timber slats until he found the loose one. Removing the panel, he studied the small space, but it was empty. Replacing the timber slat, he looked around the floor. A small pencil sat under the bed amongst the dirt. Lifting it between his index finger and thumb, he saw that it left no outline in the dust. Nor was there any dust on the pencil. Turning it over in his fingers, he returned it to where it had landed when the killer had discarded it.

Leaving the room, Clement walked back into the barn and stared at the pitchfork. If the right-handed Donald Crawford had been holding the implement at the time of his fall, it would either be outside lying in the snow or directly beneath him. Not on the floor in the middle of the barn. Clement ran his gaze along the shaft of the tool then the tines. No blood. Nothing to indicate that Donald had either been holding the fork or threatened with it at the time of his death.

Clement looked up at the deceased. Why had Crawford gone up to the loft and not waited for his wife? Unless he had been forced to? And the pitchfork had been added to make it appear accidental. Clement's gaze shifted back to the loft. Or had Donald been killed in the small annex and carried up to the loft? If that was so, then that fact alone exonerated Sarah who would never be able to lift her deceased husband, much less carry him up a ladder and throw him into the window. Such an act would require much force and great strength. He needed to know if Donald had sustained any other injuries which would indicate that death had taken place elsewhere.

Clement reached for the loft ladder and leant it against the wall beside the broken window and climbed up, the body inches from him. Even though more than two hours had passed since the man's death, Clement could smell the whisky. His gaze focused on the deep blue-purple colouring around the deceased's upper lip and cheeks. Diminished oxygen, Clement knew, caused the lips to turn a purplish blue. But it was not just the lips. Placing his forefinger and thumb on Crawford's cheek, Clement turned the face towards him. Discolouration and a mild degree of swelling extended over the forehead and cheek bones. Clement looked at the man's hands and fingers. They were covered in rivulets of congealed blood, but there was no sign of broken skin or grazing about the knuckles to indicate a struggle for life with his assailant. There were no bullet wounds, no knife wounds, neither was there any kind of blunt trauma injury about the man's body that would have caused death prior to the fall. Clement leaned closer to the man's face. Why, if Crawford had fallen backwards, was his face bruised and swollen?

Clement returned the ladder to where he had found it, and closing the barn door, walked back along the road towards the kirk. He needed to think. He no longer saw the beauty of the coastline, such was his concentration. He believed Donald Crawford had been asphyxiated, the purple-blue bruising around the mouth and nose suggested it. He had learned the technique in the unarmed combat lessons at Coleshill. The victim was approached from behind. The move usually preceded a dagger to the throat, but in this instance the murderer had not required the final assault. Why? Had Donald Crawford been completely oblivious to his attacker and, once killed, simply slumped forward over the desk? The bruising suggested it. But why had the killer moved him? Donald Crawford was not a small man. Clement began to visualize the murderer; fit and muscular with strong, capable hands and most probably not much older than forty-five.

At the intersection, Clement left the road. Walking past some headstones, he headed straight towards the large kirk door. Despite the head-wind, the walk from the barn had taken only twenty minutes. He hadn't passed anyone, either on foot or in a vehicle. He now knew that was not unusual. People didn't just stroll about in Caithness in winter. Provisions were delivered and other than a visit to *The Bell*, there was no reason for anyone to be walking along the road. Except Donald Crawford. He had walked from the shop to the barn to attend to the radio schedule. Even that was unusual. Sarah routinely did the schedules to coincide with the daily deliveries. Her lorry parked outside the barn or even driving into it would raise few eyebrows…but Clement's arrival in Caithness had changed the routine.

The kirk door swung open. No one was inside. Walking to the first pew, he knelt to pray. The cold bore into his flesh. He had been in Caithness only one day and already his mission had become complicated. In addition to the appalling death of Donald Crawford, the wireless and book had disappeared. Clement stared at the whitewashed walls, his mind searching for answers, but answers required at least some information. As a stranger, especially one who had arrived only yesterday, he felt he was in a whirlpool of ignorance and uncertainty. As was often the case when he was alone, his mind dwelt on Biblical verses; he found they gave him clarity of mind, as if the Lord was giving him guidance with his problem.

The cover name Johnny had assigned to him drifted into his thoughts. *Hope.* "'For we are saved by hope,'" Clement quoted, "'but hope that is seen is not hope: for what a man seeth, why doth he yet hope for?'". Leaning back in the pew, Clement closed his eyes. "'For what a man seeth…'" The words reverberated around his mind. What had Donald Crawford seen? Had Crawford seen his killer or learned something that exposed this man? Perhaps something that needed to be passed on? Was he killed only to prevent the radio transmission? Had Crawford even attended to the radio schedule before his killer struck? Somehow, Clement had to speak with Johnny.

An hour later, Clement left the kirk and walked towards the manse, visualizing the roaring fire in the sitting room. He hastened his step. Looking over the meadows, he could see late afternoon descending. The pastures had taken on a colourless greyish-white and the hedges that criss-crossed them now seemed like black ribbons over the fields. The smoke still issued from the chimneys at *The Bell*, but the grey car was no longer parked at the front. He checked his watch. It was only four o'clock, but the land would be in total darkness within two hours.

Rain began to fall. It seemed to come directly at him like horizontal daggers. Clement huddled into his greatcoat as the rain turned to sleet, his mind again on Donald Crawford. He didn't doubt he'd been murdered. A man with strong arms and capable hands had killed Crawford then carried him up the ladder and thrown him into the window.

Clement looked up, his gaze shifting from one rooftop to the next. Did one of these dwellings harbour a traitor? In the diminishing light of the bleak afternoon, Clement felt the killer's existence like a sinister shadow. But the proximity of this man did not mean he was a local. In fact, now that the wireless was gone and Crawford had been killed, Clement doubted the murderer would remain in the vicinity. He wriggled his toes, the scabbard of his commando knife digging into his ankle.

As Clement pushed open the gate to the manse, the beginning of a plan was forming in his mind. Either he could remain in Canisbay and wait for the police to arrive, or he could walk to Thurso and make contact with Johnny through Inspector Stratton. He hoped Aidan was at home, he needed to know when the police were expected.

Clement knocked and entered the unlocked house, but it was eerily quiet. 'Aidan?' he called, to no response. Walking into the sitting room, Clement prodded the dwindling fire, the flames leaping from the warm coals and he sat before it warming his legs and feet. Pulling his note book from his top pocket, he began to compile a list of all the men in the area he knew about. Malcolm and Stewart McCrea were on the top of the list, as was the informative Tom Harris. As farmers and fishermen, they would be fit and strong. Then there was Robert Wallace, a man Clement had not yet met and who did maintenance work at the kirk. Wallace had a reason for frequenting Crawford's barn. Moreover, if the man's wife was any indication, Wallace had a temper. Clement pondered the only other local men he knew about. Ian McAllister, who despite his evident strength, had an alibi as he was doing deliveries, and Sean Mead whose bus was apparently not in the region at the time. But whilst their alibis were strong, Clement couldn't be sure. He added their names to the list and scribbled a question mark beside each.

Half an hour later he heard the kitchen door open. Aidan came into the sitting room and slumped into the chair.

'Ian and I have lifted him down. Couldn't leave the man like that.'

Clement nodded. 'What did Thurso Police say?'

'In fact, it was the police who told us to take his body down and wrap him in a blanket. We put him on the bed in the annexe now that it is snowing. Ian will board up the window. The Inspector said they can't get here till Friday.'

'Not before?'

Aidan shrugged. 'Investigating some burglary, apparently.'

'Is Mrs Crawford alone?'

Aidan shook his head. 'No. Joyce McAllister seems to have taken charge of the widow. I'll check on Sarah again tomorrow. The funeral will be on Sunday, after morning service.'

Clement stared into the glowing embers. He was glad to hear that a woman was with Sarah, but the news that the police were not due for two days meant a long walk into Thurso. 'If there is anything I can do to help?' he asked, hoping there wasn't. 'I thought it best to leave you with your parishioners to grieve. Especially in view of what I said.'

'Thank you. You certainly put the cat amongst the pigeons, Clement. I thought we were going to have our own war there at one stage.' Aidan paused. 'Actually, they were pretty incensed about your remarks. With reflection, perhaps it would be best if you took Tom Harris's boat to Orkney tomorrow. It's a local matter and in places as small as Huna, it is important to respect their privacy.'

'Of course. If you think it best. Do you know where I can find Tom Harris?'

'His boat will be in Gills Bay, but given the weather, he will probably be at *The Bell* now.'

Clement glanced at Aidan from the corner of his eye. While he did not feel hostility, he did perceive that there wasn't the same warmth and bonhomie he had shared with his fellow cleric on the previous evening. 'Perhaps I will go now, before it gets too cold.'

'A good idea, Clement.'

He walked into the front hall and reached for his coat and hat. As he opened the door, a flurry of snow blew into the house. Hurrying, he closed the door and wrapping his coat around his body, started to walk up the road towards the village of Canisbay and *The Bell*.

A lorry was parked at the side of the building and several bicycles were leaning against the brick columns that formed the porch of the inn. Clement pushed open the door. A stale warmth greeted him as all conversation stopped. In the bar were four men and a prodigious woman with a broad face who he guessed was the publican, Jean Buchanan.

'You must be the visiting vicar, Reverend Wisdom.'

Clement smiled and nodded at the woman.

'The *Wise Man from the South!*'

It was a voice Clement didn't recognize.

'Never mind him, Reverend Wisdom. He's a heathen, so he is,' a familiar voice added. Sean Mead stuck his head around the booth and smiled at him.

Clement smiled back, but it surprised him to see the Irishman, whose bus wasn't parked outside. Sean was definitely back on his list.

'How are you Sean? I was wondering, is Tom Harris in tonight?'

'I'm Tom Harris.'

The fisherman was a short, muscular man of about thirty-something with dark hair, large calloused hands and a two-week-old beard.

'Can I buy you a drink? Allow me to buy the next round for everyone.' Clement said.

'I'll have a whisky,' a chorus of voices responded.

He smiled. 'Do you have any whisky, Mrs Buchanan?'

'Well, I might have some put aside for a birth. Or a death.'

'Small places, Vicar,' Sean said.

'Yes. A tragic and dreadful accident.' Clement stared at the faces. Looks were being exchanged.

'We hear you think it was murder?'

'Introduce yourself first, so the vicar knows who he's talking to,' Sean chastised.

'Malcolm McCrea.'

McCrea was about twenty, well-built with thick red hair, pale blue eyes and a surly expression. An identical boy beside him spoke next. 'Stewart McCrea.'

'Robert Wallace,' the oldest man among them said. It had been Wallace who had labelled him the *Wise Man from the South*. Clement stared at the face; a mature, more robust version of the adolescent Billy stared back at him. Wallace was sitting alone at a table by the window, the glass in his hand almost empty, but the man's grip on the glass was tight. Firm enough for the knuckles to be turning white. Clement stared at those fingers. Across the man's knuckles were grazes and Clement could see the power in that fist.

'And this is Danny O'Reilly,' Sean was saying, indicating a dark haired, black-eyed youth sitting beside him.

A door opened into the bar from behind the counter and Ian McAllister walked in. McAllister was wearing a long oil skin coat that was covered in black dust. Their eyes met, McAllister doing little to disguise his contempt.

Jean Buchanan poured a drink and left it on the counter. Without speaking, McAllister drunk the liquor down and left the bar by the front door.

Clement sat at a table by the door. 'I was wondering if I could speak with you, Mr Harris, about a passage to St Margaret's Hope?' Harris and a small Jack Russell dog joined him at the table a little away from the others.

'I had a Jack Russell when I was a boy. What's his name?' Clement asked patting the dog's head.

'Flip. He appears to like you, Vicar. He doesn't usually take to strangers.'

'Your good health,' Clement said, raising his glass to the room. 'And to you, Flip.'

Tom sat down, the dog at his feet, and the conversation in the room recommenced.

'When, Vicar?'

'Tonight.'

'How many passengers?'

'Just the one. Where is your boat?'

'In Gills Bay, tied up at the jetty.'

'When could we leave?'

'It won't be till late. There is almost no moon and the tide is low. Next high tide is around two. Make it three o'clock at the jetty.'

'You can't make it any earlier?'

Harris shook his head. 'The tide runs fast around Stroma Island. A sea-going boat makes little headway on an incoming tide. Besides, Pentland Firth is littered with ship wrecks and I have no intention of being the next one.'

'Very well. How much?'

'Ten shillings.'

'Two weeks' wages for some!'

'Five shillings then. But only because Flip likes you. Pentland Firth is not for the faint-hearted, Vicar, especially at night.'

'Agreed.' Clement stood. He knew the crossing would be dangerous in the dark, but Flip's acceptance of him aside, Clement still believed Tom Harris was taking advantage of him. He would pay because there was no alternative, something the fisherman knew all too well.

Clement left them to talk about him and stepped outside, the cold wind hitting his chest and face. Ian McAllister's coal delivery lorry had gone, but Clement could hear the gears as McAllister drove away through Canisbay village, turning left onto the inland road.

As Clement walked back through the snow to the manse he went through the faces of the men he had just met. The McCrea boys were fit, strong, young men.

Identical twins made for an interesting situation. No doubt the locals could tell them apart, but that required years of familiarity. It had surprised Clement to see McAllister. It was likely that Donald Crawford's death had delayed the coal deliveries to the vicinity. McAllister had been in the public bar for no more than a few seconds, but the large man managed to come and go without drawing much attention. And McAllister was strong. Clement thought back on the body of Donald Crawford. There had been no evidence of coal dust on the man's clothing, but perhaps McAllister wasn't wearing the all-encompassing coat at the time. The barn was the closest building to McAllister's garage, so the man would have to pass it even before the first delivery. Sean Mead also moved around the district easily enough, with or without his bus. And Clement had no idea about Sean's young friend.

It was Robert Wallace who worried him most. From Clement's experience men whose quick temper resulted in sarcasm and brawling usually had something to hide. Clement stared at his feet as he often did when walking. Small places. And small places close ranks. Especially from a *Wise Man from the South*.

# 9

Thursday 27th February

Lifting the blankets, Clement switched on his torch and checked the time. It was just after one o'clock. He slipped out of bed and dressed quickly. Going to the window, he pushed the curtain aside and stared into the rear garden. With almost no moonlight, darkness engulfed the scene. It would make for slow progress but at least he now had some familiarity with the terrain. His gaze lifted and settled on the thinnest slice of moon that flickered behind invisible clouds.

Clement let the curtain fall. He reached for his knife and secured it as usual to his left calf, then inserted the long barrel of his pistol into the holster on the left side of his vest. He then placed four magazines of ammunition into his webbing and pulled on his over-shirt, jacket and greatcoat. Collecting his boots and pack, he tiptoed across the room and opened his bedroom door. All was quiet. He'd said good bye to Aidan the previous evening. He glanced back at the room. Nothing of his remained.

Descending to the ground floor, he crossed the sitting room. A few coals in the grate from last night's fire were still alight, their low orange glow stark in the dark room. He closed the door to the front hall and put on his boots. Standing by the door, he stopped to listen. Nothing stirred either outside or in and Aidan had not woken. Opening the front door, Clement let himself out.

Wrapping his scarf around his face, he pulled his hat down hard against the biting wind and walked across the garden to the road, his breath condensing, his footprints leaving long stride marks in the snow. Where Aidan's front garden met the roadway, Clement turned and staying behind a hedge, cut back across the fields heading east towards Huna.

Twenty minutes later he stood beside the red telephone box, studying his surroundings. Nothing but the wind moved in the bitter early hours of morning. Before going to Tom's boat, he wanted to speak with Johnny and the only place he could do that was in Crawford's sitting room. He crossed the road and lifted the latch on the gate to the rear yard. Once inside, he scanned the space. Crawford's lorry sat parked in the centre. Passing it, he hurried towards the kitchen door and turned the handle. The house was unlocked. Frowning, he stepped inside. In the next room a clock ticked loudly. Checking the black-out curtains, he made his way to the telephone exchange. Within minutes his eyes had grown accustomed to the darkened room. Sitting in the worn chair, he flicked on his torch and studied the switch board, but of all the skills he had learned at Coleshill, switch board operation hadn't been one of them. He stared at the scramble of cables in front of him.

He swivelled in the chair, his ears straining. If Sarah had not obeyed his instructions to keep the door locked, she may not have moved into the McAllister's house either. He couldn't hear anything but he needed to know. Holding his hand over the beam of light, he made his way through the house and along a hallway that he guessed led to the bedrooms. Sarah Crawford was in the end room. He could see her lying asleep on her side, her hair loose and falling over the pillow. The sight of her made him feel uncomfortable. He was the intruder, and he hoped if she awoke suddenly she wouldn't scream. He switched off the torch and crept towards the bed. Placing his hand over her mouth, he wakened her.

Sarah's reaction was immediate; instantly awake, eyes wide and confused, fear so starkly evident, even in the darkness.

'It's only me,' Clement whispered.

He saw the woman's expression change from fright to contempt. He removed his hand from her mouth and she sat up, pulling the bed covers over her shoulders.

'I hope you have a good explanation for this intrusion?'

'Get up quickly and dress warmly. We don't have much time.'

'What's happened?'

'You're leaving. It's too dangerous for you to stay here.'

'I'm not!'

'I am insisting. Is there anyone else in the house?'

'No.'

He frowned. Whilst her being at home had made her departure from Huna easier, he was annoyed that she had not followed any of his instructions. 'Before we go, I need you to get me a London telephone number. I'll pass on what we know while you dress.'

Sarah reached for a shawl and wrapped it around her shoulders. 'Why the change of plan?'

'Because I cannot stay in Canisbay or Huna to watch your back.'

Sarah Crawford stared at him. 'And what makes you think I need you to protect me?'

He felt frustration rise in him. 'Isn't the manner of your husband's death enough for you? He was not just killed, he was brutally murdered. If the killer knows both you and your husband attended the schedules, how long do you think it will be before he strikes again?'

'All the more reason for me to stay! To show him that I am not intimidated.'

The woman's response amazed him. 'What frightens you, Sarah?'

She paused. 'Donald would have died instantly. He wouldn't have known anything about it.'

Clement shook his head. 'While I believe Donald's killer first asphyxiated him in the annexe, then threw his body into the window, I cannot be completely sure.

What if he was only rendered unconscious before being thrown...'

Clement saw her eyes widen. 'You don't really believe that, do you?'

'As I said, it cannot be ruled out.'

Sarah sat at the small exchange. Her hands shook as she placed the headphones over her ears. 'What's the number?'

He waited while she connected the call.

'Hold the line,' she said then standing passed the headset to him.

'Captain Winthorpe, please,' he said as he sat in the worn chair.

Sarah left the sitting room. He heard her footsteps disappear along the corridor.

'The Captain is not available.'

He thought for a moment. 'Nora Ballantyne?'

'One moment.'

The line crackled. Minutes passed.

'Hello?' a sleepy voice finally said.

'Miss Ballantyne, this is Clement Wisdom. I need to speak with Johnny.'

'I'm afraid you've just missed him, Major.'

'Do you know where he is?'

There was a pause. 'Island holiday. With old friends.'

Clement stared at the frayed sitting room carpet. Johnny had said he was going north, to the Faroe Islands and Norway, and thanks to Nora, he now knew it was with the Royal Navy. That could only mean Johnny was in Orkney.

'Thank you,' he replied.

The line went dead. The information could not wait. With Johnny in Scapa Flow, Clement decided against Thurso. Tom Harris could take them both to St Margaret's Hope.

Sarah entered the sitting room carrying a small bag and clutching her red tam o'shanter.

He looked up at her. 'Do you have another cap? One less recognisable than red plaid?'

'No. Besides, it's really warm. And it's dark outside. Who's going to see it?'

Clement nodded but he didn't like it.

'Where are you taking me?'

'St Margaret's Hope.'

'At this hour?'

'It's important you leave here. Besides, if you are going to do this sort of work, you'd better get used to odd hours.'

'I'm a Wireless Operator, not Mata Hari!'

Clement blinked. Never in his life had he spoken so abruptly to a woman. He felt badly about it, especially in light of what Sarah had been through in the last twenty-four hours. But right now, he didn't have the time to discuss it. 'Either way, you are leaving now and Tom Harris is expecting us at three o'clock.'

He saw her gaze around the room as though seeing it for the last time. Perhaps she was reminiscing, but her composure surprised him. He had expected greater resistance. Did she believe she would never return to the shop in Huna? Was that her intention; an opportunity to escape? Huna had, quite possibly, not been the happiest episode of her life. He glanced at the small bag in the woman's hand. Life. Could all she cared about be bundled up into so small a space?

Clement knew it could.

He watched Sarah from the corner of his eye as the woman pulled on her long overcoat and slipped her feet into a pair of boots by the back door. No tears fell from Sarah Crawford's eyes as she closed the door. In fact, she showed no emotion of any kind. He saw her turn the lock.

'Is it your habit to lock the door when you leave?'

'Why?'

'Everything must appear as if you could soon be back.'

Clement watched her thick, strong wrists as she unlocked the door. Perhaps, he thought, she did not realise the detail required for even the smallest deception. Anything out of the ordinary could arouse suspicion.

He felt the frown cross his forehead. He had watched Sarah turn a key but in his mind's eye he saw the pencil under the bed in the annexe. It occupied his thoughts as he followed Sarah into the yard. Had the pencil been deliberately left under the bed? If so, then the killer, whoever he was, was no ordinary collaborator. But for what purpose? He audibly gasped as it struck him. Clement felt the detached, calculating presence of an assassin; a well-trained enemy plant who knew exactly what he was doing. He thanked God that he had left the pencil in the dust. Had he taken it, the killer would know that someone not only suspected that Donald Crawford's death was murder, but also knew what had been hidden in the walls of the annexe. Moreover, leaving the pencil under the bed also told Clement that the murderer was watching and waiting. Clement felt a shudder run down his spine, the killer's proximity like breath on his cheek.

'What's wrong?'

Her voice jolted him back to the present.

'Nothing for you to worry about,' he said but he felt a sinister presence wrapping silently around him.

'There are two bicycles in our shed. It's easier than walking in this weather. We can leave them in the fisherman's shed on the jetty.'

'Who uses the shed?'

'No one much. Tom uses it sometimes to store his fishing nets.'

They crossed the yard to an out-building on the far side. Neither of them spoke. Opening the door, Clement wheeled the bicycles into the yard and checked the tyres. Swinging his pack onto his shoulders, he waited while Sarah placed her small bag into the handle basket and together they walked in silence towards the gate to the street.

The wind had increased and it was snowing again as Clement closed the gate to Crawford's yard. But even though he knew they were heading west into the inclement conditions, it wasn't the weather that worried him. He checked the street in all directions, his senses on high alert. Opposite was the red telephone box. He stared at it but no one was there. Swinging his leg over Donald Crawford's bicycle, Clement pedalled into the strengthening wind. Sarah was already ahead of him. He pushed hard, making up the distance until she was only slightly in front of him. He thought her pace was becoming faster. Perhaps it was the weather, but he sensed that now she couldn't wait to leave.

Ten minutes later they passed the closed and locked barn. He noted she did not glance at the building this time. Sarah Crawford. Was there no one in this woman's life she regretted leaving? If there had been ru-mours about her and Sean Mead, had he only ever rep-resented escape from her life of bitter resentment, and nothing more? Sarah Crawford was not like any woman Clement had ever met. She appeared to be totally inde-pendent, reliant on no one. Yet, in the barn, he had glimpsed a tender side to her; a side, he surmised, not much seen. Her shaking hands when she had connect-ed the telephone call also belied her air of stoic indif-ference. Perhaps it said more about Donald Crawford than it did about his widow.

They pedalled on in silence. Off to his right was Wallace's farm, but only the black outline of the farm roof and some out-buildings were discernible against the starry night. Fifteen minutes later they passed the kirk. Ten minutes after that they descended the hill to-wards Gills Bay.

Despite his heightened nerves, there was no warn-ing.

The face came out of the night.

Only the downward deflected bicycle lamp coming towards them gave any indication that anyone else was on the road. Then just as suddenly, the rider was gone, disappearing into the gloom like an apparition that melded into the night, as though imagined.

'Sarah?' came back from the cyclist.

'Don't answer. Keep going!' he whispered but Clement's pulse was racing. The sudden encounter con-firmed their complete vulnerability.

The sight of someone on a bicycle pedalling east and on the road at that hour alarmed him. He thought it was one of the McCrea boys but he couldn't be sure. There was no time to investigate it now. He needed to get Sarah away. He looked up. Ahead, Tom Harris's boat was tied up at the long stone jetty, a lit, shaded lamp tied to the mast.

Clement glanced back along the road. 'Did you recognise the person on the bicycle?'

She nodded. 'Malcolm McCrea.'

'You're sure? It couldn't have been his brother, Stewart?'

'I saw his coat and hat. It was Malcolm. He saw me and possibly you.'

In Clement's mind it wasn't conclusive proof but, perhaps it no longer mattered. He stared back into the gloom. 'McCrea may not have recognised either of us. He called out your name, but it was said as a question. It could be that he only saw your red cap and made the same assumption you did. Regardless, there isn't much we can do about it now.' They rode down the hill. Off to his left was the shed and in front was the long stone jetty. Clement swung his leg over the bike and walking it along the jetty a few yards, lifted it, dropping it into the dark waters of Gill's Bay.

'What are you doing?'

'The bicycles should be disposed of permanently.'

'But I need them.'

'Not if you're dead, you won't.'

Sarah held his gaze for a few seconds before sliding off her bicycle. He knew what he'd said was harsh, but there was no time for discussion. Without waiting for further objections, he lifted her bicycle and dropped it into the black sea. 'Can you think of any reason why either McCrea would be on the road at this hour?'

She shook her head. 'Doesn't look good, does it?'

'I think that is an understatement. If the traitor is Malcolm McCrea, you don't have a moment to lose.'

She was looking at him, her eyes wide. 'Traitor? You think Malcolm was on his way to kill me?'

'I think the killer is close by and is intent on removing anyone who could identify him.'

'I don't know who he is!'

'He doesn't know that. But he does know that someone, most probably you, also operated the wireless.'

Sarah stared out into the night.

He could see the fear on her face. 'When we get to St Margaret's Hope, stay there. I will pass on your location to Special Duties Branch.'

A burst of fast-moving air skimmed his cheek.

He recoiled by instinct and although sudden and unexpected, he knew precisely what it was. Dropping his pack, Clement grabbed her shoulders and pulled her to the hard stone jetty. 'Stay down!'

'What are you doing?'

'Don't move!' Twisting around, Clement could just make out the shed behind them about twenty feet away, too far away for shelter and in the opposite direction to Tom Harris's boat. Clement knew, by the bullet's trajectory, that it had been fired from somewhere in front of them, from across the water. Raising his head, he looked over her prostrate body and scanned the dark sea and surrounding land mass. A low light, like the glow from a candle, flickered in the night and was then extinguished. But it was enough. 'I think it came from the bell tower at the kirk.'

'What did?'

'A bullet. Someone is trying to kill you!'

A suppressed frightened gasp escaped Sarah's lips and Clement felt the strong pragmatic woman burrow into his chest.

'Stay calm and do as I say, Sarah.' He felt the woman's head nod against his chest but her whole body was shaking. He stared out across the black waters, his breathing exaggerated. How had the sniper located them in such limited visibility? Telescopic sights? Perhaps. But at night? Surely the distance was too great? He stared again into the darkness. A direct line could be drawn between the kirk and the Gills Bay jetty. Their only cover was the night.

'What do we do now?'

'He's waiting.'

'For what?'

'For us to move.'

He heard her whimper. A minute passed. Two. But no further shots were fired. Clement began to question what had happened. Had he imagined it? He had felt something. But he hadn't imagined the glimmer of light. Someone was in the bell tower. Clement's hand went to his coat pocket to retrieve his telescope, but it was metal and could reflect the limited moonlight. Was that how the gunman had located them? Had the light, for only a second, glinted on the bicycles? Nothing now must give away their location. He pushed the instrument down in his pocket.

'Just stay down, Sarah. I don't think he can see us, so he doesn't know whether we are alive or dead.'

'How did he see us at all?'

'I don't know, but he will assume if we are alive, we will seek cover near the shed, so his eye will be focused there for any movement. Thank the dear Lord that there is almost no moon tonight.'

'I cannot believe it! Malcolm McCrea is trying to kill me!'

'We must not give him a second chance. Are you wearing any metal?'

'Just my belt buckle, I think.'

'You need to be sure. Use your cap to conceal the buckle, undo it then hide it in a pocket.' He waited. There was no sound other than the waves slapping against the stone walls of the jetty.

'We cannot wait any longer. I'm going to count backwards from three. On the count of one, get up as fast as you can and run for Tom's boat. Don't stop no matter what happens. Do you understand?'

'Yes.'

'Three, two, one!'

The sound of their boots on the hard stone echoed in the night air. Clement stared at his feet. All he could see were the uneven, weathered stones beneath his running footsteps. The slabs were irregular and the danger of tripping was great. He grabbed Sarah's hand and continued running. From the corner of his eye, he could see Sarah's coat flapping as she ran towards the fisherman's boat. He knew his grip was tight, but she had not removed her gloved hand. Shots rang out, sharp and rapid, but it was not the silenced single shot from a sniper's rifle. Machine gun fire now coursed the jetty, strafing the area wildly. He felt his pulse pounding in his ears and his throat was gulping air. He prayed they would soon be beyond the machine gun's range, but the familiar spitting sound continued to punctuate the night. Short bursts of rapid fire filled his ears. Up ahead, Tom had extinguished his shaded lamp. Bullets pinged off the stones around Clement's feet. Some were wide, spitting into the water off to his right. Clement realized the firing was random, spraying in all directions and cast over a wide area. They had a chance. Tom's little dog, Flip, was barking. It was like a homing beacon in the darkness. As they ran, he glanced up and to his right at the kirk's bell tower. Yellow flashes of rapid fire spat out from the window. The barrage had not lessened. He could hear the bullets hit the water beside him and up ahead. 'Tom, start the engine!' he yelled.

A moment later the small craft's motor sprung into life.

The machine gun was still firing, the pinging and spitting intensifying. Looking forward, Clement could see the fisherman was casting off the ropes which tied the vessel to the wharf. As they approached the boat, Clement gripped Sarah's hand. 'Jump!'

They landed heavily as a line of bullets dug deep into the deck beside them, splintering the timbers. Scrambling over the deck, Clement pushed Sarah down beside the wheel house on the seaward side as the little ship pulled away from the jetty. He stared back at the dark coast, praying that the ship's engine was safe from the incessant hail of bullets. From the little window high up in the kirk, he could still see the yellow flashes of machine gun fire as the gunman continued to strafe the bay. But as the minutes passed, the ship put sufficient distance between them and the shore and the firing ceased.

The range of the weapon astounded him. Clement didn't know of a gun that had a range greater than one

114

mile. Special Units perhaps had such a weapon, but he knew nothing about that. He thought of Malcolm McCrea. If it was the lad in the bell tower, the boy was far more than a youth with a political axe to grind.

'Are you alright, Sarah?'

She was rubbing her right ankle. 'I'll live. Thanks to you.' She looked up at him. 'I still cannot believe it! Malcolm McCrea wanted to kill me. I think I can understand his prejudices, but this!' Her voice broke off.

Whilst he understood the hollow feeling of betrayal, he wasn't as convinced about the identity of the gunman as Sarah appeared to be. Did Malcolm McCrea, or someone in his clothes, have enough time to cycle to the kirk from where they passed him on the road? If so, then that meant that the weapons were already in the bell tower. 'Come below so we can look at that ankle.'

Helping Sarah to her feet, he looked back at the receding black cliffs of Gills Bay. The night had enfolded the boat in its protective darkness. The only sounds now were the waves as they lapped against the sides of Tom's boat and the slow putt-putt of vessel's engine. He and Sarah made their way into the wheel house, to its shelter and comfort. As the boat began to roll and pitch, Clement knew they had entered Pentland Firth. Mainland Britain was now behind them.

He saw Sarah glance up at Tom as the man came below into the warmth of the cabin. 'What the hell is going on?'

'Malcolm McCrea is a German spy!' Sarah said.

'What? Never!' Tom said his gaze shifted to Clement as he checked Sarah's ankle for any sign of fracture. 'More than a Vicar going to Orkney, then. And you, Sarah?'

But it was Clement who spoke. 'Innocently caught up, Mr Harris. Can you take us to St Margaret's Hope?'

'Aye. Well. We're not out of danger yet. I'm not displaying any navigational lighting. We could run into something or worse, have something run into us. And who is going to pay for the repairs to my boat?' Tom's eyes fixed on Clement.

'I'm sorry about your boat, Tom and I have no idea who was shooting at us. It seems you have two passengers now. Ten shillings after all.'

'Make it a pound and we'll call it quits about the damage. I'll get a bandage for that ankle, Sarah.' Tom went to a cupboard and retrieved a small medical pouch.

'Not hurt yourself?' Clement asked.

Tom shook his head and reached for a torch. 'I want to check the bilges for any holes, but I think we escaped unscathed. More by good luck, though. We'll be in St Margaret's Hope by dawn.'

The fisherman stared at him before leaving the wheel house. 'You can get all manner of things in St Margaret's Hope, you know, Vicar. I suppose it's because of the large number of naval men stationed around there.'

The little dog appeared at his feet.

'We could see old Eric. You like Eric, don't you, boy? Flip likes the dance music Eric picks up on his wireless.'

Clement smiled at Tom Harris. 'It could be a good idea, Tom, if you were to wait a week or two in Orkney before returning to Gills Bay.'

'Aye. You could be right.'

# 10

The little ship pitched and yawed, taking in water with every roll. Tom told them to stay below and get some sleep but Sarah had been sick and the cabin smelt of vomit. Tom remained on deck the whole crossing, his binoculars around his neck. With morning's light, Clement thought the ship's incessant rolling had lessened and he guessed they had entered the sheltered waters of Scapa Flow. He climbed out of the bunk and reached for his watch. It was just after seven.

Staring through the porthole, Clement could see shafts of pale light penetrating the grey clouds, tingeing them creamy-yellow and piercing the tranquil waters. Despite its natural beauty, the sheltered harbour was a dangerous place and the graveyard of many men as well as ships. He glanced at Sarah who was finally asleep in the bunk opposite, then went to join Tom. Stepping out on deck, he breathed in the cold sea air; it's freshness a panacea to his lungs.

Off to his right, the cliffs of South Ronaldsay appeared black, silhouetted against the eastern sky. He turned a full three-sixty taking in the barren, isolated beauty. As they rounded Hoxa Head, the cliffs gave way to treeless, green fields sloping gently down to the sea.

'Can I ask you, Tom, about the men in *The Bell*?'

He saw Tom flick a glance in his direction. 'Before last night, I would have told you to learn about them yourself, but I don't feel much loyalty to someone trying to kill me. What is it you want to know, Vicar?'

'How many people around Canisbay and Huna can use a gun?'

Tom turned to face him. 'All farmers can use a gun. It goes with the job. But I'll tell you this for certain, I don't know anyone who has a machine gun and regardless of you and Sarah seeing Malcolm on the road last night, I cannot see Malcolm McCrea being an accomplished assassin, likewise Stewart. Accomplished horsemen, aye, but not killers.'

From the corner of his eye, Clement saw Sarah sit up in the bunk below deck, but she remained there, her foot raised on a cushion.

'We're nearly in,' Tom said. 'Once we've tied up, I'll introduce you to Eric Fraser, the shipwright here. I want him to look over my boat anyway.'

Clement glanced at the hardened fisherman. Conversation hadn't flowed as easily with Tom as Clement had hoped. It wasn't surprising; the crossing had been long and rough and Tom would have been preoccupied with the possibility of enemy shipping especially with his ship partially damaged. Or perhaps he just didn't speak to *Wise Man from The South*. Yet he had noted that neither Tom nor Sarah volunteered information. Neither had they chatted about the events of the previous night. Even the subject of Donald's death had not been raised. Surely that was unusual between friends?

'What do you know about Sean Mead, Tom?'

'Not much. He's not much of a sailor, though. Told me he feels sick just looking at the sea.'

'What brought him to Caithness?'

'Some trouble in Ireland.' Tom paused. 'Ask Jean Buchanan. She seems to know him better than anyone.'

'You mean she knew him before, in Ireland?'

'No. I don't think so, but she is, like him, not born and bred in Caithness.'

'Any idea where she does come from?'

Tom shrugged.

'How long has she been the publican?'

'A few years.'

'And the Irish lad?'

'Danny O'Reilly?'

Clement nodded.

'Comes from Wicklow, same county as Sean. He's not a bad worker. Strong lad, for his size.'

Clement stared out over the flat silver bay as the early morning light turned the white sky to the palest blue. His eye fell on the grey silhouettes of Royal Navy ships some miles distant to the north and west, their hulls like enormous, dark whales against the snow-covered shores beyond. Several barrage balloons floated above them. As comforting as the sight should have been in a time of war, it reminded him that even in beautiful and remote places, the enemy is never too far away, forever lurking and ever watchful. Was that also true for Sean's fellow countryman?'

Tom followed his gaze. 'Can't go there. Get fired on. And I've had enough of that for one war.'

Clement's mind was still on Danny O'Reilly. Regardless of the lad's supposed strength, Clement believed the boy was too small to be physically able to suffocate then lift the deceased Donald Crawford. Dead men are heavy, Clement knew that first hand from the trenches, but the lad would be capable of carrying rounds of ammunition and a machine gun. That could make him an accomplice and there was only one man for whom Danny would do such things. Clement shook his head. He considered it unlikely. Sean chatted too much while on his bus routes. Despite his murky past, the man didn't have the freedom of unobserved movement necessary to commit murder. Of the other men in *The Bell* last evening, there remained Robert Wallace and Ian McAllister. Clement assessed Wallace to be a loner: strong and fit, with a temper and a liking for a fight.

'Tell me about Robert Wallace?'

'The man's a hero. True, he does resort to his fists quicker than perhaps he should, but he was decorated in the first war. Dropped a grenade into a German trench then killed five more of the bastards with his knife.'

Tom's fervent remarks surprised Clement. Were they spoken too ardently? An attempt to defray suspicion? Tom Harris wasn't completely off Clement's list but his presence on his boat last night made it highly unlikely that he was complicit in Crawford's murder.

They passed the headland and Clement could see the snow-covered roofs of St Margaret's Hope. A hunched line of grey stone dwellings clung to the shoreline. In the centre was a large barn-like building with slip rails rising up out of the sea and disappearing into the tall shed. Scanning the shoreline with his telescope, he saw no movement of any kind. He sighed. He had always thought the name *St Margaret's Hope* sounded romantic, but in reality it was cold, remote and small. He replaced the instrument, his mind on the men of Canisbay and Robert Wallace in particular. Could this man have been trained and placed as a sleeper among them? It seemed unlikely in view of what he'd just learned from Tom. Clement stared at the line of dismal buildings that grew larger by the second.

Tom cut the motor. 'We've been lucky with the crossing. We've had some bad weather lately. Last Saturday's gale was particularly bad.'

Tom's words lingered in Clement's mind. Last Saturday, Stroma lighthouse had been bombed. Why would a German fighter even be flying in a gale? He needed to speak with Johnny. The mission was no longer straight forward. In fact, Clement believed he was drowning in a web of possibly unrelated complexities. His mind returned to the men he had seen at *The Bell* and to the other man he considered fitted the profile; Ian McAllister, and his large lorry. Unless, or until, Clement could learn from Inspector Stratton about each man's whereabouts yesterday between approximately ten o'clock and midday, all it could ever be was conjecture. It also assumed Stratton would share the information. Clement also did not expect the killer to tell the truth. The man would be hiding in a labyrinth of lies.

Tom manoeuvred his boat into the wide harbour and tied up at the jetty. 'That's Fraser's Shipyard, along Front Road, there.' Tom pointed to the tall, wooden building. 'Eric Fraser is the shipwright on South Ronaldsay. His wife, Shona, will look after Sarah.'

'Thank you, Tom.' With both men supporting Sarah, they left Tom's boat and walked towards Fraser's shipyard. A large man with wild red hair came out to meet them. 'Didn't expect to see you again so soon, Tom.'

Tom introduced them.

Clement shook the massive hand. 'I understand from Tom that you have a wireless, Mr Fraser. I wonder if Mrs Crawford could use it to send a message? It is important and won't take long.'

Fraser's deep-set eyes flicked to Tom who nodded his approval and within minutes Sarah was sitting at a desk in the shipwright's office sending out a coded message to the Royal Naval Base in Kirkwall. All Clement could do now was wait.

'My wife can look at that ankle,' Fraser said and lifting Sarah under her arm he led her across the quay, towards a house opposite.

Clement turned to Tom, two ten shilling notes already in his hand. 'Thank you for the passage, Tom. And, please, remember to stay away from Gills Bay for a week or so.'

'Aye. I'll say goodbye, Vicar. Good luck to you.'

Clement patted Flip's head and watched Tom and his little dog walk towards *The Bellevue Inn*. Alone now in the shipwright's office, Clement sat at the desk, his gaze taking in the disordered space. He swivelled the chair, so that he could see out to the waterfront and beyond to the bay.

Ten minutes became twenty and he began to worry that his message had been deemed too unimportant for Captain Winthorpe. Clement stood and stared at nothing, breathing in the aromas of fresh sea air, sawdust and pitch. Standing in the doorway, he stared at a round-hulled ship on the slipway, his ears straining for any voices emanating from the wireless.

At zero eight thirty-five hours, he received the reply. Johnny was coming personally to St Margaret's Hope and would be there before noon.

Leaving the shipwright's yard, Clement walked towards the door of Eric Fraser's house. Entering the kitchen he saw Sarah, with Eric and Shona Fraser, sitting around a table drinking tea, an old dog lying beside the stove. It looked so natural. So every day. In his mind's eye he saw Mary sitting at their kitchen table peeling beans, the knife moving adeptly over the vegetables. He felt his heart thump. It caught him off-guard; it always did. Blinking the image from his mind, he drew in a deep breath and sat down as Shona Fraser reached for another cup. 'How far can your wireless pick up traffic, Eric?'

'It depends on the frequency used and the time of day. And on the weather. With favourable conditions, about five hundred miles.'

The distance surprised Clement. 'Do you ever just listen to the traffic?'

'Never. It is always turned to the emergency channels. That is the reason I was permitted to keep it. In any case, even if it was tuned to other frequencies, you would have to be in the office to hear anything and I cannot afford that luxury with ships in dock to repair.'

'Have you ever overheard a transmission that you do not understand?'

'You mean in a foreign language?'

Clement nodded.

'Plenty before the war, of course. Less so recently. However,' Eric paused. 'I have heard what I can only describe as gibberish. Jumbles of letters and strange sentences that mean nothing.'

'For example?'

'"The cushion is on the chair". Like I said, Vicar. Nonsense. But English nonsense. Or sometimes French.'

'And lately?'

'Quiet. Although, once, there was something I thought could be the Jerries chatting to each other. Or it could have been our boys in Scapa Flow, for all I know. Buster, my old dog, bumped the table and the dial shifted off the emergency channel.'

'Can you remember what you have heard?'

'Easily. It was in Morse code. And it consisted solely of letters. Like JVZQA. All scrambled and random. But now I come to recall it, it was always in groups of either four or five letters.'

Clement saw Sarah look up, their eyes meeting, but she said nothing.

'Would you mind if Mrs Crawford listened for a while?'

'It's not supposed to be on anything but the emergency frequency, and then only for a few odd hours each day.' He glared at Sarah, 'And no transmitting on other channels, the enemy can get a fix on it and I could be arrested as a spy.'

'It is important. I could vouch for you.'

'Who with? God?'

Clement smiled. 'Him too.'

Eric Fraser's stern gaze remained on him. 'Aye, well. If you hadn't come with Tom Harris I wouldn't agree.' Finishing their tea, Clement assisted Sarah to hobble across the quay to the shipwright's office.

Away from the house Sarah leaned in towards him. 'What is it, Clement?'

Her use of his Christian name surprised him. 'Would you recognise the touch again, if you heard it?'

'Of course. But it is a long shot, given the restrictions on time.'

Clement opened the little door into Eric's boatshed and they went inside. He felt ambivalent about having Sarah's arm through his. His mind went where it always did, but Sarah and his Mary were nothing alike. Perhaps it was the domestic scene in the kitchen, or that he could feel her arm through his, or even her use of his Christian name that had jolted him into the past. He felt a smile cross his lips. Maybe now he may get to call her "Sally". Drawing the chair up to the wireless, Sarah placed the ear phones over her head and reached for the frequency knob, her thumb and forefinger slowly shifting the dial. Lifting Buster's fur covered blanket from an armchair in the corner, Clement sat and closed his eyes. His mind floated and drifted. It was almost as good as sleep. Ten minutes became thirty.

'This is him!'

The certainty in her voice wakened him. He watched Sarah scribble notes. She removed the headset. 'It's different though.'

'In what way?'

'For several days it consisted of up to forty groups of five letters. Then two days ago there was a transmission morning and afternoon. That was unusual. But it is always in groups of five letters. This is very short. Five groups of five letters.' Sarah handed the note to him and he read the letters. DEGGO LIBEN HIDNT ELENU RRAWT.

'Does it make any sense to you?'

'None. As I said, you need the key.'

He leaned back. 'Why didn't you tell me about the transmissions on Monday?'

'It was before you arrived and I wasn't sure I could trust you. I intended to check on you. But then Donald was killed and the wireless was stolen before I could.'

'Do you trust me now?'

Sarah nodded. 'Sorry. But I had to be sure.'

'And you've no idea what these messages say?'

'No. I take down the letters then send them on to the Y-station.'

Clement stared at the note. 'At least he is still in place and transmitting.

'What now?'

'We wait.'

They sat in Eric Fraser's ship yard looking down the wharf and out over St Margaret's Hope harbour. Ten minutes passed, the only sound that of the rhythmic waves hitting the slipways.

'Are you alright?'

Sarah turned to face him. 'You mean Donald?'

Clement nodded.

'I suppose I shouldn't say this, but I feel wonderful. Odd don't you think, in view of his death and what happened last night. But in truth, for the first time in years, I feel alive.'

Clement smiled, but he didn't really understand it. They both had lost their spouses, but their reactions could not be more different. He would miss Mary forever.

At nine fifty-three he saw the tiny craft. He reached for his telescope and watched it as it approached. Twenty minutes later, Clement saw the familiar frame of Johnny Winthorpe step ashore and stride towards the buildings of Front Road. Meeting by the large double doors, Clement led Johnny to Eric's small office where Sarah was still listening to wireless chatter.

'I was surprised to receive your message, Clement. I gather something has happened sufficient for you both to break cover?'

Clement told Johnny about the events of the previous two days.

'Are you sure it is the same person transmitting?' Johnny asked Sarah.

'No question about it.'

'And the strength of the signal?'

'Strong, Captain Winthorpe. Possibly ten miles, but not much more.'

The sound of approaching aeroplanes halted their conversation. Johnny looked out over the waters as the planes circled above them then disappeared south and west. 'Hurricanes,' Johnny said. 'Are the signals stronger here or on the mainland, Mrs Crawford?'

'The mainland.'

Johnny led Clement a short distance away. 'We will send the latest transmission directly to our friends at Bletchley Park. I suspect it will be of greater use to them than it is to us.' Johnny looked out over the black waters. 'If this Malcolm McCrea is our enemy agent, he will know you left Gills Bay with the fisherman. Is Mr Harris still here?'

'I suggested he should stay away from Gills Bay for a week or two.'

'Good idea.'

'If you don't need me anymore, I'd like to sit inside in the warmth,' Sarah called to them.

Johnny walked back to her. 'Tell me something, Mrs Crawford. When Tom Harris told you about the ship marked NN04, did he know about your Special Duties role?'

'No. Tom still doesn't. No one knows.' She looked at Clement. There was a long pause. 'My husband knew.'

Clement saw her look down, the pockets bulging from her clenched fists.

Johnny's eyes flared. 'Your indiscretion has cost your husband his life. I hope you know this! And you would have been next if this traitor had learned that you are the operative, not your late husband. It appears to me that you have much to thank Major Wisdom for, Mrs Crawford.' Johnny paused, his thinly suppressed anger only just under control. 'There is little to be gained in telling anyone else about it now. Your husband is deceased, so it will go no further. But I must tell you that I could not turn a blind eye a second time.'

Clement could see the relief on her face.

'Thank you.' Sarah didn't wait for further comment. Turning, she hobbled back to Shona Fraser's kitchen door.

'Do you trust her, Clement?'

'I don't think she is our enemy, if that's what you're asking.'

'Total stupidity. But it does beg another question. Did Tom Harris tell others about NN04? Enemy ships operating alone, especially in the North Sea, are usually weather reporting vessels, and that would mean it has a radio transmitter and Naval Enigma Coding machine on board. Capturing one of those could turn the tide for us in the North Atlantic. The problem will be finding this ship again. The North Sea is a vast expanse of water and there are just too many fjords in occupied Norway for them to hide in. But I will inform The Admiralty. Who knows, we may just happen upon it, like Tom Harris.' Johnny stared at him. 'Speak to this fisherman and find out who else he told in Canisbay. Then send all that you have learned to Nora Ballantyne.'

'And then?'

'Go home, Clement.'

'What?'

'I am leaving Orkney in a matter of days for the Faroe Islands then Norway. Not sure when I'll be back. A few days, God willing. But I'm afraid, Clement, you are not sufficiently trained for what is now required.'

'There is no time for a Special Operations Agent, Johnny. And I am trained.'

'Clement, you have never *done* this sort of work. There is a huge difference between theory and practice. For what is now required you would need to be fit, young and, quite frankly, have a death wish. Not some-one of your years and limited abilities.'

'I may not be young, Johnny, but I'm all you have.'

Johnny shook his head. 'It is out of the question, Clement. Of course, your arrival, the death of Mr Crawford and the disappearance of Mrs Crawford, could well be enough to frighten our man into leaving, so he may not be there any more for us to find.'

Johnny's words lingered. 'It's a pick-up signal, Johnny. It has to be. It's too short to be anything else. You're right about recent events. Perhaps he believes he's in danger of being exposed. If that's the case, we don't have much time.' Clement waited. 'Like I said, Johnny, I'm all you have.'

The silence lasted a further five seconds before Clement saw the hesitation cross Johnny's face.

Johnny stared directly at him. 'As soon as you have spoken with your fisherman, leave without delay. And Clement?'

He turned to face Johnny.

'Take care. Bring him in, if you can. He could be useful to us.' Johnny paused. 'I know I've said this be-fore but make no mistake, this time you really are alone.'

# 11

Clement stood on the quay and watched Johnny leave until the launch was nothing more than a speck. His gaze fixed on the seas beyond Hoxa Head. The wind had strengthened, the water now dark grey and white crests had formed. He stared up at the cloudy sky and spoke to the freezing air. 'Have you completely lost your faculties?' Johnny's parting words echoed in his mind. He felt a sigh rise and allowed it to float away from his lips. Even though he knew he was alone, he felt the weight of his decision and the old self-doubts bubbled to the surface. '"We are in God's hand, brother, not in theirs,"' he told himself, voicing his favourite line from Shakespeare's *Henry V*.

A cold shiver ran down his back. Did he really have a death wish? He stared at the black waters hitting the stone footings of the quay beside him. Deep. Isolated. He'd said before he didn't care if he lived or died. He wasn't sure it was true. 'Well, I suspect you're going to find out, Clement Wisdom,' he said. Hunching his shoulders to the bracing wind, he walked back towards the only public house on the quay hoping to convince one of the fishermen there to leave St Margaret's Hope. Opening the door, he stepped inside *The Bellevue Inn*.

It was crowded and the air was heavy with pipe smoke. He ordered a drink and went to sit with a group of men in the corner, but the answer was always the same, no one was prepared to make the crossing. Citing the enemy, the weather, or maybe just because they were tired, Clement didn't know the true reason, and he couldn't blame them either. Leaving the main bar, he walked to the inn's front door; the heat, noise and smoke in the confined space dulling his senses.

He stepped outside and wandered away from the buildings, walking west and following the curve of the bay hoping the biting wind would clear his thoughts. Somehow he had to get one of them to take him back to the mainland. He foraged in his pockets and scraped together five pounds. A reasonable amount under normal circumstances, but few would be tempted to risk their life for such a sum. Staring out across the bay, he huddled into his greatcoat. Perhaps his body was becoming accustomed to the icy blasts, for he found the solitude of the waterfront much more to his liking than the stifling hot air of the inn.

He heard the footsteps and turned. Tom Harris was walking towards him, Flip at his heels.

'I hear you want to go back now?'

'Yes. Tom, I need to ask you a question.'

Tom Harris reached into his pocket, retrieved a pipe and began to pack the bulb with fresh tobacco. 'Well?'

'Who else did you tell about the sighting of the ship NN04?'

Tom's eyes widened, the pipe suspended in his grasp. 'I may have mentioned it at *The Bell*.'

A long sigh escaped Clement's mouth. 'How many?'

'The usuals.'

'Names?'

'The McCrea boys, and their father, I think. Robert Wallace, Sean and Danny, Jean, of course. And Ian McAllister could have been there. I just don't remember.'

Clement stared at the expansive mass of water before him, his hands in his pockets. The fact was, it no longer mattered who had been there; the whole vicinity would have known within the hour.

Tom shook his head. 'Sorry, Vicar. I suppose I spend too much time alone at sea. When I'm on shore I talk a bit. I'll keep my mouth shut from now on.'

'I should. But in light of what happened, it does raise another question, Tom. Exactly who was the intended victim of last night's shooting?'

'You think it was me?'

'It's possible. But it is more likely to have been Sarah or me. Just as many people who knew about NN04 also knew that you would be making the crossing to St Margaret's Hope, and even though initially I booked the passage for Sarah, they would have thought it was for me. Your sighting of that trawler must have caused someone alarm.' Clement watched the fisherman. He hadn't shared what troubled him most about Tom's indiscretion; that someone in Canisbay not only knew the number, they also knew the significance of the ship.'

Clement continued to stare at the snow-covered hills that surrounded St Margaret's Hope, Tom beside him, Flip at their feet. In the ensuing silence Clement watched the smoke from Tom's pipe blow away in the wind.

Tom took the pipe from his mouth. 'I'll take you. I owe you and Sarah that.'

Clement felt deep relief. 'Thank you. Could you take me to Thurso instead?'

'Thurso?'

'Is there a problem?'

Tom took a long puff from his pipe. 'The estuary at Thurso is narrow and hazardous, especially if the wind is from the nor'-west. But I owe you, so if that is where you want to go, then so be it.'

'When can we leave?'

Tom looked at his watch. 'Early hours of tomorrow. Be at my boat just after midnight. We'll get into Thurso, God willing, with the high in-coming tide just before three o'clock tomorrow morning.'

'What about the damage to your boat?'

'Superficial, so Eric says. It can wait.'

They walked back to the square in front of *The Bellevue* without speaking. Tom returned to the public house. As the door swung open, Clement heard the swell of voices carry on the air. The door closed. Silence returned.

An icy draft blew across the harbour front. With his passage secured, he now needed a plan and that required a quiet place to think. But first, he wanted to inform Sarah of his decision.

Clement knocked at the door to Fraser's house. Shona Fraser opened it. Sarah was still sitting at the table in the kitchen.

'Won't you come in?' Shona asked.

'Thank you, but no. I have no wish to impose. Could I have a word, Sarah?'

Sarah nodded. She stood and reached for her coat and cap. Supporting her arm, Clement helped her to walk outside a little way away from the kitchen door.

'How's the ankle?'

'Fine.'

He knew it was a lie. 'I'm going back.'

'I thought you would.'

'Can I ask you something?'

'How could I refuse?'

'As I understand it, with long range radio transmitters, the aerial has to be attached to the transmitter. Is that correct?'

Sarah nodded.

'And you have been picking up the enemy traffic from the barn?'

'Yes.' She looked up at him. 'He is local. Has to be. Scotland is too cold in winter for him to travel far to transmit. What is it, Clement?'

'There are no large trees and no other tall structures anywhere about Canisbay or Huna, except the kirk. Have you ever been into the bell tower?'

'Once. But I didn't see an aerial.'

'What about above it, in the rafters?'

Sarah fell silent.

'Do you always wear that red tam o'shanter when out of doors?'

'I suppose I do.'

'It could be a good idea if you pack it away. Borrow one from Mrs Fraser. Just until after the war.'

Sarah pulled the cap from her head and buried it deep into her coat pocket. 'How long have you been doing this sort of work?'

'Not long.' What Clement felt like saying was, not long enough. 'Do you know everyone around Canisbay and Huna?'

'Of course.'

'Yesterday, a few minutes after I came to your shop at ten o'clock, your husband was connecting a telephone call. Any idea who that caller was?'

Sarah stared down at her bandaged ankle. 'Anyone in the telephone box outside, I suppose.'

Clement shook his head. 'I saw the telephone booth from your lorry as we drove away only minutes after your husband connected the line. It was empty.'

'Really?' Sarah paused. 'Then it can only have been someone at *The Bell*. Or the Frew sisters. But that would be unusual. Is it important?'

'I don't know yet.'

Sarah turned, extending her hand towards him. 'Take care, Clement. If that's all, I'll go back inside. And thank you.'

He smiled, shook her hand in farewell, then watched Sarah Crawford limp away.

Returning to the public house, he arranged a room on the first floor and organised for the landlady to put some hot water and a razor in the room. With Tom not leaving till after midnight, Clement had ample time to think of a plan and to wash and shave. He also wanted to spend some time in prayer. As he passed the large fireplace in the main bar, he dropped the enciphered note into the flames; the random letters etched in his mind. Climbing the stairs to the upper floor, he saw Tom Harris glance in his direction, but he knew it was unlikely the fisherman would discuss him with anyone now.

His room was on the first floor at the front. Opening the door, he stared at the single bed. A many coloured, hand-knitted woollen blanket sat folded at the foot of the bed. He closed the door behind him. He hadn't expected a room in a public house to have such personal touches. It reminded him of the single bed in Reverend St Clair's guest room, but here the blanket was hand-knitted from the remnants of many jerseys. In his mind he heard the click of Mary's knitting needles. For one moment he permitted himself the time to dwell on Mary. His thoughts lingered over everything about her; her hair, the colour of her eyes, the touch of her skin, her slender ankles, her clothes, even her apron that hung on the scullery door to their garden and the way her hands peeled beans and carrots. He closed his eyes. The irreversible hollowness was torture.

Lifting his gaze, Clement caught sight of his face in the small mirror on the wash stand. A visage he hardly recognised stared back. He thought he looked older, but perhaps it was the stubble or the bitter cold. Removing his shirt and clerical collar, he filled the bowl on the wash stand and shaved his beard. Patting his face dry, he turned the mirror to face the wall. He didn't want to see his reflection and the sadness that inhabited his eyes.

He wasn't sure who he was any more. He was a man of God, but he didn't feel it. He was an officer in the King's Special Duties Branch, but that role was unfamiliar. Buttoning his vest, he tossed the towel over the wash stand and lay back on the bed, but even though his muscles were at rest, his mind churned. He couldn't think about himself anymore. He'd made his decisions. He pushed his doubts away and forced himself to formulate a plan. Staring at the ceiling, he began to piece together what he knew. It wasn't much. Johnny had been right. He felt completely out of his depth.

He tried to visualize the coastline around Canisbay. He hadn't seen that much of it, but he knew there were cliffs beneath the kirk that extended as far as John O' Groats to the east. Gills Bay was well protected, the mainland at its back and Stroma Island lay just off the shoreline. Tom had said that the tide raced through Pentland Firth; "a graveyard for shipping". Not the place for a U-boat rendezvous, if, that is, Clement was correct about a pick-up. And, also thanks to Tom, Clement now knew that Thurso estuary was hazardous in certain weather. He closed his eyes remembering the maps he studied. There was only one place. Dunnet Bay.

Despite never having actually seen it, he knew it was the only inlet of any size along that part of the coast and where the coastline was flat. A sandy beach ran almost the full length of the bay. Moreover, at the eastern end of the beach, the large promontory of Dunnet Head provided protection from wind and waves in the right conditions. It would be an audacious place for the Germans to rendezvous, given the proximity of the Y-station and all the military presence in the area. Perhaps that was why. Whilst the surrounding installations made it unlikely as a place for an enemy force to invade, it was ideal for a single craft to beach undetected. And it would be totally unexpected. The U-boat didn't even need to enter the bay. It could surface offshore, launch a dinghy that could row onto the beach, make the rendezvous and row back in the lee of Dunnet Head where it would be shielded from prying eyes and adverse weather.

Clement opened his eyes feeling like he had just placed the last piece in a large jigsaw puzzle. But his theory pre-supposed that the radio transmission had been about a pick-up and, further, that it would occur in Dunnet Bay. He began to think about the people who knew about the ship NN04; Jean Buchanan, Robert Wallace, Sean and Danny, the Irishmen, as well as the McCrea boys and their father, a man Clement had not met. Yet these were only those who frequented *The Bell*. What about the other inhabitants of Canisbay who remained in their homes? He remembered Sarah telling him of the Grants and the Hendersons, farming families who lived further to the south and west, people he knew nothing about.

Clement sat up in the bed. Only the people who had been in *The Bell* knew he had arranged passage with Tom Harris. He stared at his jacket hanging on the back of the door, his thoughts racing. His enemy had either been in the public house at the time or was well known to one of the men who had been there. Clement lay back down. Malcolm McCrea was someone he wanted to speak to on his return. Instinct, however, told him that neither McCrea fitted the profile. No enemy plant worth his salt would rant in a public place. 'So who?' he said aloud. Whoever this killer was, the man was strong, young enough, secretive, mobile and either in or known to someone who was in *The Bell* the night Clement arranged the passage with Tom.

Clement visualized the deceased Donald Crawford. The man had been suffocated and his corpse grotesquely displayed for maximum effect. Why had the murderer gone to such lengths? Was it only a warning to Sarah, a way of telling her that her husband's killer knew about her covert activities? Surely, if it were to frighten Sarah into leaving, then the killer had achieved his objective. So why the pick up? What else had recently happened to make the enemy plant break cover?

# 12

Friday 28<sup>th</sup> February

Half an hour past midnight, the little ship crept its way into the black waters of Scapa Flow. Above Clement a strong green light flashed across the sky in the darkness making the waters appear blacker and the land masses like a risen leviathan.

Clement stood beside Tom in the wheel house as the Northern Lights danced their celestial brilliance over the sea. 'Spectacular, aren't they? I've never seen them before.'

'A mixed blessing, Vicar.'

Clement turned to look back on St Margaret's Hope, the shoreline receding with every second. No lights could be seen anywhere ashore. He thanked God that Tom Harris had both local knowledge and a conscience. He stared at the mesmeric Lights. Their presence was more than an extraordinary spectacle, he saw that their brilliance lit up the heavens and the surrounding land. 'Could we go by way of Stroma Island, Tom?'

The fisherman's eyes widened. 'You're a brave man, there's no denying it, Vicar.'

Was it fear in Tom's voice or incredulity at his request or something else? Clement had seen Stroma Island from the kirk, but the lighthouse which had reputedly been bombed only last Saturday was not visible from the mainland. Was there something on the other side of the island he didn't know about? 'Tell me about the lighthouse on Stroma?'

'It's at the northern end of the island, above a whirlpool, and it's a place to stay away from, especially at night.'

'How does one get onto this island?'

'In daylight, by boat to the western end. Then a walk of about three miles over rocky ground passing several crofters' cottages with unfriendly dogs. It's always windy there.'

Clement shot a sideways glance at the hardened fisherman. He hadn't seriously entertained an island location for the rendezvous, but Tom's local knowledge, said almost as an after-thought, ruled it out as a feasible place to land an aeroplane, and he didn't believe Tom was lying. Why had the attack occurred? Had it been just a release of unused bombs from a raid elsewhere? But there was nowhere else around Stroma, other than the well-defended Scapa Flow and the Royal Air Force Base at Castletown, from which a squadron of fighters would surely bring down a lone German fighter. Why hadn't it been intercepted? What purpose had strafing the lighthouse accomplished? Always questions and no answers. 'When is dawn?'

'We'll see some light around six.'

'Could we hug the coastline?'

'Anything in particular you hope to see, Vicar?'

'Not really.' But he prayed the Aurora would persist for some hours because he wanted to see the shoreline between Gills Bay and Thurso, especially around Dunnet Bay.

'Suits me. But I can't guarantee you'll see much before sunrise.'

Tom didn't talk much after that. Perhaps it was the early hour, but Clement didn't think so. From the man's intense expression, Clement assumed Tom's concern was for enemy shipping, above and below the surface.

He turned his gaze on the receding land masses that enclosed Scapa Flow. While over the heavenly lights flashed, it was possible to see some distance. But without them, with only the stars and little moonlight, the sea was horribly dark.

An hour and a half later they entered Pentland Firth.

Tom pointed towards the dark shore. 'There's Gills Bay.'

Clement stared into the gloom. Taking his telescope from his pocket he trained it on the shore. The dark silhouette of the bell tower of Canisbay Kirk against the starry night sky filled the scope. Moving it to his right, he scanned the cliffs and familiar surrounding hills and jetty of Gills Bay, but all was in darkness.

It was almost three o'clock when Tom's boat rounded Dunnet Head, the massive promontory looming over the seas, the sound of the crashing waves audible across the water. Dunnet Bay spread out before them in the darkness off the port beam of the boat. He knew from the maps that the inlet was wide and faced almost due north-west. From the corner of his eye Clement caught the flare, illuminating the heavens. Above him the Northern Lights flashed their shimmering green ribbons once more over the sea. Clement reached for his telescope and trained it on the coast. Sweeping the instrument along the shoreline, he saw in the bright green glow, at the far eastern end, a dark groyne protruding into the bay. It was tucked well around, in the lee of Dunnet Head.

'Is that a pier?'

'Aye. Dwarwick Pier. Not much used now and it's not for the faint-hearted, especially in a nor'-westerly.'

Clement nodded. He heard the anxiety in Tom's voice, but Clement had no intention of asking the fisherman to take him there. He did concede that while a landing at Dwarwick Pier may be hazardous in a north-westerly wind, from its location, in an easterly or even southerly breeze, the place was well protected by the mass of Dunnet Head. It was also very well protected from prying eyes in any weather, especially if not much used. He moved the telescope along the shoreline. From what he could see, the pier appeared to be surrounded by deep water so it would be possible for a ship, in favourable conditions, to tie up there. Lifting the telescope, he scanned the surrounding countryside still shrouded in darkness. 'Are there any villages there, Tom?'

'No, just farmers.'

With no villages or public buildings of any kind in the immediate area, Clement thought Dwarwick Pier was about as ideal a place for a pick-up as he had ever seen.

Lowering the telescope, he contemplated his theory. But he had no proof for any of it.

The little ship rolled on the swell as it entered the narrow estuary of Thurso Harbour, the engine struggling against the out-going tide. The diversion around Stroma Island and Dunnet Bay had delayed their arrival into the northern port, and from Tom's concerned expression, Clement was left in little doubt that the fisherman was relieved to finally be tied up at the wharf. Thanking Tom for the crossing, Clement jumped ashore. It was just after half past six. Drizzling rain began to fall. He huddled into his greatcoat. In the early dawn light he scrutinized the waterfront. In front of him was a long building where two men sat mending nets in a doorway. Further to his left, rising steeply from the river's inlet, a street disappeared between the houses. Clutching his pack, Clement walked along the wharf and taking the snaking street, headed into town to find Olrig Street where, so Tom had told him, he would find the police station.

Clement saw the small sign hanging outside another grey stone building about half way up the street and next to a church of some size. But the police station was closed, the door bolted shut and snow clung to the window sills and around the doorway. Thurso Police Station, so a sign board told him, would not open for another three hours. Turning, Clement looked around for a place out of the weather. Finding none, he returned to the waterfront. For a moment, he considered taking refuge with the fishermen mending their nets. It was unwise; the fewer people who knew of his movements the better. People talk. He'd said that before.

From where Clement was standing on the street above the quay, he could see Tom's boat still tied up alongside the wharf, but neither Tom nor Flip were on deck. Clement wondered if Tom had decided to catch a few hours' sleep. He walked towards the boat, hopeful of a place out of the weather. Climbing aboard, he found the hatch into the wheelhouse locked. Clement turned around, his eyes focused on searching for Tom and Flip between the buildings, but other than the two fishermen mending their nets, no one was about. He hoped Tom was below or buying provisions and not gossiping in some fishermen's haunt. But while that was a risk, Clement didn't believe Tom would talk about him at all now. Tom knew just enough about the English vicar's presence in Caithness to get himself into trouble. That, surely, would keep the man's mouth closed.

Leaving Tom's boat, Clement walked along the wharf to the point and stared into the westerly wind, to a wide-open bay off to his left and beyond to the port of Scrabster. On the sand below him were several up-turned wooden dinghies. He pulled a balaclava from his pack, and tugging it over his head, jumped from the quay and walked towards the small craft. Selecting one, he crawled under it. Wrapping his coat around him, he burrowed himself into a small patch of dry sand. At least he would be protected from the rain and wind. He closed his eyes, but his thoughts were on Dwarwick Pier.

Just before nine he pulled himself out from under the dinghy, his muscles aching and the pain in his hips an instant reminder that was not a young man. Dismissing this, he brushed the sand from his clothes and looked along the beach. No one was about. He hurried back into the town.

Thurso Police Station was a formidable building. Constructed of grey stone with narrow recessed windows and a heavy entry door, it exuded deprivation and austerity. Clement pushed the heavy panelled front door open and stepped inside. Before him was a long room with a cream painted wall on one side and a long reception desk on the other. A fire, recently lit, struggled to burn in a fireplace at the end of the room. He walked towards the desk and tapped the bell.

Within seconds a man in a constable's uniform appeared. Clement recognized the young man. He had seen him with his wife on Sean's bus, the day Clement had arrived in Caithness. 'Could I see Inspector Stratton?'

The constable's eyes roamed over Clement's damp, sandy clothing. 'Well, if it isn't the Vicar going to South Ronaldsay! You're a little off-course, aren't you, Reverend? Something happened?'

Clement smiled. 'Could I see the Inspector, please, Constable.'

'Of course! Please, won't you sit down?'

Clement walked towards a row of chairs lined up along the wall. Turning the last one to face the fire, he sat and warmed his hands. Within minutes the Constable returned. 'This way, Reverend.'

Clement stood, reluctantly leaving the growing flames, and followed the young man along the corridor.

Inspector Stratton was, Clement guessed, approximately forty to fifty years of age with a ring of slightly greying, light-brown hair around an otherwise bald head. Round spectacles sat on the Inspector's nose, the small dark blue eyes darting upwards as Clement entered the office. Stratton possessed the air of a well-respected, professional man; he wore a three-piece tweed suit and Clement decided that Stratton was the kind of man that is held in high esteem by townspeople and from whom opinions are sought for all manner of things.

'My Constable says you are a Vicar? What seems to be the problem?'

Clement turned to see if the young Constable had left the room before speaking. 'I believe you know of my existence in Caithness. I am *Hope*.'

Stratton stared at him. Perhaps it was because since leaving St Margaret's Hope, Clement had decided not to wear his clerical collar, or his unexpected English accent, but from the man's blank expression Clement wondered whether Stratton had even heard him. He was about to repeat himself when Stratton jumped from his seat and rushed around the desk.

'I have been expecting you to make contact. How can I help?'

'May I?' Clement gestured towards the chair in front of Stratton's desk.

'Of course, forgive me. Please, do sit down.'

Clement could see the man's gaze assessing his appearance. 'Have you told anyone of my anticipated presence in Caithness?'

'No. I was asked not to and I am a man of my word.'

148

'Not even your Constable or Mrs Stratton?'

Stratton's face clouded. 'I have told you I have not. And there isn't a Mrs Stratton.'

Stratton's reaction surprised Clement. It certainly hadn't been his intention to offend. But regardless of Stratton's manner and whether or not there was, or ever had been, a Mrs Stratton, it concerned Clement only as far as maintaining his anonymity. But he wondered, if like himself, Stratton was a widower. Loss and grief effect people differently. 'I apologize for my appearance. I was hoping to get a lift with you when you leave for Huna today. What time will you be going?'

A frown creased Stratton's forehead. 'I hadn't planned on going there today, Reverend Hope. What makes you think I am?'

'Reverend Heath telephoned you. On Wednesday. About the death of Donald Crawford.'

Stratton was staring, the intense, bird-like eyes had not blinked since Clement had asked his question.

'You do know about the sad death of Mr Crawford, inspector?'

Stratton leaned back in his chair. 'You had better tell me about it.'

'Perhaps you should use my real name. After all, the people in Huna and Canisbay know it. I am Reverend Wisdom.'

Stratton's eyebrows lifted. It was the smallest of reactions but perhaps, like numerous others over the years, Stratton thought his name appropriate for his vocation.

'I am surprised, though, that Reverend Heath didn't telephone you about it. I suppose they think it is a local matter, but in view of the manner of Mr Crawford's death, I thought, at the very least, you should be informed.'

Stratton opened a drawer in his desk and produced a form and began to fill it out, but there were no words of surprise or regret for Donald Crawford's passing.

'Tell me, Reverend Wisdom, in your own words, what you know?'

Clement gave Stratton a detailed description of the scene in the barn and where he had taken Sarah Crawford. But he refrained from telling Stratton about Sarah's Special Duties role or the stolen wireless. Neither did Clement mention the gunman in the bell tower of Canisbay Kirk.

Stratton continued to scribble notes.

Clement watched the man's grip around the pen, the thick wrist and sturdy fingers. But the face was devoid of emotion.

'And why would Mrs Crawford be so hasty to leave, Reverend?'

'She was naturally distressed. But the people in Huna and Canisbay...' Clement paused. 'Well, small places, Inspector! I'm sure you understand. I believe Mrs Crawford found it all rather stifling. Especially after she told me that she believed the locals never liked her husband.'

Stratton stopped writing and looked up from his notes. 'You seem convinced that Mr Crawford's death was not accidental?'

'I am. For the reasons I have explained.'

'A misplaced hay fork isn't conclusive evidence of a crime, Reverend Wisdom.'

'At least you should look at the barn, Inspector, and at Mr Crawford's injuries.'

150

Stratton frowned. 'Very well. I have to go to Castletown today anyway, but I can go to Huna first.' The Inspector paused, the intense eyes on him. 'I have been instructed not to ask questions about why you are here and I'm required to provide you with whatever assistance you request. I'm not all together happy about it, but it appears I have no choice. Regardless, I won't have you interfering with my investigations. I don't care who you are.'

'Understood. Should we take the doctor with us?'

'There is no need for that. I can check Mr Crawford's injuries and confirm that death has taken place. And as so many people appear to know about it, I think I can determine the time of death accurately enough for the certificate. I'll get the car brought around.' Stratton lifted the receiver on his telephone.

'Perhaps we could meet again, after you have spoken to all concerned?'

Stratton raised his eyes and looked over his round spectacles. 'Why?'

'I would just like to know what they tell you.' Clement sat back in his chair. 'I would also request that you do not mention that you have seen me. No one is to know where I am.'

Stratton removed his spectacles from his nose and placed them on his desk. 'And where will you be?'

Good question, Clement thought. 'I don't know yet.'

Through the window, Clement saw a black car pull up at the front. Stratton stood and reached for his coat and hat. Following the Inspector along the corridor, they left the police station by the front door. A little further down Olrig Street, Clement saw a bus pull up and a few people alighted. Many of the passengers wore military uniforms of one kind or another. He remembered the Royal Air Force Base in Castletown and wondered what was taking Inspector Stratton there.

'I forgot my glasses. Get in, Reverend, I won't be long.' Stratton hurried back into the building while Clement waited in the car. Minutes later Stratton returned and they drove out of Thurso.

During the drive east, Clement learnt that Stratton had started as a young constable in Glasgow where he grew up until attaining the rank of Inspector. But after the death of his wife of only two years, he had requested a transfer to Thurso where he'd remained. Clement wanted to share with Stratton that he understood the heartache of widowhood, but he couldn't. Chatter, whether idle or well-meaning, had the potential to compromise. But he felt the lost opportunity. Not sharing the agony of grief was contrary to everything he believed.

Clement stared through the window at the passing countryside. As the miles passed, he wondered what he had learned about the character of the man sitting beside him. It wasn't much. He had seen men like Stratton before; they were used to being in-charge, above all, they reserved judgement and kept their own counsel.

The car slowed through the village of Castletown. The High Street was long with few shops. Residences, municipal buildings, a drill hall and a park fronted the street. From what he could see, the town consisted almost solely of grey stone dwellings. One shop, a General Store and Post Office was half way down the High Street, while a butcher's shop and veterinary surgery appeared to be the only other enterprises apparent. Military personnel, however, abounded on the streets and came and went from various buildings. Stratton passed no comment.

As they drove further east, Clement kept his eye on the land to his left, waiting to see the outline of Dunnet Head. As the road descended around the western end of the beach he checked his watch. It was just before ten. Twenty minutes since leaving Thurso. His eye shifted to the speedometer. Whether on the straight road or on bends, Stratton never went faster than thirty-five miles per hour. Clement wondered if the murderer had access to a car. In Canisbay he had seen only Sean's bus and the delivery lorries belonging to McAllister and Sarah Crawford. There had been a car. Outside *The Bell*. But he hadn't seen it there again. Clement's gaze returned to the passing scenery and he began to calculate how long it would take to walk from Canisbay to Dunnet Beach. A minute later they drove over a low hill. In front of him was a long stretch of road. He glanced at the few buildings that made up the village of Dunnet, his gaze settling on a two-storied building on the left. Outside a sign told the traveller that it was *The Dunnet Hotel*. His eye lingered on the building which, he knew, billeted the officers from the Royal Air Force Base just south of Castletown at a place called Thurdistoft. A car was parked outside. Beside it, Clement caught sight of several bicycles leaning against the main door into the inn.

Stratton continued on without comment, but in those few seconds as they passed the hotel, Clement glimpsed a lane that went from the main road inland, presumably to Dunnet Head and Dwarwick Pier. It was narrow and hidden to the oncoming traffic behind a stone wall with a tall hedge behind it. 'Could you pull over here, Inspector?'

Stratton stared at him, the eyebrows raised in surprise. But the man did as Clement requested and pulled the car up on the side of the road.

Clement reached for the door handle. 'Thank you for the lift.'

Stratton's face remained a study in astonishment as Clement said good bye.

Without waiting for the Police Inspector to drive away, Clement started walking towards the inn not twenty yards distant. He stared at a diminishing patch of blue sky as he walked. His instant decision had surprised even himself. He hoped it was one he would not regret. He wanted to see Dwarwick Pier and right now, he had the time. A second later, he heard the car pull onto the road and drive away, heading east. Pretending to tie a shoelace, Clement squatted on the road side and looked back. Stratton's car had disappeared from view.

Swinging his pack onto his shoulder, he walked on. As he approached the parked car, he peered through the windows. A newspaper sat on the front seat, but there was nothing inside to indicate the vehicle's owner. Leaving the front of the hotel, Clement turned into the lane that he hoped led north to Dwarwick Pier. But he wanted to know who owned the car. Making another instant decision, Clement walked to the rear of the inn as the unmistakable sound of fighter aircraft intensified in the sky above him. Looking up he could see a squadron of Hurricanes returning. Reaching for the door handle, he stepped inside.

A girl of no more than sixteen was standing at a sink washing dishes.

'Hello,' Clement said. 'Do you know whose car is parked outside?'

The girl looked up and smiled. 'Wing Commander Atcherley. He was here for breakfast, so if the car is still here, then he is too.' She nodded in the direction of the dining room.

Clement returned the girl's smile. Her frankness surprised him, but she had probably seen hundreds of unknown faces coming and going. Too many to be suspicious. Leaving his pack by the rear door, he walked through the kitchen and pushed open a swing-door into the main bar. Three men sat at a table by the window in an otherwise empty dining room.

Clement approached the senior ranking officer present, his hand out-stretched. 'Good morning.'

Two of the men stood, their hands reaching for holstered pistols.

'My name is Reverend Wisdom. Could I speak with you, Wing Commander?'

'Your business with Wing Commander Atcherley?' one of the junior officers asked.

Clement reached for his pass and handed it to the nearest officer who handed it to the Wing Commander. Atcherley studied it then looked at him for several seconds before handing it back. 'What brings SIS to Caithness?'

The young officers looked surprised.

Clement pocketed the pass. 'Are you aware, Wing Commander, that some unusual radio transmissions have been picked-up in Caithness?

Atcherley indicated the vacant chair at the table and Clement sat while the young officers exchanged glances.

'This is Captain Trevelyan and Lieutenant Pickering,' Atcherley said. 'Captain Trevelyan is our liaison officer between the Royal Air Force Base here and our Royal Navy friends hereabouts.'

Trevelyan nodded. 'It was reported and we are informed that it is being looked into. Although I wasn't expecting it to be…' the young man paused.

Clement smiled. At one time he would have elaborated. But not now. 'Is it possible that the sender is someone at the Y-Station?'

'Impossible!' Trevelyan answered.

Clement's eyes shifted to the young officer. The brusqueness of Trevelyan's reply seemed naive to Clement, but perhaps it was more surprise on the young captain's part that Clement knew of the existence of the Y-station.

Trevelyan went on. 'They have all been thoroughly screened and besides they are, without exception, decent types.'

'Excuse me, Captain, but all spies are. On the surface. That is their skill.' Clement turned to face the Wing Commander. 'Is there any time when only one person is on duty at the station?'

'Never!' Trevelyan replied.

Atcherley sat forward. 'Reverend, the only person who enters and leaves there on a regular basis is the despatch rider. I could arrange for you to meet him, if you think it necessary. But, in any case, he doesn't have access to the radio rooms and would never be left unattended.'

'And he's a bit old for such endeavours, don't you think, Sir?' Trevelyan said, staring at Clement.

Clement smiled, ignoring the slur.

Atcherley shifted his gaze, their eyes meeting but neither commented on the young Captain's remark.

Atcherley went on. 'The despatch rider's a local man. And perhaps he is a trifle older than I would like. But we are a little short staffed at present and *beggars can't be choosers*, isn't that the phrase?'

Reg Naylor flashed into Clement's mind. 'There is a small group of Pioneer Corps chaps in Wick who could be useful to you.'

'Really? I'll check them out. Thank you, Reverend.'

Clement looked at Trevelyan. 'Do you know the Y-Station personnel, Captain?'

'I've met them all.'

'Are they billeted here?'

But it was Atcherley who responded. 'No, poor sods. They live on Dunnet Head, spending their days in concrete boxes and the old lighthouse keeper's house. Only time they leave there is to take leave. Which, as I understand it, isn't often.'

'Have any been on leave this last week?'

'None,' Trevelyan said.

Clement stood. 'Thank you, Wing Commander. Gentlemen.'

'Answered your questions then?' Atcherley remarked.

Clement nodded. 'I'd appreciate it if you wouldn't mention that you have seen me to anyone?'

'Mum's the word, Reverend. Give my regards to Winthorpe, when you next see him.'

The girl wasn't in the kitchen when Clement returned. He collected his pack and left by the rear door. Once back on the dirt road, he struck out north towards Dunnet Head and Dwarwick Pier.

Clement watched his feet as he walked. His gut told him that his enemy had too much freedom of movement to be in the Services. That eliminated several thousand military personnel in Caithness but did little to discount the civilians of his acquaintance, especially the men who frequented *The Bell*.

Twenty minutes later the road bifurcated at a low stone dwelling. About fifty yards away was another crofter's cottage. He stared at the road running up to his right. The track rose steeply to a large house on Dunnet Head and although he could not see them, he knew that somewhere on the wind-swept headland were the bunker-like buildings of the Y-station.

On his left, the track descended to Dwarwick Pier and the waters of Dunnet Bay. Since leaving the main road and arriving at the junction where he now stood, the terrain had been easy; no steep hills and a distinct, albeit narrow, track furrowed by the wheels of horse-drawn carts, led down to the bay. Even the snow that lay in patches over the ground presented no difficulty, being no more than ankle deep. It had taken him just on forty minutes to walk from the rear door of the hotel to reach the pier. It would be much less if one was running and familiar with the track.

Descending to a flat area adjacent to the pier, Clement saw a small, windowless shed. It was closed and a large padlock was evident on the door. He walked along the stone promontory. Standing at the end of the pier, he stared out over the waters of Dunnet Bay. The wind was fierce. Below him the deep waters churned, slapping the pier's stone footings, the spray rising up the steep embankment. He pulled his coat around him, his body leaning into the wind. Dwarwick Pier was no place for a rendezvous in such conditions, just as Tom had said.

Clement turned and looked back at the steep hillside of Dunnet Head immediately behind him to his left. But the large house that he had seen from the track was not visible from the pier. Below him and to one side of the stone pier was a timber ramp that ran down from the flat area into the crashing waves. He stared at it as the swell came and went over the sodden timbers. It was devoid of any marine growth, scrubbed clean by regular use. Why had Tom told him the pier was rarely used? Clement scanned the surrounding fields, but no one was about today. He checked his watch. Almost noon. The morning had yielded valuable information, but now he had to leave. He estimated it would take him some hours to reach the kirk in Canisbay. He wanted to see the terrain in daylight and to reach the kirk just on dusk.

Looking east from the hill above Gills Bay, Clement could see Canisbay Kirk, the bell tower silhouetted against the gloom of a late-afternoon sky. Since leaving Dunnet, heavy rain had fallen and the temperature had decreased. Snow lay in patches around the district and the sea was grey. It was nearing four o'clock, an hour or so of dull light left in the wintry day before the invisible sun set. The walk from Dunnet Head had taken four soaking hours of inclement conditions over boggy

159

ground, the slush and wet tussock grasses and un-marked lochs making for slow progress. He had, how-ever, expected the snow to be heavier and deeper than it was. Aidan's comments about snow and wind echoed in his memory. It was true. But even with the wind at his back, walking any distance was miserable. It was not something one would do without good cause and defi-nitely not in the opposite direction. But it confirmed that if the killer intended to make a dash for the coast, he needed to be in place well before the rendezvous time. Or have access to a vehicle.

Keeping to the stone-walled fences and beech hedges, Clement approached the kirk from across the fields, coming out of the south-west. He checked the district for any movement before taking cover behind the stone wall at the intersection opposite the kirk. Nothing stirred. Crossing the road, he walked through the oldest headstones towards the kirk's front door. Lifting the latch, he paused, listening for any voices. All was quiet. He walked in, glancing at the empty pews before going straight to the small door on his left that, he guessed, led to the belfry. Opening the door, he scaled the spiral staircase. It led up to a timber-floored space where bell ropes hung like stalactites in the cen-tre.

A chill wind was his first sensation. His eye settled on three narrow, open windows. He walked towards the first, the one that faced south, and peered out. Be-low him was the intersection and road to Canisbay. He moved to the second. It had been where the gunman had stood. It looked west, across Gills Bay and the third looked east, towards Huna. Clement backed away and stood beside the barely moving stalactites, thinking.

160

The panorama was extraordinary. There was an uninterrupted view in almost every direction and a direct line of sight to the pier in Gills Bay. He returned to the window facing west. The distance from the kirk to the stone jetty in Gills Bay astounded him. It had to be more than a mile and again he contemplated both the accuracy of the sniper and the range of the weapon. Moving to the southern window, Clement stared again towards Canisbay. He could see the whole locality, from *The Bell* to the roof tops of Huna and Wallace's farm. Turning around, he scanned the floor for any casings from the hundreds of bullets that had been fired at him and Sarah, but the gunman had done a thorough job. Clement's eye scrutinized the space before him, his gaze focusing on the walls. Behind the door into the belfry from the stairs was a white painted ladder. His eyes followed it upwards to a trap door some fifteen feet above him. Turning, he returned to the window to check the roads. About half a mile away, he saw a car driving inland towards Canisbay. He guessed it was Stratton, but in the dull light, he couldn't be sure. Given that the Inspector had wanted to visit Castletown on his return to Thurso, it surprised Clement that Stratton was still in the district. Perhaps he had spent more time than anticipated in Crawford's barn. For trained eyes, the barn told a different story from the one believed by the villagers.

Stratton had probably interviewed the McAllisters and the Wallaces at length. Clement wondered what had been learned.

The car held his gaze. It was mesmerising. He felt himself frowning, recalling the grey car that had been parked outside *The Bell* on the day Donald Crawford had died, but all cars looked much the same to Clement, especially at a distance. However, other than Stratton's and the Wing Commander Atcherley's cars, the only other vehicles he had seen around the district were buses or lorries. Clement watched as it drove towards Canisbay. With no hills of any size or groves of thick vegetation to conceal it, the car was visible. Highly visible. Even during the early twilight, he realised that no vehicle of any kind could travel the roads of Canisbay and Huna in daylight hours without being seen for miles around and he didn't believe it was solely due to the height of the bell tower.

Waiting by the window, Clement checked his watch. A few minutes after five o'clock. Dusk was beginning to descend as he watched the car stop at *The Bell*. Two men got out. His hand reached for his telescope. Focusing the instrument, he stared at the forms hunched against the weather, hurrying into *The Bell*. He recognised Stratton immediately, but he couldn't identify the second man, who wore a heavy coat and hat. Clement moved the telescope and focused it on the manse, then the home of the Frew spinsters. A thin spiral of smoke was coming from Aidan's fire, but nothing was forthcoming from the Frew sisters' fireplaces. He lifted his gaze. A few stars were already visible between the clouds. It would be completely dark within the hour. Turning from the window, he replaced the telescope and reached for his knife. Placing it between his teeth, he placed his foot on the lowest rung of the ladder and began to climb upwards.

# 13

Clement pushed back the hatch and lifted himself into the dark space. Around him, pale specs of light filtered through between the tiles. It was cold and the incessant wind whistled its eerie screech through the cracks. With barely an hour of daylight remaining, he grasped a wooden beam above his head then placed one foot on the adjacent rafter, inching himself forward. Something hard hit his face. He recoiled from it but he knew what it was. Reaching out, his fingers traced along the wire until he felt several others. Placing his knife between his teeth, he took out his torch and flicked it on for one second only. But it was enough. Antennae wires, arranged like a metal bed head, criss-crossed the space in front of him and thick dust coated everything. He stared into the dark space before him. The amount of dust he had seen confirmed the antennae had not been installed recently.

Returning to the trapdoor, he placed one foot on the top rung of the ladder and descended to the belfry, his enemy's unseen presence like the pervasive icy wind. He walked towards the window facing south and looked over the villages of Huna and Canisbay. Somewhere out there his nemesis lurked. Twilight was descending. Nothing stirred. He turned and stared at the stalactite-like ropes in front of him. Still. Waiting for the hand of Robert Wallace or Ian McAllister to inform the region of invasion or the end of the war. Clement frowned trying to recall how long the nation's church bells had been silenced. He thought it was more than a year now. Was it possible the antennae had been in place that long?

Wallace or McAllister. Both men fitted his physical profile of the killer. But if not these men, there was only one other who had ready access to the bell tower. He stared at the ladder behind the door that rose vertically to the trapdoor above his head. Had Aidan lied about being fearful of heights? Clement stared at the perpendicular ladder. It was certainly not for those afraid of heights. He searched his memory about it. Sarah had also told him about Aidan's fears. Moreover, on the morning of Donald Crawford's death, Aidan had gone to visit his neighbours to pay the rent and had seen both he and Sarah conversing in the graveyard. The Frews sisters had even given Aidan a sponge cake. Clement felt the relief. Aidan was the one person who had a water-tight alibi.

He looked around the belfry. While the bell tower was the best surveillance point in the area, he knew he couldn't remain there. Not only was there a risk that the killer may return, but with the plummeting temperature, Clement needed a warmer place if he were not to freeze to death. From now on, he needed to be mobile and able to move at a moment's notice. Donning the few remaining items of warm clothing from his pack, he scaled the ladder again and hid the bag in the rafters.

Five minutes later, he descended the stairs from the belfry and let himself out. Leaving the kirk, he hurried through the graveyard and across the road, checking for any movement. Nothing. And no sound carried on the wind. Breaking into a slow run, he covered the three hundred yards to the manse in minutes. Checking around him, he scaled the low stone garden fence and crouched between the plants at the side of the manse. He could see the sitting room windows. The black-out curtains were drawn and he could smell burning coal. Keeping to the garden beds, he skirted the house and studied the snow-covered rear garden. The footprints from the kitchen door that he had seen on Wednesday had vanished under some recent snow and a fresh set now led from the back door across the field disappearing through the gate. Aidan was evidently visiting his neighbours and would return soon enough. Clement decided to wait, his gaze on the rear gate to the Frews' house.

He pondered Aidan's lie about contacting Thurso Police. Had he just changed his mind? The smell of the burning coal filled the night air. The promised warmth beckoned. Standing, he went to the door and knocked. He waited two minutes but no one came. It confirmed that his friend wasn't there and he wondered if Aidan would mind if he let himself in. Trying the door knob, Clement found it locked. He frowned. Was that unusual? He reached for his lock-picks then stopped. When Aidan returned, how would Clement explain his presence in the house? He turned, his gaze on the set of footprints that led away from the manse. He decided to wait.

Sleet began to fall and Clement felt the cold trickle run down his neck, making him shiver. He stared at the poultry shed not five yards away. There he could wait for Aidan to return. And it would be warm. Running the short distance, he turned the handle and let himself in.

The cold was unexpected. He closed the shed door behind him, and reached for his torch, flicking on the beam. The sight left him speechless. Ten hens sat on their perches, frozen to where they had died, their necks twisted, their heads flopped to one side. A cloud of condensed breath floated away from Clement's lips. He ran his hand over the dead birds. They were cold but there was no evidence of decay and not a drop of blood had been spilt.

He stared at them, a frown deepening. Why had the birds been killed? Backing away, he sat on a bale of hay on the floor at the far end of the shed and flicked off the torch. His intention had been to pass the night at the manse, but the bewildering spectacle made him uneasy. Now he wasn't so sure.

He stared at them wondering if Aidan knew. Clement had no way of knowing. Neither did he know if Aidan would return this night. A hollowness was developing in his chest, the sinister unseen presence enveloping him once more. He couldn't stay but shelter was now his major concern. He thought back to the large cattle barns he'd passed on his walk from Dunnet. The closest to the west was at least two miles distant and with night imminent, he would be travelling across fields and bogs in the dark. He shook his head. Besides, cattle are inquisitive creatures and would surely alert the farmer to his presence. Wallace's farm was closer but as Robert Wallace was one of the two men Clement now suspected, he decided against it.

He pulled his coat around him and blew warm air over his gloved hands, the gesture reminding him of the trenches. The appalling cold, the dead. Dead not from bullets but from poor shelter and inadequate clothing. But they, poor souls, had had no alternatives. In those days, the penalty for desertion was the firing squad. He chastised himself for becoming maudlin. It was the cold and the loneliness of this mission that tore at the soul. It clouded judgement, sowed doubt in the shadows. He recited the ninety-first psalm, the Lord's word giving him the comfort it always did. But right now he would have given his right arm to have just one of his former team members from the Auxiliary Units beside him.

He checked his watch. It was just after six o'clock and Aidan had still not returned. Had Sarah Crawford been at home he would have gone there, but with her away in St Margaret's Hope, the house would be as cold as the poultry shed. As much as he didn't like it, he needed to trust someone. His mind went through the people of Canisbay. There was only one whose loyalty to the people of the district was non-existent; Sean Mead…an outsider with a grudge.

Standing, Clement pushed open the poultry shed door and looked out. The twilight shadows had vanished over the rear garden and the bitter night made him shiver. He closed the door and skirting the manse, ran the short distance to Canisbay village.

Squatting by the hedge on the opposite side of the main intersection, Clement studied the inn. To one side of *The Bell* was a narrow passage with a high stone wall. Hurrying, he crossed the intersection and ran down the dark side path, the sound of raised voices audible through the blacked-out windows of the main bar above his head. At the corner of the building he paused and stared into the rear yard.

Behind the public house was an area of approximately fifty square yards. To one side, and leaning against the side fence, was a stack of empty barrels. On the other was a long out-building. He ran across the yard towards it, but heavy padlocks kept the building closed to the inquisitive. Stacked to one side of the out-building were some empty wooden crates. Squatting beside them, he checked the time; half past six. Beside the rear door to the inn was a bicycle. He hoped Sean was there, for although Clement hadn't seen Sean's bus, he knew Sean didn't need to be driving it to be in Canisbay.

Clement watched the rear door for several minutes but no one came or went. Taking a leather pouch from his webbing, he withdrew his lock-picks.

The door opened.

He stayed behind the crates and waited.

Sean Mead stood in the doorway, Jean Buchanan behind him. Clement's thoughts and apprehensions churned. He wasn't sure about Jean's involvement, but he needed help and he had no time for philosophizing. Swallowing hard, he stood and crossed the yard.

'Reverend Wisdom? Now I wasn't expecting to see you again.' Sean took in Clement's bedraggled appearance. 'Something happen?'

'Could I have a word with you? Inside?'

'Perhaps you should not make your return to us widely known, Vicar,' Jean said, closing the door behind them.

'What makes you say that, Mrs Buchanan?'

'Stewart McCrea is blaming you for the deaths of both Donald Crawford and his brother.'

'And Sarah Crawford disappearing at the same time has all the tongues wagging.' Sean added.

'Malcolm McCrea is dead?' Clement asked. 'That is terrible news.'

Sean was staring at him. 'Aye. Found on the rocks below the kirk yesterday.'

Clement felt the grievous weight of the murderer's wickedness. McCrea must have heard and seen the gunfire from the belfry and gone to investigate. That chance encounter had cost the boy his life.

'Like to tell us what is going on?' Jean asked.

He looked at the woman. 'I did not kill either Donald Crawford or Malcolm McCrea.'

'But you know who did?' Sean added.

Clement shook his head. 'Sadly, no. But I did see Malcolm on Wednesday night. Well, early Thursday morning, to be precise. I was escorting Sarah Crawford to Tom Harris's boat in Gills Bay. The lad came out of the darkness. Why was he on the road at three o'clock in the morning?'

'Why were you and Sarah Crawford?'

He heard the woman's insinuation but ignored it. 'Tom was taking me to Orkney and that was when the tide was right.'

'And Sarah?'

'Needed a place to think for a while.'

'Malcolm was on his way to Huna, to call the Veterinary in Castletown about a sick horse,' Sean told him.

'At that hour?'

'A sick farm horse is a real emergency, Vicar.'

Clement nodded. 'Who's in the bar at present?'

'Danny O'Reilly and Stewart McCrea,' Jean told him. 'So you better not go in there.'

'Mrs Buchanan, I understand you have a telephone. Can you tell me who used it last and when?'

'I did. Last Monday afternoon, to check on a delivery from the brewery. But I haven't been able to get a line until today given that neither Donald nor Sarah is there to operate the exchange. It's been a major inconvenience.'

'Did anyone else come into the bar this afternoon?'

'Just the usuals,' Jean answered.

Clement watched the publican from the corner of his eye. He wondered why she had chosen not to tell him about Stratton and his unknown companion Clement had seen from the bell tower.

'If that's all, I have work to do.'

'Yes, thank you, Mrs Buchanan.'

The woman left the kitchen, closing the door to the rear corridor behind her.

Sean went to a cupboard and took two glasses from the shelf and retrieved a bottle of whisky from behind the meat safe. 'Will you have a drink, Vicar? It looks like you could use one.'

Drawing a chair up to the kitchen stove, Clement sat down. 'Thank you. Sean, could I ask you something?' Clement took a deep breath. 'If I had to call on someone for assistance, could I count on you? As one outsider to another?'

'More than just a vicar, eh, Vicar?'

'Something like that.'

Sean stared at him for a few seconds. 'Aye. Why not? I was never one to shy away from a fight!' Sean swallowed the whisky in one gulp.

'Who was on the bus from Wick, the day I arrived here?'

Sean leaned back in the seat. 'If I remember correctly there was old Graham Nesbitt, a tenant farmer from Brabster. He falls asleep almost as soon as he is on board. Then there was the young constable and his wife from Thurso who had been to see the doctor. She's expecting. And the Veterinary from Castletown, Doctor MacGregor and his wife. Although, I don't know why he was on board. He's got his own car. Saving petrol, I suppose.'

'The Vet from Castletown, you say?'

'Aye. So you've heard about the theft. It happened while Doc MacGregor was in Wick.'

'Does he know what was taken?' Clement asked, hoping that Sean couldn't see he hadn't known about the theft.

'Chloroform.'

Clement heard the words like an explosion in his head. Donald Crawford's blue lividity, the fresh smell in the barn annexe. The lack of any sign of a struggle. It all made sense now.

'Do you know who drives a grey car?'

171

'Aye. Doc MacGregor.'

'Anyone with Stratton this afternoon?'

'Know him, do you? Why doesn't that surprise me?'

Clement smiled but he didn't answer.

'Aye, Aidan Heath. The Reverend and Joyce McAllister are taking it in turns to operate the telephone exchange and open the shop in Sarah's absence.'

Despite learning who owned the grey car and the revealing news about the theft of chloroform, Clement beamed. It was the first genuine smile that had crossed his lips since the death of Donald Crawford. Aidan's whereabouts had concerned him but now his relief was as heartening as the man's hearth.

'Well, if that's all, Vicar, I better put that empty barrel out or the landlady will start charging me board.'

'Mind if I stay here a while?'

'You can have a room, if you like. But I thought you would be staying with Reverend Heath, now that you're back.'

'It's been a long day and I wouldn't mind a few hours to myself. Besides, I think Aidan has enough on his plate without a house guest.'

'I understand. A man needs his solitude.'

Sean opened the rear door, the icy wind filling the kitchen. Lifting the barrel onto his shoulder, he disappeared outside.

Clement removed his boots and wriggled his toes, staring at the combustion stove, the heat seeping into his near frozen feet. The chloroform had been stolen on Tuesday, the day he'd arrived in Huna. Donald Crawford had died the next day, the same day Clement had seen the Vet's car outside *The Bell*. That surely was no coincidence. But while he knew the theft and the murder were linked, he didn't understand the motive. Was the Vet involved in some way? With the growing warmth, Clement's body began to feel the tiredness washing over him. Fatigue always clouded judgement and made rational analysis difficult. It had been a long walk from Dunnet to Gills Bay, especially in bad weather, but now that he knew beyond any doubt that Donald Crawford had been murdered, he couldn't ignore it. He also realized something else of importance; Donald Crawford had connected a telephone call, but as no one was in the red telephone box at the time and it had not been placed from *The Bell,* that left only one other place.

The back door opened as Clement slipped his feet back into his boots and retied the laces.

'It'll snow tonight, that's for sure.' Sean closed the door and removed his coat.

Clement stood. 'Thank you, Sean.'

'Going out? I thought you wanted a warm place to sit for a while.'

'I do. But I have to check something.'

'Here, take this then, Vicar.' Sean removed his sturdy green and brown tweed coat and tossed it to Clement. 'You'll catch your death in that poor excuse of an overcoat you wear.'

'You won't need it?'

Sean winked. 'I'm sure I'll be warm tonight. And Vicar, I'll leave the rear door unlocked for a few hours, if you want to come back here. The key cupboard's there.' Sean pointed to a small cabinet inside the pantry. 'There's no one in this evening, so take any key.'

'Mrs Buchanan won't mind?'

'What the eye doesn't see, the heart doesn't grieve over.' Sean opened the door to the main bar and left him.

Leaving *The Bell* by the rear door, Clement ran into the dark, side passage.

# 14

Clement paused at the corner. Pressing his back against the inn wall, he peered around the edge of the inn and studied the intersection in front of him. Nothing stirred and no lights were visible from any of the houses around Canisbay. He sniffed the air. The distinctive odour of burning peat came to him on the wind. Just off to his right was a confusion of footprints in the snow around the front door. Two bicycles were leaning against *The Bell's* front porch, their tracks disappearing into the night. Stratton's car had long gone but Clement could see the slush where the vehicle had pulled off the intersection to park outside the inn. He stared at his feet. The damp was beginning to penetrate the cracked leather of his old boots, but his mind was not on his increasingly numb extremities. He was annoyed with himself for letting slip that he knew the Thurso police Inspector. It was a mistake. Careless. Such inattention could cause his death. He stared again at his muddy and sodden bootlaces, praying his decision to confide in the Irishman would be vindicated.

Clement lifted his gaze, his eyes resting again on the car's tyre tracks. Although still well-defined, they were not fresh. Stratton couldn't have stayed long. But why had the man gone to *The Bell*? Had he gone to interrogate others who were at the inn? Stewart McCrea, Sean or Jean? Clement felt his head nodding. It made sense. Especially in light of the tragic news of Malcolm's death. It also explained Aidan's presence. And investigating the lad's death had delayed Stratton.

Clement lowered his head, thinking. Why had Jean not told him about Stratton and Aidan's visit? And what about MacGregor, the Vet? Questions and few, if any, answers. Perhaps it was another lesson learned about solo missions. There was no one with whom to share doubts. And even if Sean proved to be the asset Clement hoped for, he couldn't confide in the man. Neither could he count on Sean keeping his return to Canisbay secret. People talk. Things slip out in conversation. *He* was guilty of that. He bit his lip wondering if his lapse about knowing Stratton would adversely affect him. But one thing was certain; as warm as *The Bell* was, he couldn't stay there now. Not only could his whereabouts become widely known, it placed Jean in danger. He looked around. All was quiet. But finding a warm place to rest would have to wait, at least until he had seen the Frew sisters. They held a vital piece of information. He turned his mind to the pair. He knew al-

most nothing about them. Were they completely innocent, or implicated in murder? He had to know. But
one thing he did know; the call that had preceded Donald Crawford's death had been placed from their house.

Scanning the street once more, Clement crossed the
road and, opening a gate into the fields opposite, headed overland towards Huna. Keeping to the hedges, he
crossed the paddocks. From time to time, he looked
back over the ground he had just covered, but in the
darkening night his presence and his footprints were
concealed. So, of course, was anyone following. The
realisation only served to heighten his nerves. It was, he
guessed not yet eight o'clock and what there was of the
waxing moon was low in the sky. Unseen clouds came
and went, casting their brief but long, flickering shadows on the ankle-deep snow. Hugging the waist-high
beech rows, he approached the elderly ladies' house
from the front. He squatted by the dilapidated wooden
front gate and studied the building. It was a large
house, three storeys, with several chimneys. Squinting,
he stared at the stacks. No smoke was visible from any
of them and no smell of burning peat or coal lingered
in the air. No light was visible in the front rooms. It
looked neglected and bleak.

Hopping over the low, stone, garden wall he walked
up to the front door and listened. Silence. He knocked
and waited. No one came. Leaving the front porch, he
skirted the house. The manse stood silent over the rear
fence. He couldn't see any lights there either. Clement
glanced up at the rear door of the Frews' house. Beside
it was a window. He surmised the door led into a scullery or kitchen and wondered why the black-out curtains over the window weren't drawn. He stared at it,

an uneasy feeling beginning to take hold. He reached for his lock-picks when a noise, like something being dropped, came from one of the upper storey rooms. Glancing up, he waited, but the noise was not repeated.

Putting the lock-picks back in his pocket, Clement returned to the front of the house and knocked loudly, the uneasy feeling increasing. This time he heard the rhythmic fall of footsteps but still no one came to the door. Returning to the front gate, Clement stood facing the house, his eye scrutinizing the windows. All appeared to be closed, but he could see a distorted reflection of moonlight on the glass pane of the last window on the upper floor. Warped from years of rain and melting snow, Clement surmised that the window no longer closed properly. He thought for a moment. Despite not wanting to frighten the old ladies whom he had never met, breaking into the house had now become a necessity.

Looking back over his shoulder, Clement checked the fields for moving shadows, but in the darkness he saw nothing. Looking to his right, he could see the outline of Wallace's farm against the starry night sky. Hurrying through the overgrown garden, he made straight for the southern end of the house where he knew a large beech tree spread its branches over the entire end of the dwelling.

Removing one of the four magazines of ammunition from his webbing, he assembled the Welrod pistol and screwed on the silencer, then tucked the weapon into his belt. Reaching for his knife and holding it between his teeth, he started to climb. The tree had a sturdy trunk and thick branches and it felt more secure then he had expected. With his head level with the upper floor windows, and holding the branch with his left hand, he eased his head around the corner of the house and studied the window. No curtains were drawn there either but, he surmised, that unlike a scullery window, the upper floor bedroom was not in daily use. Using his knife, he prized open the pane closest to him. A small clod of snow broke away and fell from the window sill, breaking apart on impact below him. Pushing back the window panes, he swung his right hand around the edge and grasped the window's central timber pillar. With both hands wrapped around the wooden strut, he swung his right foot upwards and dragged himself over the sill. Once inside, he sat on the floor and waited in the silence. Slowly, he stood, the pistol firm in his grasp. The door to the hallway beyond was closed. With his ears straining, he untied his boots and secreted them under the nearby bed. Creeping towards the door to the hallway, he turned the knob.

The corridor beyond was dark and quiet.

He took a step forward.

The sting was instant. The only sound had been the hard cough-like thud of a silenced weapon. Wincing, he retreated to the bedroom, slamming the door closed and waited, his pistol clenched in his fist. The suddenness of the attack made his heart race. Glancing at his forearm, he saw a small amount of blood. It was not deep and he forced himself to stay alert to any noises in the corridor. Nothing. In the silence, he heard only his own pulse pounding in his ears.

Three seconds later he heard the sound of running feet, the tread too quick for an old lady. Making an instant decision, and holding his pistol before him, he threw open the door and fired along the darkened passage then drew back behind the door jam. No response. No movement. No sound. Where were the old ladies? He paused, collecting his thoughts. He reasoned that the gunman must be in one of the two rooms between himself and the staircase, but he could not understand why the gunman had not come after him. The man knew where he was, yet he had not fired again. Holding the pistol at arm's length, Clement crept around the door again. Nothing. No shot. No movement. He edged his way along the hallway, towards the staircase, his breathing suspended. Had the gunman lured him into the open? He felt exposed and vulnerable. His mouth was dry and his eyes wide open. Two seconds later he was at the top of the stairs, his back leaning on the balustrade. He glanced upwards through the stair well to the upper floor. Nothing. With his ears and eyes straining he stepped onto the top tread of the staircase to the lower floor. Stooping down, he peered through the banisters and stared into the front hall below him.

The unmistakable sound of a door opening and closing somewhere upstairs made him run. Descending the stairs, he ran into the sitting room on the lower floor and dived behind a large armchair for cover. Kneeling behind the seat and grasping his pistol, he inclined his head to one side and stared at the base of the staircase. No one descended. Why had the gunman not fired again? Not waiting to check the lower floor, Clement ran back up the stairs and thundered down the corridor to the small bedroom where he had entered the house. Kicking the door open and with his pistol clenched in both hands, he stepped into the room. A cold draught from the open window slapped his face.

Standing by the wall next to the window, he stared down at the snow-covered front garden. But even in the limited moonlight he saw only one set of foot-prints. He gasped, his breathing almost halted. A door had opened and closed but that was all. He felt the nausea welling up, adrenaline gripping his body. The killer was still in the house. Running his tongue around his dry mouth, Clement made himself think. Three sto-rey house. Servants' stairs! One of the doors he had passed must have led to the back stairs. Why had the killer not come after him? It made no sense.

He reached for his boots under the nearby bed and slipping them on, hurriedly tied the laces. Grasping the pistol, he worked his way along the upper corridor, opening every door. The last door opened to the serv-ant's stairwell. With each passing second his pulse ran faster until it thumped in his chest. But whoever it had been, he believed they were no longer there. His thoughts returned to the old ladies. Where were they in all the madness? He hadn't heard a female voice, nei-ther scream nor whimper. With his ears straining, and his Welrod in front of his face, he slowly descended the stairs and tip-toed along the hallway. Stopping by each doorway, he listened. Silence. No talking ladies. No boiling kettles. The unknown gripped his throat. A gust of cold air blew over him from the end of the hallway and he ran along the corridor to the rear of the house, his pistol raised, ready to fire.

The icy wind enveloped him and he knew the rear door to the garden must be open, but he was not going to react on impulse. He had made that mistake before. The open door didn't mean his adversary had gone. Moreover, the gunman, like himself, carried a silenced weapon. Never before had Clement felt death so imminent. He believed it had been more by divine intervention than his good management that his error had not already cost him his life. With his pistol raised, he edged himself around the kitchen doorway. Nothing but the bitter wind. Yet, Clement felt he was not alone. He crossed the kitchen and closed the door to the rear garden. Edging towards the window he drew the blackout curtains and switched on the light.

Before him, two elderly ladies were seated on either side of the breakfast table. A rope held their bodies, arms and legs to the chairs where they were sitting, their heads forward, their bodies still in death. Congealed blood matted their crimped grey hair. Swallowing hard, Clement screwed his eyes shut. His heart thumped, the pulsing gripping his throat. He made himself breathe then opened his eyes and stared at the old ladies he had never met.

The scene was grotesque. They resembled two porcelain dolls with white faces and wide pencilled eyes. He knew what kind of bullet had killed them. Subsonic bullets left little external mess. But there would be nothing remaining on the inside. How long had the ladies been seated in their kitchen? The cold delayed decomposition. Turning, he walked over to the door, his eye scrutinizing the lock of the rear door. Again, no damage to locks or handles was visible.

At his feet and beside the door sat a brown paper bag of kitchen scraps awaiting disposal and two empty bottles of gin beside it. How long had the ladies been dead? Why had the man returned this night? Clement's gaze fell on the telephone sitting on the bench beside the back door, but he knew the line was no longer connected. Sarah had disconnected it for him to call Nora Ballantyne in the small hours of yesterday morning.

Standing by the door, Clement faced the two lifeless bodies, arranged like rag dolls supping tea in a lifesize doll's house. They had been tormented, their last moments spent in terror. Such savagery was beyond assassination. And, from the lack of any evidence of a physical struggle, he knew they had submitted like lambs. Fear paralysed. He knew that. Such killings played no part in war. They were not the actions of decent men, even men who were the enemy. Placing his hand on their thin, icy shoulders, he quietly swore to their souls that he would find whoever was responsible and see them brought to justice. The obscenity of their deaths and the mockery of the tableau made him feel sick. The gunman had fired into their skulls from above. Instant death. He recited the Lord's Prayer aloud. Turning off the light, he re-opened the curtains and looked out, his eye on the rear door of the manse. Darkness had engulfed the scene, but he could still make out, in the centre of his vision, the silhouette of the poultry house not thirty yards away.

# 15

Despite the late hour, Clement decided to telephone Nora Ballantyne and Crawford's exchange was the only place. Closing the door to the elderly ladies' house, Clement stared at the footprints that ran away from the back door, disappearing through the open gate and into the manse's rear garden. What he had just experienced chilled him to the core and what had happened to the elderly ladies sickened him. He had never felt so close to evil. He had escaped with his life, but what he had seen would remain with him forever.

Clement crossed the rear garden leading to the gate in the fence. Two sets of footprints now crossed the manse's rear garden. He stared at the house, dread gripping his heart. All was in darkness. He rubbed his forehead. Everything left him confused. Nothing fitted. For all that he had seen, he still had no answers, just more questions. But one question could no longer wait to be answered. He crossed the rear garden, heading for the manse. Placing his hand on the backdoor knob, he turned the handle. Still locked and no smell of burning coal in the air.

His hand reached for the lock picks in Sean's borrowed coat pocket. It took Clement less than thirty seconds to gain entry. As the door swung open, Clement reached for his pistol. Pushing the door wide, he stepped inside, his pistol raised and his senses alert. All was still. And dark. And cold. He held his breath, his eyes were wide in dread of what he might find. Fact; Aidan Heath hated the cold. Clement closed the door behind him without making a sound, and with his left hand, reached for his torch. Flicking on the beam, he crept into the sitting room, his throat tight and his heart pounding. But no body lay sprawled before the hearth.

Opening the door to the rear hall, he crept up the stairs to the upper floor and threw open the door to Aidan's room. Nothing. No sleeping vicar and no dead body. Clement let out a long breath. Walking in, he checked the wardrobe and lowboy for the man's personal effects. Everything was in place.

Turning, he descended to the lower floor, now eager to leave. Standing on the small front porch, Clement looked out into the night, his senses alert to any noises. Nothing came to him on the cold wind. The gunman had vanished into the night. But Aidan's absence worried him. Then he remembered that Aidan

185

and Joyce McAllister were between them operating the telephone exchange. He prayed Aidan was there. Clement stared at *The Bell* some hundred yards distant. Why had the gunman not fired at him again? Another unanswerable question. He wondered if the killer had sought refuge at the inn. He needed to know. Besides, with either Joyce McAllister or Aidan operating the exchange, the call to Nora Ballantyne would have to wait until both had left Crawford's house.

Leaving the manse, Clement ran towards the public house, his mind alert for any movement in the dark. Crouching in the side passage, he studied the rear yard. He heard a door open. But it wasn't to the inn. Drawing his pistol, he waited in the shadows. A second later, he saw Jean Buchanan emerging from the outbuilding opposite. Stooping, she placed a box on the ground before bending to re-lock the out-building door. Two seconds later, she bent over and grasping the box, swung it onto her hip. Even in such circumstances, Clement felt guilty that he wasn't offering to lift it for her. But the sound of bottles clinking as she walked told him what the box contained. He stayed watching her as she crossed the yard and climbed the steps to the rear door, his mind overwhelmed by all that he had seen this night and the rapidity of events. He heard the door close.

Clement looked down at the torn sleeve in Sean's coat. With all that had happened, he hadn't felt the pain in his arm until now. He should wash the wound, and returning the coat would also give him the opportunity to question Sean about any recent arrivals in the public bar. He stood and placed his pistol back into the holster around his chest.

'Sean?'

It was a male voice.

Dropping to his left, Clement rolled behind some barrels. Withdrawing his pistol, he waited, the weapon raised. Footsteps. A man approached out of the shadows, a small dog at his side.

Clement exhaled and stood. 'Not Sean. Just borrowed his coat. Has something happened, Tom?'

Flip wagged his tail. Tom's startled eyes shifted from the pistol to the tear in his left sleeve. 'You alright, Vicar?'

'I'll live. I thought you were going back to St Margaret's Hope?'

'I was. But something's happened.'

'What?'

Clement heard the hesitation in Tom's reply. 'Maybe nothing. But after dropping you off this morning in Thurso, I saw a ship that I know entering port. Belongs to Karl Fraser, Eric's son. Karl had some interesting news. Sarah has left St Margaret's Hope.'

Clement frowned. 'Did Eric's son say where she went?'

'No. But given that every fisherman in port, except me, wouldn't put to sea for you, I'd say she is still on South Ronaldsay.'

'How long have you been in Canisbay?'

'Arrived a couple of hours ago. Why?'

'Is your boat in Gills Bay?'

'Yes.'

'Did you pass anyone on your way here?'

'No one, but then I came across the fields.'

'Can I ask you not to tell anyone you have seen me?'

'Does Sean know about your non-religious activities?'

'Not specifically.'

'Right. Well, I'll get a drink and warm up then, I think.'

'Be careful, Tom. The killer knows Sarah and I left here on your boat. Your life could still be in danger.'

'You encountered him, I see,' Tom said, his gaze on the blood-stained sleeve.

Clement nodded. 'I wouldn't want you to suffer the same fate.'

'Despite what you said, it is you he wants, Vicar. Someone else knows you are more than a vicar going to Orkney. Anyway, if someone wanted me or Sarah dead, why would they wait until now? Doesn't make any sense. I run the risk of dying at the hands of the Germans every time I put to sea. I'll take my chances here.'

'Well, if you are so determined. Could you do me a favour?'

Tom inclined his head.

'Could you find out if anyone entered *The Bell* within the last half hour?'

Tom nodded.

'And can you also learn where Reverend Heath is?'

'Isn't he at the manse?'

'No.'

'Where will you be?'

It was a good question. 'I don't know.'

Tom seemed to hesitate. 'In for a penny, I suppose. Go back to my boat. No one will look for you there. I'll be back later tonight.'

'Thank you, Tom.'

Tom disappeared into the darkened passageway at the side of *The Bell*. Clement waited until he could no longer hear Tom's footsteps before opening the rear door to Jean's kitchen. Edging his head around the door, he slipped inside. But Tom's words were ringing in his ears. "It's you he wants, Vicar."

Despite the hour, the kitchen was still a blaze of light, the black-out curtains drawn over the two windows. The room had that tidied-up-for-the-day look commercial kitchens do when mealtimes are finished. A burst of female laughter arrested him; the publican's voice. Crossing the room, Clement waited in the pantry, but no one entered the kitchen. He checked his watch. Eight thirty-five. It surprised him that the bar was not closed. But he had learned that the licensing hours in East Sussex didn't apply in Scotland. In fact, in certain parts, the inns served no alcohol at all. Wick, reputedly was one such place. A wry smile crossed his lips as he thought of Reg. From what he'd observed, no such restrictions applied at *The Bell*. He glanced around the kitchen. His coat hung over the back of a chair beside the stove. Watching the swing door into the bar, he transferred the contents of his pockets back into his own coat before removing Sean's and washing his arm in cold water. Holding his hand over the wound, he sat by the stove, feeling the warmth seep into his body and feet. It should have brought him comfort, but instead all he saw was the hideous image of the two old ladies. Four deaths. Three of them some of the most appalling he had ever seen. From the congealed blood in the old ladies' hair he knew they had not died this evening. But why had the killer returned to the house? And where was Sarah Crawford? Was she running from someone, or towards them?

He had no answers for any of his questions. His thoughts drifted to another time. Another life. One that was ordinary and safe. With Mary. Sitting by a fire, warming his feet, in his mind he heard her knitting needles clicking out their rhythmic tune as the radio told them of the cricket score in the Antipodes. Back then, he prayed more. And read his Bible and wrote sermons. Back then, he had the time for the things that were important to him. But now? It was the war. He felt an increasing bitterness for the Nazis who had taken his world and turned it upside down. The suction sound of the rubber around the swing-door that led into the bar broke into his thoughts. Leaping from the chair, he ran for the pantry, his knife in his grasp.

'Vicar?'

The Irish lilt was unmistakable. Clement stepped forward, his blade still in his fist.

'I figured you had returned.' But Sean's eyes were on the slim, long, double-bladed dagger. 'Tom was asking who came in this evening. Not something he's ever asked before. So, I figured you must have met out the back.'

'Is anyone else suspicious, Sean?'

'No. They're much too stupid for that. Besides, Tom likes to talk and everyone knows it.'

Clement smiled. 'Who's in?'

'Just Robert Wallace and Stewart McCrea now, although Ian McAllister was in earlier. It's odd really. Robert and Stewart never spoke much before Malcolm died and now they appear to have found a common bond.'

'Any idea what?'

'Misery! You know the old adage. And farming. Which, let's face it, amounts to the same thing.' Sean's gaze went to Clement's arm. 'You injured?'

'It's nothing much. I was lucky. But I'm sorry about your coat.'

Sean glanced at his coat lying on the kitchen table, the torn blood-stained hole obvious. 'Plenty of clothes nowadays have patches.'

But Clement's mind was on the men of Canisbay. 'How long have they been in the bar?'

'Stewart came in around five. Robert's been here all day. The weather's keeping most of them indoors. Bad for business, so I'm told.' Sean paused. 'You look done in, man. What about you get a few hours' sleep in one of the rooms upstairs?'

'Thank you, but no. I am sorry about your coat. I would offer you mine, but as you see, someone isn't happy I'm back in Canisbay.'

'Maybe they thought it was me, Vicar!'

Sean's remark had been said flippantly, but the thought that whoever had fired at Clement may have believed he was Sean just added to Clement's already confused assessment of events. Clement reached for his own coat and pulled it on, the dry warmth permeating his bones. It felt wonderful and for one second, he smiled. But the image of the old ladies crashed in on his thoughts and the smile fell from his face. He shook hands with the Irishman. 'Be careful, Sean.'

Clement walked to the rear door, aware that Sean was watching him. 'Has it snowed here in the last twenty-four hours?'

'We did have some flurries overnight.'

Clement nodded and opening the door, peered out. The rear yard was deserted. Pulling his collar around his neck, he hurried away. He had hoped, despite all evidence to the contrary, that the footprints he had seen on leaving the Frews' house were not fresh. But one thing Clement had learned, if Sean was to be believed, that whoever had fled through the manse's rear garden, they had not sought refuge at *The Bell*.

Crossing the rear yard, Clement climbed a fence and using the low hawthorn bushes for cover, made his way north towards the main road and the kirk.

At the intersection, Clement looked back over the fields. Slivers of pale light flicked across the pastures whenever the cloud cover allowed. On the night air he heard the low hum, the sound of a car's engine coming from the east. As it approached him, Clement wondered if he should stop the car and ask to be driven into Thurso, to inform Inspector Stratton about the Frew sisters. The sound increased as it neared. He couldn't think. The combination of the pain in his arm, coupled with his weariness and the numbing cold was dulling his senses. He could see the vehicle's deflected head lights now. Clement hid behind the stone wall adjacent to the intersection. At the last second he stood, and peering over the wall, saw a car pass not six feet in front of him. Stratton was behind the steering wheel; Aidan Heath beside him.

Clement slumped against the wall, his mind racing. He thought Stratton would have returned to Thurso hours ago. And why was Aidan in the car? Rain began to fall. Reaching for the balaclava in his pocket, he pulled it on. Standing, he checked the road in both directions grateful that the hour and the cold would keep most people indoors. Stratton's car had already disappeared into the darkness. Tom's warm, dry boat beckoned only a fifteen-minute walk away. But knowing Aidan was not at the Crawford's, the call to Nora Ballantyne could not wait. Leaving the intersection and keeping to the road, Clement headed east towards Huna.

The village looked as it always did; deserted. Withdrawing his pistol, he lifted the latch on Crawford's yard gate and slipped inside. In the darkness, he edged his way towards the kitchen door and turned the handle. The door was unlocked. He slipped inside and listened for the voice of Joyce McAllister, but all was silent and dark. He crept through the kitchen into the sitting room. The clock still ticked loudly. The room was warm and in the grate a few coals still glowed in the dark. He smiled knowing that Aidan had, indeed, been there.

Leaving the sitting room, he tip-toed along the corridor to the last bedroom. Edging forward, his hand reached for the bed, his fingers running along the cold sheets. Sarah was not there. Not that he expected her to be. Whilst her whereabouts concerned him, he did breathe a sigh of relief. Had he been wrong about her? That she had left St Margaret's Hope did not mean she was still on South Ronaldsay, despite what Tom said. Clement thought about the man's revelation. Sarah's departure hadn't seemed to cause Tom much concern. Did that mean he didn't care about the woman? Or was it that he knew where she was? More questions. Clement pursed his lips. It was time he had some answers. He returned to the sitting room and sat in the chair by the telephone exchange and memorized the current location of the cables. He didn't know which of the local phones was connected, but he guessed it was *The Bell*. Removing the cable, he attached it to the one Sarah had previously used for the London call and dialled the number. A disgruntled voice answered.

'Nora?'

'Yes.'

'This is Clement Wisdom. I need some information.'

# 16

Saturday 1<sup>st</sup> March

The sound of sizzling fat and the distinctive aroma of eggs cooking roused him. Clement's hand reached under the mattress for his knife, the action unconscious. In that instant between the oblivion of sleep and wakefulness, he had forgotten that he was on the fishing boat. Blinking the sleep from his eyes, he saw Tom leaning over the tiny galley stove, his back to Clement.

'Sleep well?' Tom said without turning around.

'Apparently too well.' Clement secreted his knife into its scabbard and checked the bandage on his arm. The blood had dried but the dressing needed replacing. He swung his legs over the side of the bunk bed and stood up.

The wind was howling through the little ship's stanchions, reminding him of the strengthening head-wind he had encountered on his walk back from Crawford's shop the previous night. Clement stared through the porthole at the grey water. Beyond Gills Bay, the turbulent waters of Pentland Firth were capped with white, while Stroma Island was all but obscured in the mist. He turned to face the fisherman. 'I thought you might stay at *The Bell.*'

'The thought did cross my mind. How's the arm?'

'I'll be alright. Do you have another dressing on board?'

'Aye.' Tom lifted the frying pan and slid an egg on-to some thick bread on each of the two waiting plates. 'Eat. I'll get the bandage.'

Clement sat at the small galley table and unwound the blood-stained compress. Tom put some iodine and a gauze pad on the table, his gaze on the shallow wound. 'You were lucky, I'd say. Now to answer your questions of last night; no one entered *The Bell* at the time you asked about and Reverend Heath and Joyce McAllister have been operating the exchange and the shop between them in Sarah's absence.' The kettle whistled. Tom went to fill the waiting tea pot. 'And I understand that Joyce is feeding Aidan. He's more helpful to the community doing that at present than sitting by his fire reading fishing magazines.'

'I agree.' Clement said securing the bandage with a pin. 'Is Reverend Heath residing at McAllisters'?'

'Couldn't answer that, but if he isn't at the manse, it is more likely he is with Ian and Joyce. It stands to reason.'

It did to Clement too. And it fitted with what he had seen last night. Although where Aidan had been going with Stratton still perplexed him.

Clement lifted his knife and fork and giving silent thanks for the food, cut a slice of egg-soaked bread. The yolk reminded him of another meal; the one he had shared with Aidan on the day Donald Crawford was murdered. Clement thought on the Frew sisters and the ghastly image. What connected the deaths? And why had it been necessary to silence the chickens? He visualized himself sitting on the hay bale in the shed, staring at the dead fouls and sacks of coal. Even Aidan couldn't enter that shed without the birds making their raucous cackle. So who had entered the shed and thought it necessary to silence the birds? Something had been hidden there. Or someone. He wanted to see the poultry shed again. 'Ian McAllister delivers coal on Saturdays, doesn't he?'

Tom sat down and began to eat. 'And Wednesdays.'

Clement nodded, licking the thick yellow protein clinging to his lips. 'Do you know much about farming, Tom?'

Tom Harris laughed. 'You're talking to the wrong man, Vicar. What's your question?'

'What do Scottish chickens eat?'

Tom stared at him, his knife suspended mid-air, the bushy eyebrows raised in surprise. 'I didn't expect that. The same as chickens anywhere I suppose; kitchen scraps and grain. Oats; there is always lots of oats. My mother fed me almost exclusively on porridge.'

'Yes. Porridge. What about hay?'

Tom laughed aloud. 'They're chickens, Vicar, not horses.'

Clement finished the egg and stood. 'Of course. Silly of me.' But he knew what chickens ate, he just wanted to know if Tom did. 'Thanks for the breakfast and the bunk, Tom. And for the information.'

'I hope you work it out soon, Vicar. Where will you be?'

'Best you do not know.'

It was nearly nine o'clock, but the dull day and white sky made it seem like early morning and Nora Ballantyne's return call was not for another twelve hours. Clement glanced up at the imposing kirk as he hurried along the worn stone jetty. No one was firing a machine gun at him today. Leaving the pier behind him, Clement took the track up from Gills Bay to the main road.

At the intersection, he paused and stared across the paddocks around him, the bleakness of the day like a shroud. Off to his left, the old kirk stood mute and omniscient. He stared at it. He began to think that the ancient building was trying to tell him something. Perhaps the cold was colouring his imaginings, but he felt driven to enter it. He glanced across the fields to the manse, checking the chimney. No smoke. Wherever Aidan was, he wasn't at home. And while Clement wanted to see the poultry shed, there was time for some overdue prayer and reflection.

Lifting the latch on the large door, Clement felt the freezing air of the closed kirk encircle him. Stepping inside, he selected a pew to the side of the entry door and knelt down. Although he recited known prayers, the words came automatically and his mind was not on them. He stopped his prayers and stared up at the white-washed wall in front of him. 'What is it You want your servant to know, Lord?'

In the silence he stared, unblinking at the wall before him, his mind suddenly calm. 'The telephone.' He said the words so silently he wondered if he had actually voiced them. Leaning back in the pew, the idea ricocheted around his brain. Was it just the telephone that linked the deaths? Had it never been about the wireless? Clement leaned his forehead into his palm and rubbed at the deepening furrows. Why had the chickens died? He drew in a sharp breath. He knew now what had been hidden in the poultry shed.

He hurried away from the kirk and crossed the road, his eyes scanning the dwellings of Canisbay some three hundred yards in front of him. Smoke issued from chimneys, but no one came or went. He wondered if people stayed indoors throughout winter or only travelled in vehicles? His mind recalled the car he had seen on his first day. He knew now that it belonged to the Vet from Castletown. But Castletown was too far away from the antennae in Canisbay Kirk. Did that exonerate the Vet?

Clement climbed over the stone fence and crouched behind the cold wall. While his eyes searched for movement in the surrounding fields, his mind was on Crawford's stolen radio transmitter. Had its theft only ever been opportunistic? Leaning his back against the cold wall, he suddenly felt the grip of sinister realization. He could almost hear the killer laughing. It was pure evil. Donald Crawford's grotesquely displayed body was a message The killer knew about the Crawfords' secret wartime role. But it wasn't why Donald

Crawford had been killed. He had died because of a telephone call. Crawford could identify the caller.

Standing, Clement glanced along the road in both directions. Still nothing. He ran along the hawthorn and beech hedges making for the manse. The wind was strong now. Nothing unusual for Caithness, but a blustering westerly made for hazardous waters in Dunnet Bay, if, that is, he was correct about a pick-up and its location.

Crouching beside a low flagstone fence, Clement could almost feel his enemy's sadistic presence. He stared at his boots, thinking about the telephone call. It was the one thing that only he and the killer knew about. Clement had seen that the red telephone box was empty at the time Donald Crawford connected the call. So how did the killer know that he, Clement, had learned about the call? He felt himself exhale. His presence in the Frews' house. There was no other reason for him to break into the old ladies' house. He felt his heart racing. But he also realised something else. Not only could Donald Crawford name the caller; he could also identify the recipient. He may even have listened to the conversation. Clement swallowed hard. He also knew now that because it was a telephone call and not a radio transmission, that recipient was local, not in Germany or on a U-boat in the Pentland Firth. But why, if the killer had a local contact, would he remain in the vicinity? Especially as now, thanks to the encounter in the Frews' house, the killer knew Clement had not only returned to the district but also had figured out the significance of the telephone call? Why had the gunman not killed him in the Frews' house?

Clement lifted his head, the manse in the centre of his vision. Running beside the hedge that bordered the road, Clement paused, crouching in the entangled branches. From his position, he could see that the black-out curtains on the sitting room windows were still drawn. Aidan, it appeared, was not at home and hadn't been for some time.

Keeping to the rose beds, he crossed the garden and skirted the house. Glancing up, he saw the Frews' home. He felt his body shudder. Looking away, he ran towards the poultry shed and opened the door.

It surprised him that the smell was not greater. His gaze shifted from the birds to the deep shelves at the other end of the shed where garden implements were stored. Two coal bags sat propped against some stacked bales of hay. Another hay bale, the one he had sat on, was in the middle of the small floor.

Turning the bale over, he could see that handfuls of hay had been removed. Pushing his fingers into the straw, his hand searched the hollowed-out cavity. Nothing. Withdrawing his hand, he knelt down and studied the space. Straw lay all around the shed. It covered the floor and the chicken perches. Had he been wrong about the wireless? He didn't believe so. Despite it not being there now, he believed it had been. He pondered who could have removed it; but there still were no definitive answers.

He needed to hear from Nora. Looking up, his gaze fell on the pipe that channelled the heat from the house. Aidan. He thought of the cleric. The footprints in the snow between the manse and the old ladies' house, the hay bale which, even though he couldn't prove it, had been used to hide Sarah Crawford's wireless, his instinct told him it had. And there was the antennae in the kirk as well as Aidan's lie about telephoning the police. Everything else could be circumstantial or completely innocent, but not that. Yet despite this, the wireless wasn't there. If Tom's information was correct, Aidan may not have even been at home for some time. Clement stared at the stone slab floor. Was it the killer's intent to implicate Aidan?

Once more Clement went through the list of men in the area. Of all the people in Huna and Canisbay, only three men knew he was again in the vicinity; the killer, Tom Harris and Sean Mead. And, both Tom and Sean could have killed him already, if that had been their intention. Therefore, neither was the murderer.

Clement sat staring at the floor, blowing warm air into his gloved hands as he thought. Was it possible that the person he'd encountered in the Frews' house was not the killer? Of the regular attendees at *The Bell*, those that remained were Danny O'Reilly, Robert Wallace and Duncan McCrea. But he already knew enough about Duncan McCrea to know that the man would be incapable of carrying either a corpse or a machine gun up a spiral staircase and would surely not have killed his own son. That left Robert Wallace and the young Irishman. Danny O'Reilly he had already discounted. And, given that Tom had said Wallace was a war hero, Clement believed it unlikely. He shook his head feeling the frustration. He needed to hear from Nora. Lifting his gaze, he stared at the two full hessian bags of coal leaning against the wall of the shed. Ian McAllister was certainly capable of lifting heavy weights. If he delivered coal on Wednesdays and Saturdays he could easily have hidden the wireless and then retrieved it at a later time and Aidan would be none the wiser. Standing, Clement opened the shed door, his mind on McAllister.

On the wind he heard the deep hum of a vehicle. The noise increased then stopped. Assembling his Welrod pistol, Clement left the poultry shed, and using his lock-picks slipped into the manse by the rear door. Glancing around the kitchen, he saw that nothing appeared disturbed. He paused in the doorway between the kitchen and sitting room and listened for any movement on the upper floor. Tip-toeing across the sitting room, he waited beside a front window. A lorry was parked in the lane beside the manse. A second later the driver's door opened and McAllister jumped out.

Clement stared at the man. It had been McAllister who had come to the manse to inform them of Donald Crawford's death. And it had also been McAllister who had helped Aidan take Crawford's body down from the window in the barn. McAllister had also been in *The Bell* the night Clement arranged his passage with Tom for Orkney and Sean had told Clement that McAllister had been in *The Bell* last evening. The man's mobility raised no eyebrows. McAllister could have placed the weapons in the bell tower at any time, especially as the man was one of the two church maintenance men.

Clement watched as McAllister walked to the rear of his lorry, lifted a full sack of coal onto his shoulder and turned towards the rear garden. Moving through the house, Clement positioned himself next to the pipe that funnelled warmth into the shed, his ears straining. He heard the shed door open and the sound of shuffling feet. Why, if two full sacks of coal were already in the shed, was McAllister there at all?

Hearing the shed door close, Clement peered through the kitchen window. McAllister was returning to the front of the manse. Hurrying through the house, Clement stood by the front door and peered through the window. In each of McAllister's hands were two dead chickens.

# 17

Clement watched from the front window of the manse as the coal delivery lorry drove away, heading south towards Canisbay. He stared after it long after it disappeared from view, his mind on Ian McAllister. Everything about McAllister fitted with the profile Clement had created for the murderer. He began to think back. On the day Crawford was killed, McAllister had driven past him and Sarah while they stood in the graveyard. Therefore, it was likely that McAllister had seen Donald Crawford enter the barn. And McAllister had ready access to all homes where he delivered coal twice every week. Could the man have gone to the Frews' house under some pretext of needing to use the telephone? No one other than the old ladies and the telephone operator would know. McAllister could also have timed the call for when Sarah was known to be doing deliveries.

The evidence was circumstantial. What Clement needed was proof.

Leaving the manse, Clement waited by the front gate. Up to his left he could see the coal delivery lorry parked outside the public house. A few seconds later McAllister jumped out. Clement watched as the man lifted a sack of coal from his lorry onto his shoulder then enter the building. Leaving the manse, Clement ran for the field opposite and hurried overland towards the rear door of *The Bell*.


Jean Buchanan was standing at the kitchen sink when Clement entered. She turned suddenly as he walked in, a long-bladed kitchen knife in her hand.

'Everything alright, Mrs Buchanan?'

Jean nodded then reached for a cabbage and chopped the vegetable in half with one swift strike.

'Is Sean here?'

Jean shook her head. 'Left first thing this morning.'

'Any reason?'

'Work! And before you ask, he cycles into Thurso. It takes him a couple of hours. More when the weather's bad.' Jean scooped the sliced cabbage between her hands and dropped the vegetable into a saucepan of boiling water.

'When is he due back?'

'Tonight. He drives the bus from Thurso via Halkirk to Wick then returns through Castletown by the inland road.'

'There's another road to Thurso?'

The woman turned, her brown eyes fixed on him. 'We may seem remote to you, but like other parts of the world, there usually is more than one road to your destination.'

'Of course.' He felt stupid. And from the expression on Jean's face, she evidently thought him dull-witted. 'What time do you expect him?'

'Nine.'

'Do you know when the funeral for Donald Crawford is to take place?'

'There isn't going to be one.'

'Really? Do you know why?'

Jean reached for the knife again and started to gut some fish. 'With the grieving widow gone, people just don't see the need to farewell the dearly departed.'

Clement ignored the sarcasm. 'What's happened to Mr Crawford's body?'

The woman met his gaze. 'Inspector Stratton took it with him to the mortuary in Thurso.'

Clement felt such relief he almost smiled. No wonder Stratton had remained in Huna for so long and taken Aidan with him.

Jean placed the fish into a hot pan. 'It's not that people are unfeeling, but with Sarah absent, a roster has had to be arranged to open the shop and operate the exchange. To say nothing of food and postal deliveries. Life goes on, you know.'

Clement nodded. He understood the community's frustrations, especially during the cold, inclement weather, but Jean's total lack of sympathy for Sarah was about something else. And from her expression, he could see she hadn't finished.

'It's unfair of Sarah to leave. People have enough to do with their own work without having to accommodate her.' Jean threw the knife into the sink. 'You should eat. I have enough for an extra plate.'

Jean had turned away from him during her outburst to retrieve some plates from a cupboard above the sink and her offer of food had been delivered without even making eye contact.

'Thank you, Mrs Buchanan. I'm afraid I don't have my ration book on me.'

'We'll manage without it.'

He watched the thick capable wrists of the publican. She was a prodigious woman, he could see that, and, he surmised, not just physically. He'd never known a female publican. The woman's self-assuredness made him believe she was completely self-sufficient. Men for Jean Buchanan were obsolete for all but one task. Perhaps that was what attracted Sean.

'And after, you should get some rest. You can have a room upstairs.'

Clement thought for a moment. 'Thank you. That is most kind. I must ask you please, not to mention that you have seen me.'

Jean held his gaze. 'Suits me. You're not the most popular person ever to come to Canisbay.' Wiping her hands on her apron, she walked into the pantry and took a key from the small cupboard.

Robert Wallace's description of him being a *Wise Man from the South* was, evidently, a commonly held opinion. Placing the key and the dinner on the table before him, she left him to finish the meal.

Ten minutes later, he washed the plate and cutlery, returning them to the cupboards from which he had seen Jean take them. Taking the key, he walked into the rear hallway to find Room Ten.

The room was on the first floor at the far end of the hall. He placed the key in the lock and opened the door. Another utilitarian room greeted him. But Jean had given him a room at the corner of the building which had an expansive view from its double aspect windows. The scene west was of snow-covered fields and several large barns where cattle were housed until the spring thaw. Clement wandered towards the other window and leant on the sill. In the centre of his field of vision was Canisbay Kirk, about five hundred yards distant to the north. Turning around, he sat on a chair in the corner of the room and removed his boots. Placing his muddy footwear under the bed and removing his webbing, he pulled back the bed covers and lay down.

He didn't sleep. He hadn't intend to. The bed was nothing more than a warm place to think. The image of Ian McAllister carrying dead chickens filled Clement's thoughts. The hunched shoulders and firm grasp, a man used to carrying weight. Whichever way Clement thought about it, McAllister had opportunity and fitted the physical profile Clement had envisaged. But he had to be sure about the man's guilt. He contemplated how to confront McAllister. Particularly from a position of weakness, given that the man, if it had been him in the Frew's house, knew Clement had returned to the district. He closed his eyes, reliving the encounter. Could Sean have been right? Could the gunman have mistaken him for Sean? Clement swung his legs over the side of the bed and slipped his feet back into his boots. Even if McAllister had thought him Sean, Clement couldn't think of a reason why McAllister would want to kill Sean. If there was one, it was surely personal. But still something nagged. Something didn't fit. He had to be certain. And whilst remaining at *The Bell* had been a kind gesture, one loose word from Sean or the publican could spell Clement's death. From now on, until either he or his adversary was dead, no one local could know his exact whereabouts.

Clement returned the room key to the cupboard in the kitchen and left by the rear door. Checking the yard first, he left *The Bell* and staying close to the fences and hedges, headed overland, making for the one place where he knew he held the advantage. Twenty minutes later, he stood by the little window in the bell tower observing the scene below him.

Off to his left were the shops and houses of Huna. In front were the manse and the home of the Frew sisters. Further distant were the houses of Canisbay and *The Bell.* He stared at the smoke rising heavenward from *The Bell's* two chimneys. Always rising. Unending. He glanced at the home of the Frew sisters and the manse. Both houses stood mute and still in the cold Scottish day. What was missing from the scene before him were people; the routine ebb and flow of daily life. The icy wind whistled around his head as his eyes scanned the fields. No farmers tilled the soil, no vehicles worked the land. Was the weather the sole reason people stayed indoors? Even the road below him was devoid of activity. And no reconnaissance fighters flew in the skies above Canisbay. He crossed the belfry and leaned on the window sill, staring out across Gills Bay, his eye on Tom Harris's boat still tied up at the jetty.

Something was going on around him. He sensed it even if he couldn't see it.

Checking the view of the district one more time, Clement squatted on the timber floor and removed all his weaponry, lining it up before him. Pulling his great-coat around him and placing his hand on the butt of the assembled Welrod, he closed his eyes and allowed his mind to drift. Sometimes trying to empty the mind helped to crystallize facts. What was the old saying? *Can't see the wood for the trees.* Too much information confused. Facts needed to be separated from suppositions. As his friend from East Sussex, Chief Inspector Morris of Lewes Police, had said, "the proof is in the detail". Maybe so, but right now Clement felt swamped by information. If Arthur Morris was to be believed, it would be something so insignificant it would be overlooked.

'Go back to what you know,' Clement muttered. Fact; Donald Crawford would have known the caller, and most likely the recipient of the call. Perhaps more importantly, he had found nothing out of the ordinary in the caller placing the call. Clement paused. Was that true? Could it have been the reverse? Was the placed call so unusual that Crawford had listened to the conversation? Had Crawford overheard something? Or was it that the telephone number had aroused Crawford's suspicion and the man had gone to the barn to inform the Y-station about it?

Clement blinked several times, his brain exploring possibilities. He felt like he was walking on quicksand. The facts were before him, he just couldn't arrange them in the right order. He knew the murderer had an accomplice because of the telephone call and therefore,

211

he knew that the murderer was close by but the accomplice wasn't. Castletown and Dunnet; the Royal Air Force Base and the Radar Station. And Doctor MacGregor, whose grey car Clement had seen on the day Donald Crawford died. The Vet was based in Castletown and would, as a professional man, surely be known to Wing Commander Atcherley? Clement contemplated speaking again with the Wing Commander, but it was already after two o'clock. Night would fall before he could reach Castletown and return, and he didn't relish crossing the bogs and negotiating the lochs in darkness.

He wrapped his arms around his body as the temperature fell. 'Perhaps it is best.' Within four hours it would be dark and bitterly cold in the bell tower. He closed his eyes, the return call from Nora Ballantyne still seven hours away.

Clement heard the hard, heavy click of the kirk's main door opening. He replaced his pistol in his belt and knife in the strap around his calf. Then he crossed the belfry, descended the stairs and, rotating the door knob silently, opened the door to the nave. Staring through the crack, he saw Sarah Crawford sitting in one of the pews. She didn't appear to be at prayer. Gently closing the door again, he hurried back up the stairs to the belfry and went straight to the land-side window and looked out. In the mid-afternoon light he saw a man walking down the road from Canisbay. He did not appear to be in any hurry but even without seeing the man's face Clement knew who it was. Flip was trotting along beside his master. Clement waited, his eyes riveted on the fisherman as the man crossed the road. Within minutes Clement heard the heavy kirk door open.

Without waiting he hurried down the stairs again and re-opened the door to the nave just a crack. In the stillness of the kirk, he listened.

'Sarah?'

'Here.'

'Are you alright? How's the ankle?'

'I'll live. But I was cold last night. What's happening?'

'That visiting vicar knows you left Orkney.'

'How?'

'I told him.'

'Why?'

'I had to. I told him I was returning to St Margaret's Hope. I couldn't think of anything else to say. But I did say you were probably still on South Ronaldsay.'

'Does he suspect?'

'I don't really know what he knows, but he is injured.'

'How?'

'Shot, apparently.'

The pair remained silent for a minute.

'When will *he* be here?'

'Later tonight.'

Sarah looked around the empty church. 'I wish *he'd* never come. Do you have some food?'

Tom Harris emptied his pockets, passing the contents to Sarah. 'Not much longer. And then we can be away from here in the wee hours.'

Clement watched Tom leave. A few minutes later Sarah also left, a walking stick in her hand. Clement ran up the stairs to the belfry and rushed to the land-side window. Sarah was limping through the graveyard, heading east. Tom was nowhere to be seen. Clement crossed the belfry to the seaward window and looked out. He could see the fisherman striding along the roadway making for his boat in Gills Bay.

Returning to the southern window, Clement watched Sarah until he couldn't see the woman any longer. But he knew there was only one place where she could hide and was almost guaranteed not to be disturbed. He visualized the single bed in the annexe of the stone barn. No doubt, she had been there the previous night, while he had occupied the spare bunk on Tom's boat. And Tom would know Sarah was unlikely to be disturbed by any wandering vicars in the dark. Clement didn't like their deception but he felt one step ahead of them now that he'd overheard their conversation. He suspected that Sarah had come from St Margaret's Hope on Karl Fraser's boat and boarded Tom's boat in Thurso, sometime after he, Clement, had left Tom, which explained why Tom's boat had still been tied up there.

Clement leaned against the white washed wall and slid down it, squatting on the floor. For some time he stared at nothing. He felt betrayed by Tom Harris and Sarah Crawford. A sigh escaped his lips. Why would they have any loyalty to him, a man neither of them had even met until a few days ago? He closed his eyes. Who was the man they were waiting for? At least he didn't have too long to find out and he didn't need to move from the belfry. He went over in his mind what, if anything, he had learned from overhearing their conversation. Firstly, there was more to the relationship between Tom and Sarah than he had initially believed.

But despite the enigmatic conversation, he did not believe either of them had been the killer in the Frews' house. But it reinforced his opinions about the illusory calm of Canisbay and Huna.

Clement stayed by the southern window. Nothing could induce him to leave the bell tower now. From time to time he stood and stamped his stiff, numb limbs as the temperature plummeted. He checked his watch. Half past five. In the cold evening air, he heard a motor.

# 18

Leaning from the window as far as he could, Clement could just make out the moving, pale shaft of light from the deflected headlights of a vehicle driving west. Its progress was slow in the poor light, but the sound was distinctive. He'd heard the oddly syncopated gears before. Running, Clement descended the circular stone steps as fast as he could, praying he was not mistaken. Opening the door to the nave a crack, he checked the kirk's interior before rushing through the building towards the main door. Flinging it open, Clement ran through the graveyard and waited on the road for the bus to stop.

The door opened and Clement stepped aboard, first glancing along the seats. 'No one on board, Sean?'

The Irishman shook his head. 'As you see. I only had three from Wick. Two I left in Hastigrow. And as I only had old Farmer Nesbitt on board after that, I took him home to Brabster. It's a village not far from here. What is it, Vicar?'

Clement took a deep breath. 'I realise that I am making an assumption, Sean, but would it be fair to say that you know how to use a pistol?'

The man's eyebrows raised, but it was the only reaction. 'Aye. But I've always been better with my fists.'

'I need your help, Sean.'

Sean switched off the headlights and engine.

Taking the front seat on the left, Clement rested his feet on the warm wheel arch. 'Sean, there is something I feel obliged to tell you before you make any commitments.'

'And what would that be?'

He told Sean about the Frew sisters. Clement suspected not much rattled Sean Mead, but learning how the Frew sisters had died had turned the Irishman pale. 'And it is not impossible that I was mistaken for you.'

The man ran his hand over his chin before speaking. 'Forgive me for asking the obvious but I suppose I would like to hear it confirmed, Vicar. Would I be right in thinking that your presence here in the north is more to do with secret war business than any religious matter?'

Clement nodded. 'I cannot tell you any specifics, Sean. Were you aware that Sarah Crawford has returned to Canisbay?'

'I wasn't. But I'd like to know how it is you know that.'

217

Clement told Sean of the conversation he'd over-heard in the kirk.

'And you think Sarah is involved in some way?'

'It would appear so.'

'Who do you suspect?'

'Ian McAllister.'

Clement watched Sean for any reaction, but the Irishman's face had not shown much surprise.

'Why him?'

'He is male, strong and more importantly, mobile. He was also in his lorry on Wednesday, the day Donald Crawford was murdered.'

Sean's head was nodding but he hadn't spoken.

'You appear not to be surprised, Sean. Any reason?'

'I had a bit of an altercation with the man some time ago.'

'About?'

'Sarah Crawford, as it happens.'

'Really?

Sean paused. 'He accused me of having an affair-of-the-heart with Sarah.'

'Was he right?'

'Of course not. And despite what you say about Sarah and Tom Harris and whoever this other man may be, Sarah Crawford is a good, hard-working woman who has,' Sean corrected himself, 'had an abusive alcoholic husband.'

Clement looked at the man. He considered Sean's anger had more to do with the past. But whatever Sean may or may not have done in Ireland, it was not Clement's current concern. At one time, Clement would have been shocked by his own complacency. The war had changed everything. He had said that before. But whatever reason had led Sean to leave Ireland, Clement believed the Lord had placed Sean Mead where the man was most needed. And right now, that was with him.

Clement continued. 'If Ian McAllister is the man I'm looking for, then I need more proof than him being in the right place at the right time on Wednesday. But we must be careful. And invisible. I don't suppose you know about the man's past?'

'I've never asked. I prefer not to know too much about people. It makes leaving easier.'

He met Sean's gaze. The Vicar in him wanted to reach out to Sean and what troubled him, but it would have to wait.

'What do you have in mind doing, Vicar?'

'I want to see inside his lorry.'

'Is there anything else you care to tell me about before I sign up?'

Clement could feel his eyebrows rising. There was so much he had not confided to Sean.

Sean interrupted Clement's thoughts, no doubt seeing his hesitation. 'It's alright, Vicar. If it's a fighter you want, or someone to watch your back with no questions asked, then I'm your man. I don't need to know the whys and wherefores. Actually, I prefer not to know any more than I already do.'

'Thank you, Sean.'

'What's the plan?'

Clement thought for a moment. 'Tom said they would leave in the small hours and I know from experience that Tom will not put to sea before the turn of the tide. On Wednesday night the outgoing tide commenced at two o'clock. Tom adds an hour to allow for the outgoing current to be swift and the tides shift here by about half an hour to forty minutes a day. That puts their departure around four o'clock in the morning. So why are they meeting the third person later tonight? To do what?' Clement stared at Sean, hoping his question wasn't rhetorical.

Sean shrugged his shoulders.

Clement wasn't convinced that Sean was telling him all he knew. He thought of his old team in East Sussex. Men he could trust. He dwelt on Reg, who, although in Scotland, was miles away. Regardless, he was grateful for Sean's assistance. But there would be no discussing thoughts or plans beyond what was necessary. As Johnny had told him, he was alone. Clement lowered his head, thinking. 'Is there somewhere around here you can secrete the bus?'

'Aye. There is a large disused barn on the old Mey road.'

'How far from Gills Bay jetty?'

'All being well, and with the wind at my back, around twenty minutes' walk. Will they meet up in the kirk?'

'I'm guessing it will be here, where Sarah and Tom can wait out of the weather. But regardless of the location, we must take them before they get onto Tom's boat.'

'And then?'

'We take them into Thurso Police in your bus.' Clement thought for a minute. 'Will the bus company wonder where you are, Sean?'

Sean shook his head. 'Bus schedules can't be accurate in weather like this.'

'And Jean?'

'Same reason. Besides, we don't have that sort of relationship. What do we do until then?'

Clement checked his watch again, it was just after six. 'While you secrete your bus, I want to see inside McAllister's lorry. And Sean, please don't be tempted to visit *The Bell* for any reason. No one can know you are in the vicinity. Jean's safety and yours depend on it. I'll meet you back here at seven o'clock. When you arrive, go straight into the kirk. On the left is a small door. It leads up to the belfry. Wait there by the landside window. There is no glass in the window so you can hear anyone approaching, even if you cannot see them. And, by the way, it's cold up there.'

'And if you haven't returned by seven?'

'Then McAllister has killed me.'

Clement stepped from the warm bus and the door closed. Jumping the adjacent stone wall, he waited until Sean started the engine and drove away, the vehicle heading west. With his ears straining, Clement stood and checked the road in both directions, as usual, nothing stirred. And no sound came to him on the wind. Crossing the road, he entered the churchyard. With the wind at his back, Clement hurried through the graveyard, the only sound that of his own footsteps on the gravel.

It was colder now, or so he thought, but perhaps it was just his heightened nerves. He reached into his pocket for his balaclava and pulled it down hard on his head. Hunching his shoulders from the icy draughts, he picked his way through the head stones, the cold boring into his flesh. Shivering, he tried to remember when he was last warm. It had been on his first night in Canisbay; the night he and Aidan had sat in front of the fire at the manse. His eyes focused on the bulge in his left sock as he walked, at the double-edged blade strapped to his calf. Wearing it was second nature to him and he no longer felt it against his skin, but the arsenal of weaponry he wore about his body was a constant reminder of his current situation. Initially, he had thought he wouldn't need his knife for this mission, much less his assassin's Welrod pistol with four magazines of ammunition. But now, he knew a confrontation loomed. He felt the inevitability of it. It was just a matter of time. And when it did, it would be close and deadly.

At the end of the walled graveyard, Clement paused. In the night air he could smell the smoke from Wallace's farm, even if he couldn't see it. Above him, thousands of distant stars gleamed between scudding clouds and a thin moon lay sideways as though lazing in a celestial hammock, oblivious to the turmoil below. Off to his left, Clement caught the sudden green glow of the Northern Lights flickering their disinterest over the world below them. For one moment, he stopped to enjoy it. The heavens were spectacular. But not everything in Caithness was so natural. Behind closed doors something sinister was happening around him. Unseen, yet all pervasive. Who knew? Was it a closely guarded secret, or a conspiracy? Standing, he held his gloved hands to his mouth and blew warm air through the woollen weave over his fingers. Running through the gate, and keeping close to the graveyard wall, he returned to the road, Huna about a mile away.

# 19

Twelve minutes later Clement opened the door to the red telephone box and stepped inside, the shelter a welcome respite from the wind. Keeping the road in front and behind him in his peripheral vision, he studied Crawford's wide shop window. His gaze shifted to McAllister's garage door. Everything appeared to be closed up for the night and no lights were visible at either premise. Checking the road again, he left the telephone booth and ran across the road.

Reaching for his torch, he examined the simple barrel lock on the doors to McAllister's garage. He sprang the catch easily then switched off the torch and, pushing the door ajar, slipped inside. All was dark. A strong and enticing smell of baking chicken greeted his nostrils. Off to his left he could hear muted voices, a man and a woman. He slid the front doors to and crept towards a small door that separated him from the voices.

'I can't imagine why you did it. You take too many risks.'

'And you worry too much, woman! Besides, he won't be around much longer.'

A door somewhere inside slammed closed. Clement waited but the conversation did not resume. He stared into the cold air. Were they talking about him? If McAllister knew Clement had returned to the area, then it had been McAllister in the Frews' house. The conversation implied it. And Joyce was his accomplice. He visualized her strong wrists pouring tea in Sarah's sitting room the day Crawford died. Those hands were certainly capable of wringing the necks of chickens. But Clement wanted tangible evidence. Something that was irrefutable.

Lifting his gaze, he scanned the freezing dark garage. The lorry occupied the centre of the large, high-pitched roofed building. All around it were motor parts of one kind or another. Leaving the door to the residence, he skirted the vehicle, walking towards the rear of the garage. The inviting aroma of baking chicken was replaced by the smell of coal dust. He flicked on the torch. Behind the lorry, and off to one side, was a large pile of coal ready for bagging. He placed the edge of his overcoat over the latch and lifted the handle on the lorry's rear door. A metallic click sounded brief and hard. Switching off the beam, he fell to his haunches and, grasping his knife, hid beside the front wheel arch, but no one came to investigate the noise. Remaining by the wheel, Clement waited a full five minutes before returning to the rear of the vehicle. He climbed in, pulled the doors closed behind him and flicked on the torch again.

The space astounded him. It was easily big enough for large weapons. He moved the torch beam over the lorry walls and floor. Three full coal sacks were leaning against the front wall of the vehicle. Climbing in, he walked towards the sacks, and lifting each in turn looked behind them. Something about one of the sacks caught his eye. It had a long curved edge bulging through the hessian. His eyes shifted to the other bags. These contained only the distinctive small spherical lumps of coal. Holding the torch in his mouth, he opened the odd sack and felt for the unusual shape. It was metallic and round, about eight inches in diameter. Withdrawing it, he stared at the drum. Although now empty, the metal container had once held approximately seventy rounds of ammunition. Brushing the coal dust from the surface with his fist, he read the words stamped into the top. *Maschinengewehr Modell 34.*

He felt disgust for the man, but not just for his treachery. McAllister was a ruthless killer. In Clement's mind the man had become his personal adversary and had taken on a satanic visage while still unidentified. But the face of Ian McAllister belied the man's brutality. The image of him sitting on Aidan's velvet uphol stered chair drinking whisky flashed in Clement's memory and he chastised himself for such naivety. The professional always looked innocent. And who would suspect the person who came seeking assistance? Turning the drum over in his hand, Clement wondered whether to take it with him as confirmation of McAllister's guilt. But that was no longer necessary. He pushed it back into the sack and retied the bag. Johnny had instructed him to bring the traitor in, if possible, and for that Clement didn't need the physical evidence beyond this moment. He replaced the sacks as he had found them, his hand reaching for his pistol, his mind on confronting McAllister and his wife. Better now, he thought, in their home, without others around. And it would be quiet with Crawford's shop and residence unoccupied next door.

He drew in a long breath. If the McAllisters surrendered quietly, he could take them next door and telephone Inspector Stratton, but he knew that would never happen. McAllister was a ruthless killer and brutal to the point of evil. There was no honour in such a man. Surrender would never be considered. Clement reached into his coat for the silencer and screwed it into position.

But what part did Sarah and Tom play? Was it McAllister they were waiting for in the kirk? Clement's instinct told him it was. And if so, Sarah and Tom would hang as accomplices to murder as well as treason. He needed to know exactly who the pair was meeting before confronting McAllister.

Placing the pistol into his belt, he rubbed the coal dust from his hands against his coat and checked his watch. He had been in the garage about twenty minutes. Switching off the torch, he jumped from the rear of the lorry and pushed the doors to, leaning on the handle and twisting the latch closed. As he crept past the door to the house, he listened but he couldn't hear anything. Stepping outside he relocked the doors and hurried away.

As Clement walked west towards the kirk and his rendezvous with Sean, his mind played with timings. Everything pointed to McAllister's guilt and his cover was perfect. No matter which way Clement thought about it, McAllister was in the vicinity for all four murders. Was the face of evil to be found in a strong, seemingly dependable neighbour? A woman and a man with a dog? Why had McAllister let him live after their encounter in the Frews' house? It made no sense to Clement then and it still didn't. He had also slept on Tom's boat. Three times Clement could so easily have been murdered. So why had McAllister not taken advantage of the opportunities? The man would have known that Clement intended to sail for St Margaret's Hope with Tom Harris in the early hours of Thursday morning because Tom would have informed him. What neither Tom nor McAllister knew was that, at the time, Clement had booked passage for Sarah, not himself. Regardless, he and Sarah were both there. Was that why he had not been killed when so many bullets had been fired? Had Sarah's presence with him on the jetty and with Tom on the boat guaranteed his safety? And with him on South Ronaldsay, Clement would be unable to return, as no fisherman would bring him back. So why had Tom? Surely, if his theory was correct, Tom would be the last fisherman to make the crossing. Perhaps Tom had agreed only because Clement had asked to go to Thurso, not Gills Bay? A gnawing doubt lingered in his gut. While the ammunition drum was damning evidence of McAllister's guilt, it wasn't conclusive.

Staying on the road, Clement hurried past the high graveyard wall, arriving at the kirk on the stroke of seven o'clock. He hadn't passed anyone, but it didn't stop his eyes and ears straining for the sounds of the ever-present risk of running into company. Pausing at the kirk door for only a few seconds to listen, he went straight to the belfry.

'Sean?'

'Aye.' Sean stepped from behind the door.

'Anything?'

'Not sure.'

'Meaning?'

'A car.'

Clement waited.

'I heard it approaching and saw the shielded head lights turn off the main road. The engine was switched off a few minutes later.'

'Which direction?'

'Coming from the west.'

'When was this?'

'About twenty minutes ago.'

Clement walked to the window and stared over the fields, but all was dark now.

'I lost sight of it after it turned off the main road. I could have a look about, if you like.'

Clement looked at Sean. 'We go together. But you should be armed with something,' Clement reached down to his left calf and unsheathed his knife from its scabbard.

Sean beamed a wry grin. 'Like no Holy Father I've ever known. I hope it's a new trend. I think I like it.'

Clement smiled, but Sean's remark had stung. At one time, Clement would have spent time philosophizing about his actions and his compromised values. He mourned the loss of such times. Now, there was only time for survival.

Clement handed the blade to Sean. At least, Clement thought to himself, this way he would be sure about Sean's loyalties.

Pushing back his coat, Clement took the Welrod pistol from his belt. He saw Sean's eyebrows rise but the Irishman passed no comment about the weapon.

'I could go alone, Vicar?'

'No. I don't want any more deaths because you were in the wrong place at the wrong time.'

Descending from the belfry, they left the kirk and crossed the road, jumping the stone wall into the meadow. Clement was beginning to know the snow-covered fields opposite the kirk well, even in darkness. Remaining by the hedges, they ran towards Canisbay and the rear door of *The Bell*. A strong smell of coal smoke was coming from the inn. It was like a homing beacon in the night. Within minutes they were in the rear yard, crouching behind some empty barrels. In the gloom the kitchen door opened. Framed in the doorway, and lit from behind, Clement could see the red hair of Stewart McCrea. The lad walked out into the yard carrying an empty beer barrel on his shoulders. Within seconds McCrea had disappeared into the darkness, but they heard the barrel being stacked with the others in the side passageway. A minute later Stewart returned to the kitchen, closing the door behind him.

'Not too strict about observing the black-out regulations, are they?' But Clement's question was rhetorical. He reached for his lock-picks. 'Watch my back, Sean.'

'Aye.'

Hurrying across the yard, Clement approached the rear door and inserted the lock-picks, rotating them, the barrel slipping back easily.

Sean was beside him in seconds. 'Not going in?'

'Not yet. Stay here, Sean. Watch, but don't go in.'

'What are you going to do?'

'I want to see if the car is parked at the front.'

Sean nodded.

Clement ran down the side path. Pressing himself against the wall at the corner of the building, he peered around the edge. A vehicle was parked at the front. Without waiting, he returned to the rear of the inn.

'Is it there?'

Clement nodded. 'It's Stratton's.'

# 20

'Why is Stratton here again, do you think, Vicar?'

'Good question.'

'What do you intend to do?'

'Ask Jean. But you stay here, out of sight.'

Clement stood and, reaching for the door knob, opened the door a crack and looked in. The black-out curtain was pushed back and although the light in the kitchen was on, no one was there. Warmth radiated from the kitchen stove. He slipped inside and went straight to the pantry where he could wait without being seen. A minute later the swing door from the bar to the kitchen opened and Jean walked in.

Clement stepped forward.

The woman's surprised reaction lasted no more than one second. Putting a tray of dirty glasses on the sink, she turned to face him. 'He's not here. I told you he wouldn't be before nine. But Stewart McCrea is.'

Clement nodded. 'Who's been in this evening?'

'The usuals. And Stratton.'

'Did Inspector Stratton say why he is here?'

Jean emptied the tray and reached for some clean glasses. 'Brought Reverend Heath back. Stratton isn't staying though. Says he has to be in Thurso for an early appointment.'

'Do you know what about?'

She met his eye. 'The Inspector and I are not on such friendly terms. Anyway, why did you leave the room? Don't trust me, eh?' Jean lifted the tray of clean glasses and swung it onto her hip.

'I didn't think it right to expose you to any trouble.'

The woman held his gaze. 'You anticipate trouble here?'

'I'd rather not involve others. Safer all round.'

Jean shrugged and left the kitchen.

Clement stared after the woman. He thought she wouldn't be so disdainful if she knew a killer stalked Canisbay, but he had neither the wish to alarm her nor the time for discussion. Dismissing it, he left the kitchen and slipped outside.

Sean stepped forward from the shadows. 'Well?'

'Brought Reverend Heath back. But Stratton's not staying.'

Clement was glad Aidan was back. He wondered if the man had discovered his dead chickens. Clement looked up across the darkened fields. Perhaps he should tell Aidan about the Frew sisters. They deserved to be buried honourably and not left bound to their earthly indignity. He ran the idea around his mind, but until this night was over, and McAllister was safely in custody, Clement's presence had to remain secret from all but Sean and Jean. There was nothing to be done for the old ladies now.

'What now, Vicar?'

'A few hours in the belfry, I'm afraid, Sean.' Somehow the long cold hours ahead had lost their sense of dread now that Sean was with him. Besides, even though Sean didn't know it, within two hours Clement needed to be in Crawford's sitting room to receive the call from Nora Ballantyne. Pulling his coat collar high around his ears, they struck out across the fields making for the kirk.

'Makes you feel young again, doesn't it, Vicar?'

Clement recalled Johnny's words about young men with death wishes. If there were young men who routinely did such work for "C" then Clement admired their stamina as much as their bravery. But perhaps, for Clement at least, it wasn't so much bravery as escapism. He wondered if it was the same for others who worked for "C". He had agreed because he didn't want to face a life without Mary. Right now, he would settle for just staying alive.

Scaling a flagstone fence, Clement paused and peered over the stone wall at the manse. Even in the limited moonlight, he could see the outline of the building and smell the burning coal. He smiled, visualizing Aidan fanning the flames into life. He envied the warmth and he felt an odd sense of satisfaction that Aidan had returned.

Five minutes later they were in the bell tower.

233

Clement lay on the floor with his arm under his head and closed his eyes. It was just before eight o'clock. Forty minutes rest would be welcome, even in the cold, draughty belfry. In the distance, he could hear the steady rhythm of the waves crashing into the cliffs below in Gills Bay. So much had happened in so few days and he had to remind himself that it was only Friday. He had been in Caithness less than a week, but it had been like no other week he had ever known. Everything had seemed so confused. But now he knew the identity of his enemy, his mind and his mission were clear. He listened to the insistent rhythm of the waves; coming, going. He drew in a long breath and listened to his own breathing. It was only a matter of time now, he thought.

Heightened nerves and uncertainty with every step, coupled with the bitter cold, was an exhausting combination and they eroded resolve. Was he right about McAllister? Clement chastised himself. It was the numbing cold that confused, he told himself. A frown creased his forehead and in the freezing air a realisation dawned that almost made him stop breathing. *Everything really was confused.* Every time he thought one way, something would happen to bewilder which inevitably led to procrastination and delay. What plans he'd had, had been abandoned until he no longer had a plan. Events moved rapidly and kept changing. Had he been so reactive to events around him that his enemy had been controlling his movements from the beginning?

He sat up. 'Only a matter of time.'

Time. Not weather. Or was it time and weather?

Was that the reason for McAllister's delay in leaving the region? Since the day Clement arrived in Huna unusual things had been happening around him. Secret liaisons. Clandestine comings and goings. People, for the most part unseen, leaving their footprints criss-crossing the district, confusing the everyday with the covert. Was that how his enemy remained one step ahead? Clement stared at the bell ropes in front of him. His presence in the district was known by the one man Clement had hoped to evade. Should it also be presumed that McAllister knew his true purpose in being the district? Clement blinked several times. Was he being kept alive for fear that another more able would replace him before his enemy's planned escape? *Better the devil you know.* But how much did he know? Clement realised that while his opponent knew everything, he, Clement, knew almost nothing. And what he did was mostly conjecture. Clement could feel his shoulders drooping. He felt like an amateur. Doubt again had taken hold of his thinking. He needed to remain focused or he and Sean were dead. That, too, was probably only a matter of time.

Clement rolled his head to the right. He guessed Sean was not asleep. 'How well do you know the people here?'

'How well do we really know anyone, Vicar?'

'Indeed.' Clement said, knowing the truth of Sean's remark.

'Anyone in particular?'

'It occurs to me, Sean, that I have been led on a wild goose chase from the moment I arrived in Caithness.'

'Is that what you think?'

He turned to face Sean. 'Yes. What do you and others in Canisbay and Huna know that I don't?'

The Irishman paused. 'Small communities, Vicar. When they fall out amongst themselves it is usually pretty vitriolic. Heated words. Long held resentments. But that is about the strength of it. But when someone from outside rattles the chain, enemies become friends.'

'The enemy of your enemy?'

'Something like that.'

'You think Donald Crawford and Ian McAllister became friends?'

'There are two people hereabouts with the surname McAllister. Just as there were two with the surname Crawford.

'Sarah Crawford and Ian McAllister, you mean?'

'There is another combination.'

'Joyce McAllister and Donald Crawford? Are you're saying that Donald Crawford's death was a crime of passion?'

Sean shook his head. 'I'm not saying anything of the kind. But you, like me, are not the only one who isn't, or wasn't, local. It takes time to build trust. You should know that, Vicar, if you lived in a small village.'

'What are you saying, Sean?'

'The Crawford's came to Huna ten years ago. About the same time I did, if you catch my drift.'

'The Crawford's are still considered outsiders?'

'Aye. Although they had a head start.'

'Meaning?'

'Joyce McAllister is, or rather was, Donald Crawford's sister.'

Clement felt Sean's words like a blow to the head. 'What?'

'They fought like only relatives can, but I don't believe it includes killing kin.'

Clement looked into the space before him. If McAllister wasn't his enemy then who was? 'What about the Frews?'

'I don't know about that. A terrible thing, what happened to them. But I do know they weren't well liked. Kept to themselves. Considered themselves superior and wouldn't hear any argument about transferring the barn to the McAllisters.'

'But you said Joyce was a Crawford.'

'Didn't matter. She married a McAllister and as far as the Frews were concerned, that was enough.'

'And where do you stand in all of this, Sean?'

There was a long pause before Sean responded. 'Why did you choose me, Vicar?'

'I pegged you as an outsider. And someone who, and perhaps I got this wrong, was not loyal to anyone?'

'It's true I don't get involved. But all that aside, what I know is second hand. And we all know not much truth is spoken in a pub. But for what it's worth, Vicar, I don't think Ian McAllister is your killer.'

'So I ask my first question again, Sean; what do you and others know that I do not?'

Sean stared at the roof above them. 'It would be best coming from Sarah.'

'Sarah?'

'They'll be here soon enough, if you are correct about the third member being McAllister.'

The Irishman turned on his side.

Clement closed his eyes. He felt like he was in a maze, where everyone was outside in the sunshine and only he remained on the inside feeling trapped and

237

frustrated. What had Mr Churchill said in his speech to the parliament? That Britain would fight on, if necessary, alone. Alone. A wave of desperation, or was it defeat, swept over Clement. He felt cold and weary, more weary than he had felt in years. Since the trenches. But he had come through that and it had been life changing for him. He had pledged his life to the Lord's service. He had returned from the mouth of hell on earth and found life and love. Defeat was not what he wanted. The people of Caithness may be collectively thwarting his mission, but a more sinister enemy lurked within their midst, even if they did not know it. He needed Sean. And he needed the man to understand.

'Sean. I am only interested in one man. Or perhaps two. They are German infiltrators, enemy spies and murderers. These men are the enemies of your community and of our nation. What I am not interested in are local disputes. If you are here to mind me, or to thwart me, then I would ask you, as the decent man I believe you to be, to leave now.'

The Irishman rolled over and faced him. Clement could see the blue eyes weighing up options. 'Alright, Vicar. But I'll fight for the King of England if McAllister is your man.'

'Talk to me, Sean.'

# 21

Clement should have realised what they were doing. Everyone in Canisbay and Huna knew. It was how Jean always had whisky and how Aidan had more coal than his ration and the Crawford's shop had fresh fish and meat. Clement hadn't seen sugar or bacon, but he guessed it was there. And he also should have guessed when he saw the contents of the barn. No wonder it was always locked. It surprised him that he had not made the connection. His home town of Rye in East Sussex had, in centuries passed, been a haven for smuggling, but dealing in the black market in wartime was a punishable offence and one which carried a severe sentence. Small surprise, then, that he had been treated with suspicion and labelled *The Wise Man from the South.*

'And if they knew about the Frew ladies, there would be a mob on the look-out for you, Vicar. They don't believe you are a man of the cloth, by the way.'

'Well I am. What I am not is an excise man. But why did no one mention that Ian McAllister and Donald Crawford were brothers-in-law?'

'Perhaps they didn't think it your business or maybe they didn't want you prying any more than you are.'

Clement stared at the stalactite bell ropes. While getting people to talk was a skill he had learned as a vicar, it had always been because those people had wanted to tell him about themselves and their problems. But eliciting information from unwilling sources was another matter entirely and he felt a sudden admiration for the men who worked for "C" who could. As bad as black-marketeering in wartime was, their deceit had not only complicated matters, it had very nearly cost Ian McAllister his life.

'But if not McAllister...' Clement's voice trailed off...he thought of the ammunition drum in McAllister's lorry. The evidence was compelling. The complexity of subterfuge astounded.

'You can ask him, soon, if you are right about his involvement with Sarah and Tom.'

Clement checked his watch, the call from Nora Ballantyne due in less than half an hour. 'I have to go. I want to check something.'

Sean sat up. 'Go? Where? Why? What happens if they come before you return?'

'Best you do not know where,' he said standing. 'If they are neither traitors nor murderers, as you believe is the case, then you have nothing to worry about.' Clement checked his pistol. 'I'll be as quick as I can.'

Clement hurried down the steps and out of the kirk. He guessed Sean was watching him from the belfry window but he knew the night would engulf him within minutes and the strong westerly wind would carry any sound of his footsteps away in seconds.

Keeping his feet on the solid road surface, and with the wind at his back, he headed east. It was dangerous; the night, the road, Caithness and its people and there was a real possibility that he would walk straight into McAllister coming the other way. If he was correct about McAllister being the ring-leader. It was a risk Clement had to take. As he ran, he thought of Sean's words about people. It was true. People are never quite what they seem, even people you think you know. This war, even more than his twenty odd years as a vicar, had taught him that.

Twenty-five minutes later, Clement opened the rear door into Crawford's house and tip-toed into the sitting room. All was dark. He listened but there was no sound. Checking the house, he returned to the sitting room and sat at the exchange waiting for Nora Ballantyne's call. Right on nine o'clock the phone rang. Even though anticipated, the sound of its insistent call made him jump in the still air.

'Hello?'

'Who is this?'

'*Hope.*'

'It has taken us some doing to compile this in the time, Major. I hope it has been worth the effort.'

'Thank you. Please go ahead.'

'Donald Crawford was in the Merchant Navy in the last war as a Signals Operator. He was medically discharged. No history of any criminal activity. In fact, other than the Irishman, Sean Mead, who is wanted in Ireland for beating a man to death in a bar room brawl, no others on your list have a criminal record of any kind. But there are some anomalies.'

'Go on, Miss Ballantyne.'

'Robert Wallace does not have a medal for bravery. Or anything else, for that matter. He was in the first war in France, but he disappeared at the Somme. Believed missing or dead, he resurfaced in '19 claiming he had been a prisoner of war. It seems Mr Wallace returned to Britain on a fishing boat. As we are not in a position to check his claim with the German authorities, we are none the wiser. However, there is no record of any case brought against him for either desertion or cowardice, but as I said, there is no medal.'

'And Doctor MacGregor?'

'A well respected Veterinary Surgeon and a Justice of the Peace. No record of any wrong doing.'

'Anything else?'

'The registered publican of *The Bell* is not Mrs Jean Buchanan.'

'Who is?'

'Allan Stratton.'

Clement sat back.

'Concerning Mrs Jean Buchanan; we have checked with the Scottish Records Office but I'm sure you can understand that without anything to go on, like a place of birth, it is well-nigh impossible to identify her. There are over two hundred Jean Buchanans living in Scotland currently. Some information is necessary, Major, even for us. But regardless, it will take more time than you have given me to conclusively identify her. If this information is vital I can send someone to Scotland to wade through censuses and parish records. One more thing, Major, Reverend Aidan Heath was born in Denmark, but was educated in Scotland and attended Seminary School in Glasgow. It appears he never returned to Denmark. Other than these, everyone else seems rather normal and home grown.'

Clement thought for a moment. With all he'd heard he needed time to think. 'Don't worry about Jean Buchanan at this time. If it is important I will call again. And thank you, Miss Ballantyne. You have done wonders.'

'It's what we're here for, but you don't need to be so formal, Major. After all, we have been introduced.'

Clement heard the line go dead before he could respond. Her final comment had taken him by surprise and he wasn't sure if Miss Ballantyne was endeavouring to show she was human after all. He severed the connection and reset the exchange cables then left by the back door, slipping out of Crawford's rear yard.

He checked the road in both directions, the wind tearing at his coat. The red telephone box stood mute in the night. Behind him, McAllister's garage was closed and dark. He pulled his balaclava over his head and stared to walk. Robert Wallace. The heroic story had been an invention. A lifetime of covering up the disgrace of desertion would make a man solitary. It could also explain his quick temper and liking for the bottle. As Clement walked, he thought back to those years, to the first war with Germany. The penalty for desertion then was the firing squad. While Clement knew the trenches and understood why a man would desert, he couldn't condone it. Indeed, those who had been injured in a non-life-threatening way, like himself, were considered the fortunate ones. He remembered it all too well, the gasping agony of torn flesh that produced pain like he had never before experienced. He had seen what happened to men who had been in the trenches for months on end without respite. Was this why Robert Wallace, the soldier, had disappeared into the night? Or had the man found refuge in Germany and been converted to the Nazi cause?

Clement stopped walking. Away to his right Wallace's farm stood silhouetted against the starry night sky. If he applied his original criteria, then Robert Wallace was a perfect match. Clement visualized the man's white knuckles, the hands wrapped around the beer glass. Had they also been wrapped around Donald Crawford's neck? Anger was a dangerous force. He resolved to question Sean on his return to the bell tower about Robert Wallace.

Clement leaned into the head wind, his mind on Nora's other revelations. Doctor MacGregor he dismissed from his list of suspects. Then there was the revelation that Stratton was the licensee of *The Bell*. Clement did not know for certain if it was illegal for a policeman to own a public house. And Jean Buchanan's identity couldn't be confirmed. Jean had said she was not on friendly terms with Stratton. Perhaps they quarrelled about the running of *The Bell*? But one thing was certain; questioning Sean about Jean was not going to be easy.

And lastly there was Aidan, but being born in Denmark did not make the man his enemy. The Danes were their allies and had been cruelly treated by the Nazis. In any case, Nora had told him that Aidan had been educated in Britain and had not returned to Denmark.

Clement saw the graveyard wall beside him. He hadn't seen or heard anything since leaving Crawford's. Within minutes, he lifted the latch on the kirk's door and went straight to the belfry door.

'Sean?'

'Here.' Sean stepped from shadows. 'What's happening?'

'How well do you know Robert Wallace?'

The hard metallic sound came out of the night like a pistol shot. Clement turned at the sound. It was the heavy metal latch on the kirk's main door. Flicking on his torch under his coat he checked his watch. Just before half past nine.

Withdrawing his pistol, and with Sean behind him grasping the knife, they descended the stairs. Rotating the door knob, he opened the door a crack. Sarah Crawford stood in the body of the church holding a lit kerosene lamp. In its glow he could see her face. She was wearing the red tam o'shanter. He felt the corners of his mouth draw together in disapproval. Beside her was Tom Harris. An icy wind blew across the nave and flickered the lamp's flame. In an instant Sarah extinguished the lamp, plunging the kirk once more into darkness. Clement heard the scuffling of feet on stone flagging. Then the main door opened. A second later, a single shot blasted in the silent church, the sound reverberating off the stone walls in the cold air. He heard a shriek. The main door banged shut.

Holding his breath, Clement waited, his ears straining. He had reacted to everything so far by instinct and he believed his enemy could be manipulating him again. He wanted to know Sarah and Tom's location and if they were unhurt.

'What now?' Sean's voice whispered.

Clement held his hand up and mouthed the word, 'Wait!' He had made the mistake before of thinking that a closed door meant the gunman had left. His adversary could just as easily be on the other side of the door, or in the kirk. Clement held the Welrod in front of his face as he dropped to his knees and pushed the door wide. A second later, he slithered into the nave on his belly. Out of the darkness another shot rang out, the deafening noise ricocheting around the kirk's stone walls. He heard the groan. Somebody fell.

Clement lunged forward and lay flat on the floor, his eyes on the base of the front door that was visible from under the pews. The main door opened again. In that instant, Clement saw boots running through the door.

'Tom?'

It was Sarah's frightened whisper.

Clement waited. If the gunman was still in the kirk another shot would surely follow.

'I'm here.'

Tom's reply.

'Then who fell?'

'Sarah, light your lamp, hurry.'

Tom again.

Standing, Clement ran for the belfry door. On the stairs to the bell tower Sean Mead lay on his back in a pool of blood.

Clement turned to see Tom and Sarah standing beside him. Sarah was shaking, her eyes wide in alarm. Tom Harris, ashen-faced was staring at Clement.

'You killed him?' Sarah said.

'No. My pistol has not been discharged. Did you see who left the kirk just now?'

Both Tom and Sarah shook their heads, but both were staring at Sean's prostrate body.

'Tom, help Sarah to your boat and wait there.' Clement ran towards the front door.

'What about...?' Sarah paused, staring at Tom. 'We can't leave without...?'

'Are you waiting for Ian McAllister?' Clement demanded.

Neither spoke.

'Answer me! All our lives now depend on it.'

Sarah nodded.

'Could that have been Ian McAllister who just left?'

Clement could see their astonishment. The fact was that none of them knew who had fired the shot and, if it wasn't McAllister, then Clement had only a few seconds before the killer disappeared into the darkness.

Running into the kirk's front yard Clement stopped, pressing himself against the cold kirk wall and listened. He stared into the night, his ears straining for any sound. But the gunman had gone, engulfed in the night. On the wind Clement caught the sound of running footsteps on the gravel path leading from the graveyard. Holding his pistol, he hid behind a headstone and waited. A man was running towards the kirk door without any attempt to disguise his footsteps.

Clement was behind him in seconds.

McAllister rushed into the kirk. 'Sarah?'

'Here!'

In the glow of the kerosene lamp, Clement saw three people huddled around the body of Sean Mead.

'I heard the shot from along the road,' McAllister was saying.

Tom told him what had happened.

'So how much does this vicar know?'

'Enough,' Clement called from the door.

The three turned to face him. 'While I find your illegal activities reprehensible, it is not why I am here.'

'You killed him?' McAllister demanded.

'No. Sean was working with me, not against me. And for your information, I did not kill either Donald Crawford or Malcolm McCrea. As Sarah knows, I could not have killed young McCrea, or her husband, as I was with her on both occasions. Besides, contrary to public opinion, I am a vicar and do not randomly kill innocent civilians.'

'Is this true, Sarah?' McAllister asked.

'Yes.'

Clement waited to see if anyone mentioned the Frews, but their names were not voiced.

'Did you see anyone outside just now?' Clement asked McAllister.

'No. I heard the shot and came running.'

Lowering his pistol, Clement walked towards Sean and crouched beside the Irishman's body. Sean had been shot through the chest and would have died instantly. Another death. The burden of it weighed heavily, especially as Clement knew for whom the bullet had been intended. He placed his hand over the Irishman's eyes closing them, his left hand reaching for the knife that lay on the step beside Sean's body. Slipping the weapon into its scabbard, Clement stood.

Clement looked into their alarmed faces. 'We need to talk.'

'I told you, at *The Bell*, that it was you the killer wanted, Vicar. But how did the gunman know you were here?'

'That is a very good question, Tom.' The truth was that no one knew Clement was hiding in the belfry except Sean. Had the Irishman been seen or followed after secreting the bus?

'What do we do with him?' McAllister asked.

Clement needed to think. He remembered the chickens. 'Why did you take the dead chickens?'

McAllister's startled expression told Clement that the theft had not been shared with anyone other than the man's wife.

Sarah and Tom turned to face McAllister, their faces confirming Clement's suspicions.

The big man hung his head. 'Temptation. They were already dead and it would have been wasteful not to cook them. Besides, how many chickens can Aidan eat?'

'Sarah, do you always do the deliveries around ten o'clock?' Clement asked, ignoring McAllister's attempts at justification.

'Yes.'

'And everyone knows this?'

'Of course.'

Clement looked at Sarah. The woman's routine was so predictable. Too predictable and too well-known. 'On the few occasions you were out on deliveries and Donald was in the barn, who minded the shop?'

'Joyce.'

With Joyce minding the shop, it left the garage unattended for however long Joyce McAllister was in Crawford's shop. And as anyone behind the counter was visible from the street, one didn't even need to enter the shop to know when the garage was unattended.

Clement sat on the pew, Sean's lifeless body in his peripheral vision. He felt sick with remorse for Sean, but the awful truth persisted. Despite five deaths, he still could not identify his adversary. Clement leaned forward, his face resting in his hands and rubbed at his aching eyes. Mental as well as physical exhaustion was gripping his body. He had to think. It was up to him. It always had been, but a little help wouldn't go astray, he thought, hoping the Lord was listening.

'Perhaps you should get some sleep, Vicar. There's a bunk for you on my boat, but we will have to get moving soon. There are things to load before we can leave Gills Bay.'

Clement looked up at Tom, aghast. How could the man talk of sleep, much less what the trio were doing? Did Sean's death mean so little to them? But it was a question for another time. A killer waited somewhere in the shadows and there would be no rest for Clement until either the man was caught, or one or both were dead. He took in a long breath. As tempting as the comfort of Tom's boat was, just being there now made him an accessory to their activities. Clement shook his head. 'It is best you do not know where I am. But I must say this; as long as this trip is your last, your secret is safe with me. I must have your word on this. In return, I would ask you to keep my secret. Do not tell anyone that you have seen me.'

'Agreed.'

'And Sean?' McAllister asked again.

Clement looked at the lifeless man who had so readily agreed to help him and who had asked nothing in return. He would never have the opportunity now to thank Sean nor to ask his questions about Robert Wallace or Nora Ballantyne's other revelations. Clement walked over and knelt beside Sean. Gently he placed his forefinger on the man's forehead and made the sign of the Cross. 'Can you take him with you, Tom? Bury him at sea. Somehow I feel Sean would approve. He always felt like an outsider here. "In the midst of life we are in death",' Clement began. '"He that believeth in the Lord, though he were dead, yet shall he live." May your spirit be with God in Heaven, Sean. In the name of the Father, the Son and the Holy Ghost. Amen.'

'Amen.' Clement heard the others say.

He watched them leave the kirk, Sean's body lifted over McAllister's strong shoulders. Clement knelt in prayer. He felt bone-weary but above all, he felt responsible. Looking up at the cross, he prayed aloud. 'Dear Lord, I need your help now more than I can say, for I fear I will not be able to catch this evil man before it is too late.'

He sat back on the pew, his eyes aimlessly staring at the wall opposite. How had the killer learned of his presence in the kirk? Clement let out a long sigh; there was only one answer. Sean must have left the kirk during the time Clement had gone to speak to Nora. Or, he had been followed.

Clement looked up at the high pulpit that towered above him. He prayed again for help, for clarity of mind. Where had the killer gone? He guessed his enemy had heard, and possibly even seen, McAllister running towards the kirk. Waiting. Watching. If his enemy had remained in the graveyard and not disappeared into the night, then the man would have seen not only McAllister but also himself re-enter the kirk.

Clement sat forward. What if the killer was still outside? He would had seen McAllister leave with a corpse over his shoulder. Clement stared at the white washed wall in front of him. Would the murderer follow the group to learn the identity of the deceased? Clement sat up, a shudder coursing through his body. Clement felt his pulse race. If the killer was watching, he may check the kirk before going to Gills Bay jetty. Clement's eyes searched for another way out. His ears strained, listening for any sound, especially the sound of the front door latch.

Behind him was the door to the vestry. Running up the short aisle, Clement opened the door. Inside was dark, the smell of recently burned coal lingered in the room. Off to the right was a small door that he guessed led outside. Turning the knob, he found it locked. In the darkness, he fumbled for his lock-picks, his heart pounding. Pulling the glove from his hand, he inserted the instruments and rotated the barrel. The old-fashioned lock was easy and it opened within seconds. Clement paused. If his enemy waited outside, Clement would not survive this time. Keeping his eyes on the door, Clement sank to the floor and reaching up, turned the knob. The wind pushed the door wide but no one entered. He waited. Nothing. Lying on his stomach Clement inched forward over the doorstep, the cold hard stone beneath his belly being replaced by damp grass. The wind groaned around the building, the cliffs and the open sea just yards off his right shoulder. The howling wind and crashing seas made it impossible to hear if anyone crept in the shadows. He stood. Staying close to the kirk wall, he edged his way around the western end of the bell tower. Waiting only a few seconds, and with his pistol in his grip, he ran the short distance around the kirk to the roadway.

Clement ran through the gate onto the road, his feet pounding the hard surface. Darkness would have to be his cover now, but if the killer was waiting, he had moments to live. Breathing hard, Clement ran west along the road as fast as he could, his head down, his feet beating out the frenzied rhythm. For some unknown reason he began to count as though with every second life became more certain. By the time he reached one hundred, the kirk was well behind him and he was heading west towards the junction with the track down to Gills Bay.

Still alive, he thought. At five hundred he stopped beside the road, his chest heaving and his breathing exaggerated. Adrenaline had kept him going and he hadn't finished yet. He turned around a full circle, his mouth gulping air, his eyes wide and scanning everything. He wasn't sure how far he had come and in the darkness he had no way of knowing. But no one had fired and only his own desperate breathing filled his ears. Then, between his own gasps for air, he heard it.

It came to him on the wind. Swallowing hard, Clement held his breath and listened. A muffled sound. He searched his memory for any shelter in the immediate area, but he knew there was none. The sound was louder now. Falling to the ground, Clement stared up into the night air, trying to focus on the source and nature of the noise. His pulse pounded in his ears and his chest felt as though it may explode from the freezing air, but the noise of an engine was irrefutable. Logic told Clement that he was about a mile from the kirk. He had to be near the track down to Gills Bay. He paused, and closing his eyes listened again for the sound. It had to be Tom's boat's engine. Standing, he started to run, his feet gathering pace, his eyes on his only guide; the roadway beneath his footsteps. Within a minute the bitumen curved to his right and he knew he was at the intersection with the road to the pier. He stopped. Something wasn't right. Tom's boat had a diesel engine. This was different. And with every second, it grew louder not fainter.

Lights.

Then the distinctive syncopation.

Two spears of muted light penetrated the darkness for one long second then were extinguished. Falling, Clement rolled into the grass and held his breath. He waited, face down and flat on the edge of the road, but there was no hail of bullets. Lifting his head, he stared into the night. Sean's bus was stopped at the edge of the road, blocking the descent to Gills Bay. A second later the headlights flickered again and the driver's door opened. Then the tread of footsteps on hard gravel. Swallowing hard, Clement lay motionless. His hand silently gripped the pistol as the footsteps neared.

# 22

Sunday 2<sup>nd</sup> March

Clement closed his eyes and waited, unable to even breathe. He wanted to be thinking about Mary when death came for him. He thought of her ankles, slender and fine. Her hair, her fragrance. He thought he may have called to her, but in the fear of the moment, he couldn't speak.

'Clement? Where are you, man?'

His eyes opened, jolting him back to the present, or was it the past? Raising himself silently on one elbow, he slowly brought his right hand up, the pistol clenched in his fist. He stared into the gloom. He wasn't sure if he was hallucinating. Exhaustion and adrenaline were playing tricks on his mind and body. Staying low in the grass, he drew his knees up and rolled onto his haunches.

'God's teeth, Clement, don't you know me?'

The voice was like a thunderbolt.

'Get in the bus, man, before you get us both killed.'

Clement struggled to stand, his breathing suspended, his eyes wide. Before him, in the darkness stood his former comrade and neighbour, Reg Naylor. Clement ran towards the bus. Within seconds they were both aboard. Reg twisted two wires hanging beneath the dashboard and the engine roared into life.

He sat on the seat behind Reg, his breathing rapid. Overwhelming relief mingled with a thousand questions. But for now they would wait. 'I don't think I've ever been more delighted to see you, Reg. You are a real answer to prayer.'

'Just keep your head down, Clement, while we get out of here.'

Turning the vehicle around, they headed west, climbing the hill away from Gills Bay. As they drove away, Clement peered through the bus's rear window, but he knew the kirk and his enemy had been swallowed up by the night.

'How did you know I was here, Reg?'

'I didn't. We were seconded from Wick. No rhyme or reason given. But then I never knew what we were supposed to be doing in Wick anyway. Probably a mistake, you know the Army. Anyway, the next thing I know, I've replaced some old codger driving despatches around Caithness. Speaking of age, Clement, I would have thought you too old for what I think you're involved in.'

'You're right about that. How did you know where to find this bus?'

'I was at Mey Castle delivering a message when I saw the bus being driven into a derelict barn. Very suspicious behaviour! So I followed him. He was in a hurry too. If he hadn't been, I may have given up following him. I tracked him for about twenty minutes, then I saw him go into the church. So I waited. Imagine my surprise when I saw you enter it not long after. I figured he was doing something for you and I surmised you wanted the bus for something. You just didn't want it seen, so when night fell, I decided to bring the bus closer. Three hours later and there are people all over the place! Then I heard a couple of shots. What's going on?'

'Did you see anyone else following the bus driver?'

'No.'

'I wish I had known you were there, Reg. Did you see anyone enter the kirk other than me and the man you followed?'

'Yes. Three people went in. But not together. First a woman then two men.'

'Then what?'

'I heard a shot. Then a second. Then I saw someone leave the kirk. Seemed to be alone and in a hurry. Initially I thought it was you, but then three people came out, one of them the woman and this time one of the men was carrying something. I hope you can make some sense of it, Clement, because it looked like a revolving door to me.'

'The person who left alone; did you see where they went?

'Couldn't be sure, but not to Gills Bay. Nor did whoever it was who passed me on the hill. What was the man carrying?'

'The body of a brave man.'

'Who?'

'The bus driver. The bullet was meant for me.'

Reg exhaled. 'Bad business.'

Clement saw Reg's eyes flick to the rear-view mirror. 'I know it sounds harsh, Clement, but don't blame yourself. Innocent people get killed in wartime. We both know this.'

Clement nodded but the comment didn't alleviate his guilt.

'Where are *they* going?' Reg asked tossing his head in the direction of Gills Bay.

'Not sure, but they are smugglers, not murderers.'

'I know where they're headed then. Dwarwick Pier. I overheard something in the Mess last night that is beginning to make sense. Do you know some of these officers have bacon with their eggs?' Reg paused. 'You look exhausted, Clement and you could do with a bath and a good night's rest.'

'No question about it, Reg but it will have to wait. Can you remember anything about the person who left the kirk alone?'

'Sorry, Clement. He just vanished in the night.'

Several seconds passed as Clement listened to the syncopation. 'How flexible are your duties?'

Their eyes met in the mirror again and Clement saw the boyish grin. 'Anything I could get into trouble for?'

'More than likely.'

'Dangerous?'

'Certainly.'

The grin became wider. Reg drove west, following the main road until the village of Mey came into view. Pulling off the road, Reg parked the bus in a grove of Sycamore trees and Clement told Reg all that had happened.

'No wonder you look done in, Clement. But I'll tell you something about that radio traffic. I spent yesterday with the elderly despatch rider I replaced. Nice old chap, George, but too talkative, especially with a whisky in his hand. He said the lads on Dunnet Head, at the signals station, have spoken of little else but those radio transmissions. And I hear it has been going on for a little while now. But even with the best fingers on the dial, they never could pin down his location. They were pretty sure it was the Jerries though. Always in Morse, always enciphered and never at a regular time. They were getting reports from an out-station operator in the area who was also picking up the traffic. Then a few days ago the out-station operator failed to transmit. It was all reported, of course. Since then, there's been only one transmission intercepted.'

'Did they ever get a fix on the transmitter?'

'No, but it could be a U-boat in the area. The signal is strong, apparently, so probably less than ten miles.'

'You've learned a lot in two days, Reg.'

Reg smiled. 'Now I know who to thank for getting me and the lads out of Wick. Do you know the pubs there don't serve alcohol?'

'I did know.' Clement smiled but he was thinking about young Captain Trevelyan. Even though the aged despatch rider had been replaced with Reg, Trevelyan had made a fundamental error; men not considered a threat learn things.

'Who have you told about this, Reg?'

Reg chuckled. 'No one to tell, Clement, until now. But I keep my eyes and ears open. And let's face it, if Castletown is anything like Wick, then it is full of military personnel and gossip is the glue in any closed community. Especially in wartime.'

Clement stared through the front window of the bus. Closed communities. And a closed community does not share information with a *Wise Man from the South*. He thought on Sarah, Tom and Ian McAllister and the people of Canisbay and Huna who all knew about the black-market activities in their midst. Clement had thought the illicit trade had been used to disguise the traitor's true activities, but perhaps that wasn't quite correct. It wasn't so much used to conceal as it had been to confuse. And, if Sean was to be believed, McAllister was not his enemy. Clement felt a sigh rising. But, if not McAllister, then who? It was the same familiar question that refused to be answered. And, like the wave on the sand, it always receded just as he felt he was getting closer. 'What's your opinion of these signal operators at the Y-station?'

'I've only met them twice, but I can't see any of them as your man - or woman. Besides, they are always on Dunnet, either at the station or in their billets. No time to wander about the countryside murdering people.'

It confirmed what Atcherley had told him. In the icy darkness Clement felt the pressure of failure.

Silence settled.

Tiredness and cold had contrived to confuse and thwart him. His adversary had all but won. The man had made good use of the bad weather to make Clement run around like a wild goose, exhausting himself. Now he was so debilitated he could no longer think. But a confrontation was inevitable. His enemy knew it and so did Clement.

'I was sorry to hear about Mary, Clement. Very bad. Old Reverend Battersby informed the village. I suppose he's still there. Doing a good job for his age. But they all asked about you.'

'What were they told?'

Clement listened as Reg told him about the village. People he knew, lives he'd shared. He missed them all, even the post mistress whose ability to invent gossip from very little had always annoyed him. He pictured the buildings. The vicarage; his vicarage. But mostly he envisaged Mary. He could see her hand peeling beans and hear her knitting needles as they clicked their way into producing a pair of socks. He wanted to cry. He wanted to let the tears stream down his face until he couldn't grieve any longer, but he couldn't do it. Not until it was over, one way or another.

'That you were injured and sent to the west-country for an undisclosed duration of time.'

Clement wiped his arm over his face, removing the salty tears and sat listening to Reg's reminiscences of Fearnley Maughton. 'At the time it caused some speculation. But like all gossip, it soon died away. And as far as I know that was the end of it. I haven't been home myself since Christmas. I sent Geraldine away, she's in Australia with Charles, our boy. She says she feels like a fish out of water. The Medical Corps have the house now, requisitioned as a hospital. Broke her heart to see them pulling out the rose garden. All things considered, it's best she is away. So, what now, Clement?'

Clement let out a long sigh and watched his condensed breath float away. 'My theory, such as it is, is that this man has a local accomplice and is planning to leave Caithness as soon as the weather abates, with or without the accomplice.'

'From Dwarwick Pier?'

'It would be my guess.'

'And you don't believe your man is one of the smugglers?'

'Not any more. Neither, it would appear, is it someone at Dunnet Head Y-station. But I'll tell you this, Reg, from first-hand experience; it is very difficult with all the bogs and lochs to walk, much less run, across country to Dwarwick Pier without several hours' notice. And knowing that, whoever this person is they will have to be in place well before the rendezvous time, if the pick-up is by boat or submarine.'

'Couldn't be any other way?'

'This country may be flat enough for radio transmissions, but I cannot see an aeroplane landing. Too many military installations and natural hazards. It could only land at a prepared strip or airfield and that is hardly likely.'

'Dwarwick Pier it is then.'

'And that means he will have to be hiding out somewhere in the lee of Dunnet Head well in advance of the allotted time. But all this can only be done if he knows the exact date and time of the pick-up.'

'Another radio signal?'

Clement shock his head. 'Another transmission is too risky. He is local, and therefore will know about the signal station on Dunnet Head. And in view of recent happenings he will know we are onto him. Do you know much about radio transmissions, Reg?'

'Almost nothing.'

'To get the location of a rogue transmitter, a wireless operator needs either a direction finder, or there must be three wirelesses which can be triangulated to get the fix on the location. I know the out-station in Huna did not have a direction finder. While I believe the killer knew about the existence of the out-station, I don't believe he knew where the wireless was located. But once he saw it in the barn, he knew it was only a matter of time before he was exposed. That's why he stole it. And that's why he's leaving.'

'There is another alternative, Clement. Could he have learned something so important it couldn't be transmitted?'

'You could well be right,' Clement said thinking of the lone fishing trawler, NN04.

'So why is he waiting?'

'I can only think it is about the weather and, therefore also about time. Time or timing is the key.'

'So how will he know when it's the right time?'

Clement stared through the bus's front window stifling a yawn. 'Good question! An event, I suppose. The man then knows he has a finite time to get to the pier.'

'You should get some sleep while you can, Clement.'

He nodded. 'You are probably right.'

Clement opened his eyes and sat up. Light was tingeing the land off to his left, the gentle glow shining through the mist illuminating the tussock grasses and casting long shadows. He looked at the bus windows. The

263

strengthening rays of sunlight were making the condensation on the glass panes twinkle.

'Morning! At least you've had a good rest, Clement.'

'What time is it, Reg?'

'Not yet nine. Looks like it may be a nice day. We could sure do with some decent weather.'

Clement sat up and rubbed the moisture from the window with the heel of his clenched fist and stared at the pale day. On the roadway beside him a patch of snow was slowly melting. 'Of course! Staring me in the face!'

'Clement?'

'The weather, Reg. For the pick-up to take place, he needs calm seas and fair winds. And as you just said, the weather has broken! It is what he has been waiting for.' Clement turned to face Reg. 'The raid on Stroma Lighthouse! It was a rehearsal run.' He stood and watched the increasing light of day, his mind racing. 'The kirk! It can be seen for miles. And once hit, the killer takes off from wherever he is for Dunnet Head. Dear Lord. Today is Sunday. The kirk will be full of people.'

# 23

'How do you want to play this?'

Clement stared at his old friend for what seemed like eternity.

'Here.' Reg handed him a canteen of water and a ration pack. 'I imagine you haven't eaten for a while.'

'Old habits, Reg?'

'Lessons learned.'

Clement bit into the dried, salty meat. It tasted delicious in his dry mouth. 'Morning Service is at ten. I must return to Canisbay to warn them.'

'What do you want me to do?'

'After you drop me off, drive back to the Royal Air Force Base in Thurdistoft and scramble some fighters to intercept the bomber.'

'No need, Clement. Any enemy plane will be picked up on radar and tracked. They will scramble Two-One-Three Squadron anyway. But if we're going back, we don't have much time.'

Clement paused. Time. It had always been about time. Now he needed to think clearly. '*He* has to be somewhere close enough to the kirk to see the attack. Then he'll leave and go to Dwarwick Pier.'

'Shouldn't we just go to the pier and wait for him?'

'I have to warn them, Reg otherwise a lot of innocent people will die.'

'You're a decent man, Clement. Given that someone there is doing everything possible to kill you, no one would blame you for leaving them to their own devices.'

'I have to, Reg. It's how I am.'

'I know. What do you have in mind?'

'I am making an assumption that an attack will occur today and, if that is the case, then the pick-up will also be today. It is the first good weather we've had in a week and given how quickly it can change here, I cannot see them passing up this chance. Whether by boat or submarine, the pick-up will most likely happen at the high tide. And I know today's high will be around four this afternoon.'

'Limited visibility by then.'

'Almost perfect - for him, that is. High tide, little moon and fading light.'

Clement looked away to a line of trees in the distance. 'Can you take me back to about a mile this side of Gills Bay? I don't what anyone seeing the bus.'

'And then?'

Clement thought for a moment. 'Drive to the Dunnet Hotel and park the bus around the back. Then go to the cottages near Dwarwick Pier. If you can, evacuate all the people who live there. Then occupy the cottage with the most commanding view of the bay and the pier. Put your cap in a window so I know where you are. I'll join you there.'

Reg nodded and started the engine. Sitting on the long back seat, Clement checked his knife and pistol, and running his hand over his webbing, felt for the magazines of ammunition. He knew they were no match for bombs or the guns of a fighter aircraft but the action was automatic. As the bus pulled onto the road heading east, Clement thought about the people who would soon be walking to church. He prayed he had time to warn the innocent people of Canisbay. In his mind he saw the pale-faced child, Mary, and the boy, Billy, who had seen enough for his tender years. If he was too late, his friend and fellow priest, Aidan, along with the people he knew from the villages, would be blown to pieces while at prayer. Clement squeezed his eyes, a frown furrowing his brow. Something was nagging him. He had never been a superstitious man and he didn't believe in premonitions or luck, but his inner voice was bothering him. He sat up. 'Why didn't they shoot down the fighter that attacked Stroma Island last week?'

Reg's eyes flashed to the rear-view mirror.

Clement knew the question was rhetorical, at least for Reg who had been in Wick at the time. 'What am I missing, Reg?'

'Clement?'

Time. It had always been about time. He knew that. Days spent waiting for the weather to clear. Since the death of Donald Crawford, Clement had always believed the killer was the enemy spy he had come to investigate. Moreover, he had deduced that the man had an accomplice who did not reside in either Canisbay or Huna. But what if it was the other way around? What if his enemy was distant and the accomplice was local? Had the call placed by Donald Crawford even originated in Huna? Clement searched his mind. Crawford had told the caller to hold the line. That Donald Crawford had connected a call was all Clement knew for certain. He leaned forward, his elbows resting on his knees, his face in his hands. It was possible that the call had been placed to someone doing a scheduled delivery at a pre-arranged time at the Frews' house. Was that so unusual that Donald Crawford had listened to the call? There was no way of knowing. Perhaps it no longer mattered.

Twenty minutes later Reg slowed the bus just before the hill leading down into Gills Bay.

'Can you get your hands on a couple of Sten guns, Reg?'

'Already thought of that, Clement. Leave it to me. You just get to that pier before four o'clock this afternoon.'

'God willing. And thank you, Reg.' Clement smiled and grasped his old friend's hand in farewell. Standing at the side of the road, he watched Reg turn the bus and drive away, heading west.

Clement stared at the morning sky. Low whitish clouds in long bands stretched over the pastoral scene that spread out before him. In places the sun was shining through and small patches of blue sky were making themselves visible. He looked up. A light south-easterly breeze blew into his face. In the sunshine the snow glistened and where it had melted, colour came to the meadows of Canisbay. Off to his left, Pentland Firth looked bright blue in the morning light. It lit up the land and buoyed the spirits. His eyes roamed over the gentle, green and white undulating hills. In front of him, he could see people entering the kirk. He imagined Aidan already in the vestry putting on his robes. In peacetime, the inviting sound of church bells would be ringing in the crisp air.

He started to walk. Morning service had not yet begun. On the breeze Clement caught the sound, faint and still some miles distant; a pulsating hum, like a malevolent gnat. In horror, Clement stared into the sky, his eyes widening as the sound intensified. A black shape appeared through the clouds and within seconds descended out of the morning glow.

Then the squeal.

As a lone fighter thundered overhead, Clement threw himself under the beech hedge at the edge of the road and rolled under it, wrapping his arms over his head. The menacing noise roared above him. Then two detonations in quick succession exploded the tranquil morning. Opening his eyes, Clement stared up through the branches. He could hear the plane above, banking and turning. Another run. He held his breath, but he heard no strafing.

The plane rose above him, its sinister shadow passing over him as the sound of its engines roared then diminished. Several seconds passed while he waited. The rustle of the leaves above his head from the wind in the branches was all he could hear.

Then he heard the screams coming from the direction of the kirk. Seconds later came the sound of other engines in the skies. He prayed it was Two-One-Three Squadron. Rolling sideways out from under the hedge, he stared up. Three Hurricanes criss-crossed above him, the Nazi plane banking east, heading for the open sea, the Hurricanes in pursuit. Within seconds they all were nothing more than specks in the sky. He clambered out of the hedge and stood up.

Dust and smoke had engulfed the kirk. Through the haze he could see the shattered stones and bricks. People stumbled over the rubble as the dust cloud spread out. From where Clement stood, he could see that most of the nave appeared unharmed but several of the windows had blown out with the blast. The bell tower, however, had taken the brunt of the attack. Through the dust cloud he could see smoke rising. Low flames were beginning to take hold in what was left of the tower.

Within seconds, people started stumbling through the rubble, dazed with confusion. From where Clement stood, he recognised Kathleen Wallace standing on the road. Beside her, Stewart McCrea's red hair gleamed in the intermittent sunshine. He appeared to be unhurt. The lad was holding the child, Mary, in his arms. Clement dropped into the long grass at the side of the road and propped himself on his elbows. Reaching for his telescope, he steadied the instrument, focusing it on the child. Blood was flowing down Mary's leg, but she was alive. Clement focused the instrument on the mother, the fragile Kathleen Wallace. She was crying, her face contorted with fear. Then she appeared to be screaming. Suddenly, she rushed forward, stumbling over the rubble and tossing stones in every direction. Clement scanned the scene again, realizing she must be looking for her husband or young Billy, but he could see neither. Clement prayed they would be found alive.

Lifting the telescope, he scanned the wider scene. He recognised Morag McCrea, a woman he had met only briefly on his first day in Canisbay. She appeared to be completely still, stuck in a moment of horror, unable to move. Not far away from her, Clement recognised the elderly farmer from Sean's bus who had fallen asleep on the trip north from Wick. The old man was sitting on a headstone, holding a handkerchief to his blood-stained forehead.

Clement continued to watch the devastation, hoping that Aidan would walk out of the debris. But there was no long white robe covered in dust or stained with blood. From inside the nave, a woman emerged and picked her way through the carnage. She headed straight into the graveyard, walking away from the devastation. Joyce McAllister. She appeared unhurt and was hurrying towards Huna, Clement hoped to telephone the ambulance in Thurso. Training the telescope again on the growing group of people who staggered from the wreckage, he searched again for their minister, but as the minutes passed the smoke increased and flames devoured the kirk. Clement felt his heart sinking, but his anguish would have to wait. The attack was not only a signal, it was a distraction. Putting his telescope to his eye again, he started to scan the locality, looking for a lone man walking away from the destruction. On the road from Canisbay to the kirk he saw three men running. One was Danny O'Reilly, but

Sean's friend and the two others were running towards the devastation.

Slowly Clement guided the telescope over the fields looking for anyone walking west. The manse came into view, but he knew Aidan would have been in his vestry and it, along with the bell tower, had taken a direct hit.

Lifting the instrument, Clement scanned the home of the Frew sisters. Nothing had changed there and no one was in the yard. Away to the left he could see Joyce McAllister hurrying along the road. She had almost reached Huna, but Clement knew now she was not his enemy's accomplice. Shifting the telescope further to the south, the village of Canisbay came into view. The two storied *Bell Inn* loomed over the intersection. A figure he knew stood in the window of Room Ten.

Jean Buchanan was holding some binoculars. Keeping his telescope trained on her, Clement saw her turn away. Within a few minutes, Jean was running along the road towards the kirk, a bag with a large red cross on it in her hand. Moving the telescope further to the south and west, he studied the road, lingering on the hedges he had used to disguise his presence. No one walked or ran anywhere other than towards the devastated kirk.

'I know you are here.' Clement could almost smell his adversary.

The clanging made him lower the telescope. Two ambulances from further west, Castletown or Thurso maybe, were rushing towards the kirk, their sirens piercing the morning. They had arrived more quickly than Clement had expected, but perhaps the pilots of Two-One-Three Squadron had radioed back to base.

Lifting the telescope again, he once more scanned the scene. Everything within Clement wanted to be with those people. It seemed so wrong to be just watching the events unfolding. But it was not his role. He lowered the telescope. Even though he couldn't see his enemy now, Clement knew where the man would be at four o'clock this afternoon.

Rolling over, Clement replaced the telescope in his webbing and stood by the beech hedge. His eye searched the land off to his left. Avoiding the road, and keeping to the hedges for cover, he crossed the fields heading west. He wanted to keep the road on his right within sight.

On the rise above Gills Bay, Clement turned and stared back at the kirk, a scene of tragic activity. People were helping one another while others carried stretchers. A figure stood beside one of the ambulances. Clement reached again for his telescope and trained it on the man. Inspector Stratton stood beside the open rear doors of one of the ambulances, a clip board in his hand. Clement was relieved that Stratton was there. The Inspector would bring order to the chaos. Jean Buchanan was sifting through the debris, not a pleasant job, but Clement believed that of all the women in the district, Jean, along with Joyce McAllister, was probably the most capable in a crisis. Returning his telescope to its pouch, Clement turned away and started to run, his mind now on Dwarwick Pier.

# 24

Clement watched the ground as he ran. His determination to catch his adversary was now obsessional. What would induce a man to commit treason? Yet it was only treason if his enemy was British. He pondered Robert Wallace. He visualized the man's wife's frantic searching. Perhaps it had been for her son, not her husband? Perhaps Wallace didn't attend kirk. It fitted with what Clement had learned about the man from Nora Ballantyne. The vicar in him wanted to tell Wallace that ignoring God's forgiveness for sin only prolonged the torment, something he felt sure Kathleen Wallace would be pleased to see resolved. People and their secret motives. Clement repeated the well-known saying about the devil being in the detail. He knew so little about Wallace, but as he had often said before, how well does anyone know their neighbour's inner-most thoughts? He did know that his enemy was no hired assassin. The man was ruthless to the point of inhuman cruelty. What had Clement missed that would identify the man beyond any doubt? There had to be something. So small a piece of information that he had either dismissed it or hadn't questioned it. And, more significantly, his enemy had either overlooked it or wasn't concerned about it.

On the easterly wind, the sound of an approaching vehicle broke into Clement's thoughts. It was still some way behind him. He hurried on, crossing the fields, moving closer to the main road. Looking back over his shoulder, he could see one of the ambulances driving west, but the siren was not blaring. A bad sign. One that usually meant the occupants were deceased. He wondered if he should stop the ambulance and request a lift to Dunnet, but he knew he wouldn't reach the road in time before it passed him. He lifted his arms and began to wave in the hope that they would see him. The vehicle slowed and stopped by a copse of sycamore trees on either side of an elaborate iron gateway. It had been where he had sat with Reg in the bus earlier that morning. He started to run, but as he did, he saw someone get out. They walked to the back of the ambulance and opened the rear doors.

Clement paused and waited beside a low tree. A moment later, a second person alighted from the ambulance and joined the other at the rear of the vehicle. With both back doors wide open, Clement couldn't see what was happening. Minutes later the doors closed.

Both people returned to the vehicle and it drove away. Clement frowned. Their actions made little sense.

Running over the fields, he reached the roadway adjacent to the gate. Before him was a low stone wall that formed the front perimeter fence of Mey Castle. Crossing the road, he stood at the large ironwork gate and peered down the long driveway. The gate was closed and no one was at work in the fields. Sitting on the perimeter stone wall, he looked across the surrounding meadows wondering why the ambulance had stopped there.

On the other side of the wall the ground dropped away to a grove of short, contorted trees and in the distance he could see a high red-brick wall. Beyond that, some distance away, was the castle. Clement lowered his gaze and stared into the copse. Below him, under the trees, were two hessian sacks. Something about them troubled him. Swinging his legs over the wall, he jumped down.

As he neared them, he knew what they were and his heart sunk. He reached for his knife and cut the bags at the top. The first was a face he knew, but the sight made him recoil. Robert Wallace's visage was still ruddy from the manual labour the man had done in all weathers, but his clothes bore testimony to the manner of his death. Burns. Clement opened the sack further, his stomach retching at the sight of the charred flesh, the oozing fluid that escaped the skin and would never now form blisters. He looked at the massive hands, red and black, the fingers and palms stripped of flesh from trying to smother the flames.

He turned away, memories of his time as hospital chaplain at St Thomas's in London following the Great

War bursting from the past. He opened the second sack. The boy, Billy, gazed out, his wide-eyed stare fixed in death, but the lad appeared almost completely uninjured. Explosive forces could do that, Clement knew. He lowered his head and recited The Lord's Prayer. Any death was tragic, but the death of a child was dreadful. He covered their faces again and climbing over the iron gate sat on the wall.

What the ambulance drivers had done appalled him. He gazed out at the fields. Why would transporting the injured to hospital not take precedence? He stared at the contorted trees around him, the rustling wind the only sound. Surely the removal of the bodies of Robert Wallace and his son could only be to make room for someone else, someone alive and who was already on the road heading west.

Clement's head spun. The man's escape had been well planned and it involved more than two people. Did that include the ambulance drivers? Or had these men been made to stop in the copse by someone hiding there? Clement looked along the road heading west towards Dunnet. Standing, he began to run, the ruthlessness of his enemy spurring him on. Despite what was unfolding around him, Clement again thanked God for Reg's presence and the other blessing; the tide.

"Time and tide." Clement recited Geoffrey Chaucer's famous quotation. "They wait for no man." But the reverse was equally true. As Clement broke into a steady pace, he felt the wind at his back, urging him on.

As *The Dunnet Hotel* came into view, Clement slowed. He checked his watch. Two o'clock. Two hours before the high tide. No cars were parked outside today and only one bicycle leant against the door post.

Hugging the wall, Clement crept around the building and peered into the rear yard. No one was there, but parked under a tree was Sean's bus and beside it, the ambulance. He scanned the yard. The door into the kitchen was closed and all appeared quiet. He took his knife from its scabbard and ran towards the vehicles. The bus was empty. Glancing over his shoulder, Clement opened the rear door to the ambulance and climbed inside, pulling the door to. Except for two low benches that ran along both sides of the vehicle, the ambulance was empty. He stared at the benches, wondering if the vehicle was used solely for the transportation of corpses. It did explain Stratton's early arrival, as Clement knew the mortuary in Thurso was attached to the police station. His mind returned to the ambulance drivers. It was possible they, too, were traitors. If that was the case, he faced a confrontation with more than one person.

Clement stared at the floor, his mind racing. There were only two possibilities when it came to the ambulance drivers, they were either dead themselves or involved. His gaze shifted to the kitchen door. Encountering them could mean his capture, and failure to apprehend his enemy. He checked his watch. Either way, there was no time. His speculation about the ambulance drivers would have to wait. Jumping from the rear of the vehicle, he left *The Dunnet Hotel*, his priority now to find Reg.

Twenty minutes later Clement slowed as he approached the crest of a low hill. He knew the terrain and what lay ahead. Up to his right, the track rose steeply. Before him, over the crest of the hill, were the few cottages beneath the massive Dunnet Head. Approaching the crest, Clement dropped to the ground and began to crawl his way forward. On the brow of the hill, he lay in the grass by the side of the road, his telescope scanning the fields. A low-roofed cottage with several attached out-buildings was nestled into the landscape in front of him. The home was about a hundred yards distant and close to the intersection of the road he was on and the one that led up to Dunnet Head and down towards Dwarwick Pier. He trained his telescope on each of the cottage's windows. All the curtains were drawn bar two - one in front and one on the western end of the cottage. Both had narrow gaps between the curtains. It was possible the curtains didn't close properly, but Clement considered the gap was enough for an eye or a muzzle. He studied each window again. No cap was visible in any of the front windows. Nothing stirred. The cottage appeared vacant and no farm workers were in the adjacent fields.

Clement looked back over his shoulder and checked the view in all directions. Whilst this cottage had an expansive view south, back along the track he had just taken, it had no view of the pier and while he knew Reg would never have chosen the cottage for their purposes, Clement believed it to be the ideal cottage for his enemy. Time and tide. These his enemy already knew. No need for a view of the bay. The perfect cottage for Clement was to his left. He trained his telescope on the building. Reg's cap sat on a window sill at the southern end of the cottage.

# 25

Clement crawled the short distance to the rear wall of the cottage, reached up and knocked on the window. A minute later he heard it open. Standing, he glanced back over his shoulder but saw no one.

'What's been happening, Clement?'

'Tell me about the other cottages?' he said climbing in and closing the window behind him.

'There's only two this side of the road in from Dunnet; this one and the one at the intersection. A farm hand answered the door there. He said the farmer and his wife were in Castletown. Wasn't too keen to talk, almost slammed the door in my face. But he did say he would stay indoors for the next few hours.

There is one person here though, also not inclined to leave.'

'Who?'

'The owner, Mrs Ferguson.'

The door to the room opened and a stern-faced woman of late middle-age stood facing him.

Clement smiled at the woman. 'I apologize for our presence in your home, madam.'

She nodded in Reg's direction. 'He said you'd be coming.'

Clement held the woman's gaze. 'I must insist you leave now, Mrs Ferguson, before it gets dark. I have reason to believe that a very dangerous man is in the area and I cannot guarantee your safety if you remain.'

The woman grunted, glancing at Reg. 'As I told this one. My home, my rules.'

The woman's square jaw closed. Clement could see there was little use in arguing. But while he didn't want another senseless death, he also didn't have the luxury of time for debate. His gaze shifted to Reg then back to the woman. 'Very well. Is there anyone else in the house?'

'No.'

Something about the woman's quick reply troubled him. 'Are you expecting someone to return today? And by that, I mean tonight as well?'

The woman's lips pursed, as though she had been caught out. 'My daughter will be home when she's finished washing dishes.'

Clement knew whom she meant; the girl at *The Dunnet Hotel*. But there wasn't enough time to warn her to stay away. And, he couldn't spare Reg. He prayed for a full Mess.

'A cup of tea would be appreciated, Mrs Ferguson, if you have any?'

'I suppose I could spare some.'

The woman turned on her heel, Clement staring after her.

'Don't mind her, Clement. It's nothing personal. Did you know there are about ten thousand military personnel in Caithness at present? The homes and lives of locals have been disrupted, that's all. I know what it's like to see strangers trample through your home. I took the bus to *The Dunnet Hotel*, by the way.'

'I saw it. Were there any other vehicles there?'

'No. I telephoned the base at Thurdistoft before leaving the hotel though, to warn them about a possible submarine sighting to coincide with the high tide this afternoon. That had them running. And something else, Clement. Wing Commander Atcherley, the Commanding Officer at the Base, was in the hotel for lunch. He was meeting with the local Home Guard. I gather you and he met?'

'Yes, briefly.'

'When I asked for the Stens, Atcherley ordered some of the Auxiliary Unit lads from the Home Guard to hand over two. You must have made quite an impression. I thought I'd have a real battle on my hands.'

'You may well yet, Reg.'

'I know this will sound bad, Clement, but I'm looking forward to this punch up. I also managed to get them to part with a few grenades. They wanted to be involved, of course, but I suggested they man the big forty-seven incher deck gun that's mounted at the west end of Dunnet Bay and await that submarine. As much as they seem good lads, we cannot have them interfering now. The two of us can handle things this end. Unfortunately, there isn't a large amount of ammunition. Neither did they have any sniper rifles with them, but I'm happy with the Stens.'

Clement looked up at Reg. The man was beaming. Reg had always been inclined to impetuosity but Clement held no concerns now. Reg would take his orders.

'Is there a view of the pier from the front rooms?' Clement asked.

'Yes. There's a boat tied up there. The old girl says it's been there all day. I suspect she knows whose it is, but she isn't saying.'

Leaving the rear bedroom, they walked along the corridor to the northern end of the house. Clement went to the window overlooking Dunnet Bay and peered through the lace weave curtain. 'That's Tom Harris's boat.'

'Your smugglers?'

'Have you seen them?'

'Haven't seen anyone.'

Clement checked his watch. 'Well, we will soon enough. The high tide is in half an hour. Let's see those Stens, Reg.'

The woman reappeared. 'There's a pot of tea on the kitchen table.'

Clement smiled. 'Thank you, Mrs Ferguson.'

She left the room, her annoyance barely disguised.

They walked into the kitchen. While Reg retrieved the Sten Guns from behind the wood heap, Clement checked the scene from the window above the sink. The view beyond was of the intersection and the other cottage. Clement focused his telescope on the window at the western end of the cottage. The gap was still no-

283

ticeable but he couldn't see inside and nothing appeared to have changed.

Returning the telescope to its pouch, he poured the tea. It was hot and welcoming. Reg put the Sten guns on the table alongside two grenades and a magazine of ammunition for each weapon.

Finishing the tea, Clement reached for his Welrod pistol and tucked it into his belt. Then he put the magazine of ammunition for the Sten gun into his right coat pocket and a grenade into his left. He flicked a glance at Reg. He thought his old comrade had more weaponry than was needed, but Clement didn't say anything. He knew what lay ahead. He had cheated death twice before and he didn't believe it could be avoided again.

'Do you remember the hand signals, Reg?'

'As well as riding a bicycle.'

The woman re-entered the room.

'Once we leave, Mrs Ferguson, please stay indoors. And keep your door locked. Admit no one. Thank you for the tea.'

The woman nodded.

Checking the view of the intersection again, Clement and Reg left the cottage by the rear window and ran along the western side of the house, on the Dunnet Bay side, crouching at the north-western corner. Off his left shoulder he could hear low breakers crashing onto the rocks below. In front, Tom's boat was tied up at Dwarwick Pier, but no one appeared to be aboard. Taking his telescope from his webbing, Clement focused it on the vessel. The door to the wheel-house was shut and he could see the padlock in the closed position. Returning the instrument to its pouch, Clement inched forward and peered around the building, his eye on the other cottage. Nothing moved.

Signalling to Reg, they crawled forward over the grass to a low flagstone fence. Clement reached for his telescope again and scanned the immediate area. Twenty feet in front of them, and slightly down the hill, was a dry-stone wall about waist height. Up to his right, the low-lying cottage near the intersection was still quiet. His gaze lingered over it and its curtains. Already the distinctive light of dusk was beginning to settle. He scanned the scene again from Dwarwick Pier and out to sea across Dunnet Bay, the sun now low in the sky. With the onset of evening the wind had picked up. Taking his woollen balaclava from his pocket, Clement pulled it on, the warming prickle of the coarse wool rubbing his unshaven stubble. In the failing light, they crawled forward and Clement lifted himself over the wall and dropped to the ground on the far side. Reg was beside him in seconds.

Clement lay in the grass, taking in his surroundings. Beside the pier was the flat, cleared area bounded by a steeply rising hill on the eastern side, flattening out to the south where the road led away from the jetty and up to the cottages. Nestled into the hill and off to one side was the padlocked fishermen's hut. Clement reached for his telescope once more and focused the instrument on the shed. A dim glow was just visible under the door. He lowered the telescope. With the increasing darkness, the lamp would be a beacon. He pondered Tom's whereabouts, but there was no time now to search for the fisherman.

Using hand signals, Clement and Reg descended to the flat ground where, on their left side, two overturned dinghies sat on a grassy knoll adjacent to the ramp. Advancing over the sloping ground, they took up a position behind the small boats.

'I want a closer view of the shed. Keep your eye on me, Reg.'

Hunching low, Clement ran across the road and upwards to the grassy hill, circling the flat area and approaching the shed from behind. To the rear of the hut, the hill rose up steeply. Keeping to the higher ground, and approaching it from above, Clement slid down the bank towards the building, wedging his foot between a rock and the shed wall and pressed his ear to the wooden walls. Inside, he heard scuffling.

He wondered who was inside. The ambulance drivers were his guess. At least they were conscious and able to breathe. But why would his enemy want hostages?

He heard footsteps.

Distinctive on the gravel, and more than one person.

He checked his watch. Just before four o'clock. Edging himself forward, he peered around the shed wall. Two men and a woman were walking across the flat open area heading towards the pier. Even in the diminishing light he saw the red tam o'shanter, the long coat and knee-high boots. She walked between two men, both of whom he recognised by their clothing as Tom Harris and Ian McAllister.

Clement breathed hard. Their presence complicated things. If the killer suddenly arrived there could be a blood bath.

He stared at them as they walked onto the pier, cursing himself for allowing them one last trip. Climbing back up the hill, he signalled for Reg to join him. Clement crouched near a low shrub and trained his telescope on the group.

Less than three minutes later Reg was beside him, the Sten in his grip.

In the early dusk light, Clement watched the trio below him, but something about the group troubled him.

Reg signalled "What's happening?"

'Call it gut,' he mouthed the near-silent words. 'But two things aren't right. The tam o'shanter. I once told her not to wear it and after what happened in the kirk, I don't believe she would do that willingly.'

'And?'

'Where is Tom's dog, Flip?'

'You saying these are not the smugglers?'

Clement stared at the group. He swallowed hard, wondering if it was what he wanted to believe.

'I am,' he said at length. How sure was he that the two men were not Ian McAllister and Tom Harris? And who was the woman wearing the red tam o'shanter, if not Sarah Crawford? He watched them climb onto Tom's boat, but McAllister remained on the pier.

'Reg, could you shoot just one of them from here?'

'Easy.' Reg raised the Sten.

'Climb higher and circle around. Get as close as you can without being seen. And Reg, be ready. If I am right, the dog is tied up in the shed. Once I release him, he will identify his master. As soon as I've checked the shed, I'll signal one flash of my torch. Take out the man the dog does *not* run to. If you see two flashes it means take the woman as well. Three means all of them.'

'Understood.'

As the twilight descended, Reg scrambled higher up the hillside and disappeared behind several clumps of low beech hedge. In the low light, Clement could no longer see him. Sliding down the damp, grassy hillside, Clement squatted beside the shed and listened. The scuffling was more energetic now. Reaching for the grenade in his pocket, Clement pulled the pin and hurled it as far as he could towards the ground on the other side of the clearing, near the two upturned dinghies. He had four seconds. Running around the shed to the front, he slammed the butt of the Sten into the padlock, broke it and threw open the door.

A sudden but intensely loud detonation exploded twenty yards away and shards of broken timber flew into the air.

In that instant he saw Flip tied to an anchor chain, the little animal's jaws bound together with tape. He glanced up through the open shed door at Tom Harris's vessel. With the explosion, everyone had jumped onto the boat, their attention diverted. He had seconds only. Using his knife, he cut the animal free. Flip burst through the door and ran along the pier, making straight for Tom. Within seconds, the dog was beside his master. Grabbing his torch, Clement flashed it twice. Immediately, two short bursts of rapid gunfire ripped through the dusk.

One body fell.

The other went backwards into the water.

Running from the shed, Clement leapt onto the stone pier his feet pounding along the uneven paving towards Tom Harris.

Harris was standing, anchored to the spot, fear and shock on his face. 'Thank God it's you. How did you know?'

But Clement couldn't wait. Before him, on the stone pier, a prostrate body lay face down. The clothes told him it was McAllister, but he knew by the size of the torso that it couldn't be the coal delivery man. As much as Clement wanted to know who lay dead, it would have to wait. The woman was below him, somewhere in the waves, but Clement knew it wasn't Sarah. He'd seen the woman walk to the pier and jump onto the boat when the grenade detonated.

No one with a sprained ankle could do such a thing.

In the shadow of Dunnet Head and the darkening landscape around him, Clement jumped from the pier onto the sloping ramp. The light was diminishing and the water and land were merging into a dark mass. His eyes frantically searched the area, but he couldn't see the woman. With his ears straining, he listened for footsteps, but the waves hitting the timber ramp were blanketing all other sound.

Out of the darkness, he felt a knife slice into his already wounded left forearm. He winced; the salt water stinging the raw flesh. Clement reeled backwards. Slipping the catch on the Sten gun, he let off a volley of shots, but he knew the strobing yellow flashes from the muzzle pinpointed his location. He threw the Sten upwards towards the pier and lunged sideways into the waves and grabbed his knife, his ears straining over the noise of the crashing waves for his enemy's location. Edging forward and with his knife poised, he moved his way up the ramp on the land side.

With the submarine rendezvous imminent, Clement calculated that his enemy had only minutes to be aboard Tom's boat and be heading for the open sea. Standing at the water's edge, Clement waited and braced himself, ready for attack or the tell-tale sounds of splashing or running feet.

Out of the darkness, his attacker lunged again, the blade slicing through the air in front of him. Clement jumped away to his right, to higher ground. He stood on the timber ramp, his knife poised.

A volley of shots splintered the night. Clement swung around uncertain of the direction. But there was no sound of the bullets hitting or spitting across the water. A diversion? Reg. He heard the sound of some-one in the water in front of him. Clement lunged forward. In the darkness he felt whoever was before him fall backwards. He grabbed at his adversary, catching an arm. But his attacker broke free, disappearing again in-to the waves. In that second, Clement knew his enemy was no woman. Clement waited, swinging the blade in front of him. He stood, his senses alert, his eyes wide, the blade slicing the air. Without warning, he felt a vice-like grip on his collar, dragging him backwards, the fabric of his coat twisted and tightening around his throat. Swinging his uninjured right arm backwards, Clement stabbed his blade into his attacker's thigh. The stranglehold released and Clement fell forwards. Gulp-ing air, he turned, his blade poised, his knife swinging right and left, his ears straining.

From behind and off to Clement's right the man lunged again, a massive hand grasping and pushing him under the crashing waves. Gulping water, Clement thrust his knife forward at the man's legs. He saw the man step sideways, away from his blade, and then there he was, in front of him, ready to strike the final blow. Clement's eyes widened; he saw the blade lifted high. He swung his wounded left arm up to block his opponent's thrust, at the same time he punched his right knee high, into the man's groin. Above the sound of the sea he heard the breath leave his assailant as he staggered back.

Clement rushed forward, his knife slicing through the air, the man no longer before him.

Bracing himself against a further attack Clement twisted around in widening circles, his ears straining.

Then the sound of someone running through shallow water.

Silence.

Out of the night the man fell on him from the pier above, pushing him down into the water. In that second, Clement reversed his grip on his knife and swung the blade backwards, plunging it into the soft flesh of the man's thigh and wrenching the knife upwards.

The man reeled backwards. As he fell screaming into the cold waves, Clement saw his hand move inside his saturated coat. Clement threw himself sideways into the deeper water of the bay and rolled beneath the waves, submerging into the freezing water as, off to his left, a shot rang out, the noise hard against the stone walls of the pier behind. Lifting his head above the waves, Clement heard two more shots. Then a light.

'Drop it or you're dead,' Reg called from the pier.

Three seconds later the man dropped the gun into the waves.

Clement reached for his Welrod and pointed it directly at the man's head. The glare of Reg's torch cut through the night, lighting up the face of Clement's attacker.

# 26

Clement watched Reg jump from the pier. Within seconds he had disarmed the man and was holding his Sten gun against his back.

Clement lowered his Welrod. 'Stratton, you are not only a traitor but a coward!'

As he walked out of the water clutching his left arm, Clement saw Tom with Flip in his arms walk to the edge of the ramp. He met the fisherman's gaze. 'Who is it, Tom, on the pier?'

'Jean Buchanan.'

A myriad of questions bubbled in Clement's mind, but they would have to wait. He turned to face a killer. At Clement's feet Sarah's red tam o'shanter floated at the water's edge. He bent to pick it up. 'You are contemptible and the worst, the lowest form of life. What is Jean Buchanan to you?'

'My ex-wife.'

Clement glared at Stratton. He wasn't sure if he believed it. Not that Clement believed Stratton would tell him the truth anyway. 'Did you kill the Frew ladies as well as Donald Crawford and Malcolm McCrea?'

'That's for me to know and you to find out, *Hope*. Hopeless!' Stratton's grin spread across his face.

Clement stared into the cold eyes. What he saw was maniacal ruthlessness, but what he felt was anger at a deception that had lasted years and from a man held in high regard. Clement looked away. Perhaps Stratton was trying to provoke him. Regardless, death by the hangman's noose was unavoidable for Stratton.

'Don't take your eyes off him for a moment, Reg. Tie his hands and feet and gag him.'

Clement turned to face Tom. 'Where are the others?'

'Tied up in the cottage. The one near the intersection. But don't go in. The door is wired! They expected you.'

Reg pulled the gag tight around Stratton's mouth. 'I'll deal with it, Clement.' He tied Stratton's hands and feet together then pushed him down on the hard ground. 'Take my coat, Clement.' He shrugged it off. 'You can't stay wet in this temperature.'

Clement removed his sodden greatcoat. 'I'm grateful. Thank you, Reg.'

Tom stood beside Clement, stroking Flip's fur. 'They were planning to use me and my ship to take them to a rendezvous off the coast, you know, Vicar. They would have killed me, wouldn't they?'

'Without blinking an eye.'

'What about the submarine?'

But it was Reg who answered. 'The authorities already know about it, so it won't be the rendezvous the Jerries are expecting.'

Clement withdrew his Welrod and held it on Stratton. 'Before you go and check on the hostages, Reg, would you retrieve the other Sten from the pier? And could you and Tom carry Mrs Buchanan's body to the shed? I'd rather she wasn't seen until this whole matter is resolved.'

Reg and Tom walked back towards the pier and together lifted the corpse of Jean Buchanan. The woman's death was tragic, but he hoped his pity was not just because she was female. He thought back on the few times he had spoken to the woman. Although her manner had, for the most part been brusque, she had shown kindness to him in providing food and a place to rest. He thought about Room Ten and its expansive views over Canisbay. Had she been trying to tell him something? He would never know. She had become entangled with her former husband and, Clement believed, had been used and manipulated in the cruellest way.

Clement heard the shed door close.

'I'll go now and check on the hostages,' Reg said, joining him.

Clement watched Reg disappear into the night.

Tom appeared at his side. 'Can he do it, Vicar, without setting off the explosives? Who is he anyway? I had no idea, you know!'

'To answer your questions in order, Tom; yes, a friend, and I believe you.'

'Did you suspect her?'

'No.'

Clement had surmised there were two people involved but he had not expected either of them to be Allan Stratton or Jean Buchanan. He had realised, too late, his mistake that the accomplice was local and the killer distant. A long sigh escaped his lips. The adrenaline of the night was wearing off. His arm felt heavy and he was cold and weary. Despite the warmth and thickness of Reg's heavy greatcoat, his arm was throbbing painfully. His injuries would wait. He wasn't taking his attention from Stratton.

They stood beside the shed, the only sound the crashing waves. Then they saw it. The flash of a torch light from across the water, then another. Then nothing. A moment later two more flashes. Clement saw Stratton's head lift but it was his eyes that spoke. The submarine would not wait more than its allotted time and his chance of escape had gone.

'Was that the submarine?' Tom asked.

Clement nodded, but his eyes were on Stratton.

Then a boom from across the bay, deafening in the night air. Clement looked out over the water. A bright and intense light filled the night sky. Clement remembered the large gun Reg had told him about at the western end of Dunnet Bay. But there was no subsequent explosion indicating that the gun had struck its target. Regardless, the submarine would not remain.

Clement watched Stratton. He had expected to see dejected resignation on the traitor's face, but Stratton was smiling. Clement wondered about Stratton's reaction. Was it bravado? Or was Stratton's allegiance to the Fatherland sheer fanaticism to the point of self-sacrifice?

Twenty minutes later Reg reappeared. 'It's a ruse, Clement. There are no explosives.'

Clement held the gaze of the man he had known for twenty years. 'You're sure?'

'I've been around every door and window half a dozen times and there isn't a wire anywhere and there is no sign of recent disturbance in the garden that would indicate the presence of a mine.'

'Thank you, Reg. Who told you it was wired, Tom?'

'Stratton.'

Stratton gurgled through the gag. The former police inspector; despite his injuries and impending execution, appeared to be laughing. More than that, he seemed to be enjoying the situation. Clement had never met anyone like Stratton. His true character had been completely concealed, and the man showed not the slightest remorse for what he had done.

Clement also realized that it had been Jean in the Frews' house. The woman was no murderer. Women murderers, so Clement had been taught, killed only to remove a threat. It made sense to him now why he had not been pursued that night. In fact, Jean had gone out of her way to avoid an encounter with him. He understood now. She had been ordered to get something hidden upstairs in the house. He had been correct about Sarah's radio transmitter being in the poultry shed, but it had been the machine gun and sniper rifle hidden in the Frews' house. Jean had removed them, just like Sarah's wireless, piece by piece every time Jean went to the house. Stratton then could collect them on his occasional visits to *The Bell*. Clement visualized the neat kitchen where the old ladies had died so horribly. Everything in its place, even the tea cosy sitting on a tray on the bench by the back door. He remembered the empty gin bottles awaiting collection. Jean came and went just as easily as McAllister. Jean had left the Frews' house and used the rear garden of the manse as the shortest route to and from *The Bell*. That the footprints leading from the Frews' house to the manse implicated Aidan was icing on the cake for Stratton. Clement also believed it had been Jean and Stratton in the ambulance. But why would Jean still be involved with her ex-husband? What hold did Stratton have over her?

Clement knew he may never know the answer now that Jean was dead, but he also understood how Stratton had always been one step ahead of him. "Comply with any instruction from a man named *Hope*," Clement recalled his conversation with Stratton in Thurso Police Station. He had been expected and Jean had provided all the information Stratton needed about Clement's movements in Canisbay. So much made sense now.

'Reg, there's an ambulance in the rear yard of *The Dunnet Hotel* parked next to the bus. Put Stratton in the back and make sure he cannot escape. No trips to the lavatory, no food, no water. Nothing, until he is safely behind bars. Take him to Wing Commander Atcherley. No one else. I'll see to the others. And thank you, Reg. I couldn't have done it without you.'

'Nonsense, Clement. I just held a gun on a piece of scum.'

Clement smiled, but he knew that without Reg's presence, it all may have had a very different outcome.

Reg untied the leg restraints and dragged Stratton to his feet. 'And don't worry about the woman, Clement. I'll arrange for some of my men to get her body tomorrow morning. Good to work with you again. I better report in or they'll think I've deserted.'

Clement reached for Reg's hand in farewell. 'May the Lord bless you and keep you, Reg. Oh! And don't forget your coat.' Clement began to remove the borrowed garment.

'Keep it, Clement. I can get another easily enough. And I'll collect your old one tomorrow when I return. You can do something for me, though, if you would.'

'Anything.'

'Put a good word in for me with whomever it is you work for. Got to be more useful to the war effort than riding a motorcycle and digging latrines in Caithness.'

Clement smiled.

Reg pushed the muzzle of his Sten gun into Stratton's back and they made their way up the hill away from Dwarwick Pier.

# 27

Clement waited until Reg and Stratton had disappeared from view. 'Did you dispose of Sean, Tom?'

'Aye. Just as you requested. Sad business. Sarah has the few possessions we found in his pockets.'

'Why were you all still here? You left Gills Bay over twelve hours ago?'

Tom didn't answer.

'I have to know, Tom. Everything.'

'We bring bacon and meat in and collect whisky and brandy and sometimes sugar from the shed, but it wasn't there. We waited an hour or two then Sarah went to see Anne Ferguson, who works at *The Dunnet*, while Ian and I waited on my boat. What with that Nazi plane and Two-One-Three Squadron overhead, we had to keep low.'

'Does the alcohol and sugar come from *The Dunnet Hotel*?'

Tom nodded. 'Those officers live like kings. Anne drops a bottle from time to time, cold tea, actually, and brings the whisky and brandy home, a bottle or two at a time. They don't go without. Venison, mallard, all kinds of luxuries.' Tom paused. 'But when Sarah came back several hours later, she wasn't alone.'

'What happened then?'

'We were escorted from the boat up to the cottage and tied up. We thought Stratton had arrested us for black-marketeering. He took us at gunpoint and we submitted like lambs. We had no idea.'

Clement believed Tom, but their naivety had been exploited and not just this night. 'Who's in the cottage?'

'A young farm hand along with Sarah and Ian. Aidan Heath is there too.'

'Aidan is with them?'

'He's injured. Shot in the shoulder. Only superficial though. It was a clever plan. Reverend Heath was on the ambulance. Apparently, Jean held him at gunpoint, marching him from the vestry into the graveyard while the Stuka attacked. Then when the ambulances arrived to transport the injured and dead from the raid, Stratton convinced the ambulance drivers to stay and look after the injured while he drove the deceased to the mortuary in Thurso. It's behind the police station, you know.'

'I did know. And Reverend Heath?'

301

'His presence was to provide a reason for Jean to go on the ambulance. She was to look after his injuries while on the journey.'

Clement felt the frown crease his forehead. 'But the Nazi bomber didn't do any shooting. It dropped two bombs and left. Of course. Very clever of Stratton. If Aidan's injuries had been seen by the real ambulance drivers, they would have recognised them as gunshot wounds. No wonder they wanted him on the bus. And, no doubt, they forced him to assist them.' Clement thought of the bodies of Robert Wallace and the boy. But at least now, with Aidan alive, the father and son would have a decent burial.

'It amazed us all. Especially Aidan. We all knew Jean was strong, but we never imagined she could do that.'

They stood outside the low-lying cottage where the hostages waited. 'Do you know, Tom, if they have any weapons in the cottage?'

'Not any more. Stratton threw the farmer's rifle into Dunnet Bay.' Tom stroked his little dog. 'You saved my life, Flip. And you, Vicar.'

'Just honour your vow to stay away from the black market.'

They approached the cottage from the front. Everything was in darkness.

Clement called out to them. 'It's Reverend Wisdom and Tom Harris. You are safe to come out. There are no explosives. Stratton has been apprehended and Jean is no longer a threat.'

The door opened, slowly at first. McAllister, with Sarah and Aidan, walked towards him, Aidan's left arm in a sling. 'Are we glad to see you, Clement. It's been a Sunday to remember.'

'I am pleased to see you, too, Aidan. Sean's bus is parked behind *The Dunnet Hotel*. If you can manage to walk there, perhaps Mr McAllister would drive us back to Canisbay?'

'It's the least I can do, Reverend Wisdom.'

It was nearly an hour before they sat in the bus.

Sarah handed McAllister Sean's keys. 'Found them in his pocket.'

Clement would always feel responsible for the Irishman, but he thanked the Lord for Reg Naylor. His presence in Caithness had been a real blessing; divine intervention and an answer to prayer. And the man, resourceful as ever, had acquired some useful skills, particularly when it came to starting engines without keys. McAllister shifted the gear stick into first and drove into the lane beside *The Dunnet Hotel*.

'Where are we going, Vicar?' Tom asked.

He glanced over to where Tom was sitting. 'To *The Bell*. What you all do after that isn't my concern, but it must not include the black market.'

Sarah leaned forward. 'And you, Clement. Where are you going?'

'Home!' But even as he said it, he wasn't really sure where that was. 'If it's alright with you, Aidan, I could use a bath and a bed before leaving Canisbay.'

'My pleasure, Clement. Stay as long as you want. With my arm in a sling, I'm sure you will be of more assistance to me than I will be to you.'

The bus crawled passed *The Dunnet Hotel*, the gravel crackling under its wheels. McAllister flicked on the head lights and pulled out onto the main road in the quiet darkness, heading east. As they did so, Clement saw several bicycles leaning against the wall, all grouped around the entry to the inn. The officers were returning to their billets after a long day on duty somewhere. That was the interesting thing about public houses. In one way, they were always open. People came and went all the time.

But he couldn't get Stratton out of his mind. What the man had done was beyond evil and his after-hours visits to *The Bell* had belied his true purposes. Details. Little things. Clement recalled Chief Inspector Morris's advice and the small acts of kindness exhibited by the Reverend St Clair of Inverness. Details and inherent kindness. These were the indicators of character more than anything else. But while Clement knew Stratton to be treacherous, he felt nothing but sadness for Jean Buchanan.

He thought back to the night he'd encountered her in the Frews' house. She had fled to *The Bell* but had entered the inn through the rear, after she'd hidden the machine gun and the pistol in the out-building. She'd even taken a crate of bottles before returning to the bar to defray suspicion. And, Clement believed, it had probably been Jean who had secreted the ammunition drum in McAllister's lorry while the man was doing deliveries at *The Bell*. Clement visualized Jean standing at the window of Room Ten. He knew the view from that room was extraordinary. Every detail planned for and expected. He knew now, everything was peripheral to *The Bell*, standing as it did in the middle of Canisbay, with views extending in all directions. And Stratton could use a portable transmitter with a six-volt battery which he connected to the antennae in the bell tower when he needed to make contact with the enemy. It would be unlikely that he would be discovered there, given that Aidan rarely used the vestry for anything other than robing on Sunday morning and never climbed the ladder in the belfry. In light of what Clement now knew, he regretted not asking Nora to pursue her enquiries with the Scottish Records Office.

They drove into *The Bell's* back yard. It was nearly midnight. The lazy moon still lay in its celestial hammock as shifting clouds came and went. Reaching for his lock-picks, he unlocked the rear door to the inn and bade farewell to Tom Harris.

'I'll help you with Reverend Heath, Vicar. It's the least I can do for you,' McAllister said.

At the gate to the manse, Clement said good bye to Sarah Crawford and Ian McAllister. Clement wanted to leave the area the next day. His plan was to drive Sean's bus back to Thurso and, after seeing a doctor about his injuries, catch the train south. He stood on the doorstep of the manse while Aidan opened the door, and watched McAllister and Sarah Crawford disappear into the night.

Inside, the manse was cold. He remembered the inviting warmth on his first day. In reality it was only eight days ago, but it had been the longest week of his life.

'Are you hungry, Aidan?'

'No, thank you, Clement. Given the hour and all that's happened, I think we both could do with sleep more than sustenance. You look exhausted and I haven't asked if you are injured in any way?'

'Just superficial. Nothing serious. The greatcoat took most of the damage. But if you had a bandage I'd appreciate it.'

'Of course, but I'm afraid you will have to put it on yourself.'

Aidan fetched a clean rolled bandage from the kitchen and handed it to him.

Stifling a yawn, Clement took off Reg's greatcoat and pushed back his sleeve, winding the cloth around his arm. He knew he should wash the wounds, but he was too tired. Tomorrow he would have time for such things. All he wanted was the panacea of sleep. He could allow himself that now. It was over and Stratton was safely in custody. 'Is there anything you want, Aidan, before I retire?'

'Nothing. I'll be good as new in no time. But I'm sorry there won't be any hot water for your bath until tomorrow.'

'I'm too tired anyway.'

Clement closed the door to his little room and threw Reg's coat over the chair. He fell onto the bed and began to remove his webbing and boots. Unbuttoning his jacket, he tossed it on the foot of the bed, unable and unwilling to stand up again, then unbuckled the Welrod's holster from around his chest. He ran his hand over his woollen vest. It felt surprisingly dry. The layers of coarse army clothing had most probably saved his life, as had Reg's dry coat. He glanced at his friend's greatcoat on the chair and smiled, thinking of his old comrade. Removing his knife, Clement tucked it and his pistol under the mattress and lifting his feet, lay back on the bed, the muscles in his body finally relaxing. Once he had thought the bed hard, but now he didn't care if it had nails. Exhaustion coursed through his body, making his limbs feel heavy and useless. Lying back on the pillow, he stared through the window. He knew he should close the curtains, but he was too exhausted to get up.

# 28

Monday 3rd March

The dawn light woke him, the soft whitish light of a grey, overcast morning intruded through his window. Clement reached for his watch. Seven o'clock. Early. Too early to get up. Pulling the blankets over his shoulders, he allowed the warmth to permeate his body, but his arm was throbbing. Rolling over, he pulled back the sleeve on his vest. The bandage on the wound inflicted by Stratton was stuck with thick, congealed blood. He knew without looking at the wound that it would scar. Clement pulled his sleeve back over his arm and decided he should get up and redress the wound.

Swinging his feet over the side of the bed, Clement sat up and pulled on his shirt. He stared through the window at the early morning sky. Everything seemed quiet and still. 'The illusory calm of Canisbay,' he muttered. Standing by the window, he saw the Frews' house. He stared at it. In his mind he saw the horrible image of the elderly ladies. He felt both sadness and rage for what Stratton had done to them, as well as to Donald Crawford and young McCrea. Even the man's endeavours to kill Clement had not just been an attempt at a fatal wound. Deliberately inflicting further injury to an existing wound was a contemptible act.

Clement rubbed his hand over his beard. He needed to shave and bathe and a change of clothes would be nice. He hoped Aidan would not mind if he borrowed some, as he remembered his pack had been destroyed in the bell tower. He thanked God that Aidan's life had been spared. Aidan had told him how Jean had taken him out the side door of the vestry and into the graveyard at gunpoint. There they had waited for the raid, during which she had fired the shot that injured his upper left arm. He had been forced to remain behind a large headstone until the ambulances arrived, when Stratton had joined them in the graveyard, ostensibly looking for bodies.

Clement drew in a deep breath and slowly exhaled his exhaustion. It had been one of the most difficult times of his life but with God's providence, he had survived.

Clement slipped his feet into his boots and wrapped the greatcoat around his aching body then opened the door to the corridor. He glanced up; Aidan's bedroom door was still closed. Clement decided to light a fire and make a hot cup of tea.

He tip-toed down the stairs and opened the door to the sitting room. It was bitterly cold. Seeing there was insufficient coal in the scuttle, Clement opened the rear door and stepped outside. It wasn't raining, but the intensity of the cold bore into his flesh and he shivered. It surprised him that after being in Caithness through one of the most physically and mentally challenging times of his life, he now felt the cold so keenly. Perhaps it was just that he had the time to feel it now. Opening the door to the shed, he swung a sack of coal onto his shoulders and returned to the kitchen door, but the large house behind him refused to be ignored. He turned and stared at it. At least, Clement told himself, he had honoured his pledge to the elderly spinsters.

Entering the manse, he decided to discuss the Frew sisters with Aidan, when the man awoke. There would be so much for his friend to do. Small communities always felt such loss acutely. There were funerals and memorial services to arrange and even with a damaged kirk, it had to be done if the villages of Huna and Canisbay were ever able to come to terms with the recent events.

He swung the coal sack down beside the fireplace. Of all those who had died, Clement would always feel heartache about Sean. The elderly farmer from Brabster, the only passenger on Sean's bus, had altered Sean's usual bus route, something Jean Buchanan had not known.

Kneeling in front of the fireplace, Clement opened the sack and emptied the coal into the scuttle beside the grate then reached for the brush. Cold ash fell through the andirons onto the bricks beneath as he swept the white ash aside. Turning, he looked around for some paper to light the fire, his eye falling on a local newspaper left on the velvet chair. Tearing off several pages, he twisted the paper into lengths and laid them in the grate, then piled some kindling on top. Reaching for the box of matches beside the coal scuttle, he lit the paper and watched the flames take hold. Taking some pieces of coal, he laid them over the twigs and waited. The orange flames rose quickly, the paper blackening and burning away, a twig catching the flame and glowing red. Standing, he went into the kitchen, filled the kettle, set it on the stove and returned to the sitting room to add more coal. He watched the flames dwindle, the kindling failing to ignite and he realized the twigs must have been damp. Clement looked around.

Behind him was a bookshelf filled with neatly stacked magazines. With no more newspaper he hoped that Aidan wouldn't mind sacrificing one of his fishing magazines for their comfort. He took the top one from the nearest pile. A wide-eyed fish stared back at him and he remembered seeing the magazine with the lead article about the breeding habits of the North Atlantic Cod. He smiled, wondering if given the events of the last week, Aidan would ever again read such mundane matter. Opening the magazine, he tore off the back few pages and scrunched them, poking them between the kindling and waiting for the fire to take. Staring into the flames, he waited while the kindling crackled and the fire took hold.

Putting the brush and matches aside, he closed what was left of the magazine. A small square of paper fell from between the pages. Without much thought he picked it up and glanced at the jumble of letters and numbers arranged in columns. Frowning, he stared at

311

the note. The lists resembled a puzzle. Laid out on the slip of paper in the shape of a rectangle were eight columns of letters. Above them was a line of numbers; 1,8,3,4,2,6,7,5 and beneath each number was a letter that spelt the word *breeding*. Beneath this were three lines of eight letters each in random order.

Clement's mind raced. On the lower edge of the note were five groups of five random letters. He'd seen them before. The encrypted message Sarah had taken down while sitting in Eric Fraser's boat-shed. He felt the blood draining from his head and he forced himself to think. What had Sarah said? That a key known to both the sender and the recipient was essential to decipher the message. Clement's gaze fell on the only intelligible word on the page; *Breeding*. He turned the magazine over in his hand. *Breeding* was the verb in the magazine's lead article. His eye returned to the note. Was it the key to deciphering the scrambled message? But no matter which way he read the letters, he couldn't make out any other word.

He stared at them, his eyes going from the transmitted groups of letters to how they were formed. The transmitted message followed the vertical column in the numerical order above the key word. The letters were read horizontally. His eyes returned to the rectangle as he saw it. He began to spell out the letters. They were not random. They were German. Across the bottom line he recognised one German word contained within the encryption.

In his head Clement was plunged into his past, to a time more than thirty years ago, when he worked as a youth on a farm in Romney near his boyhood home and before the first war. The farm manager had a dog whose name was *Weiler*. In his head, Clement could hear the farm manager's wife calling the animal now, the way Germans pronounce *W's* like *V's*. But it wasn't the pronunciation that now made Clement's blood run cold.

He knew what *Weiler* meant.

*Hamlet*. A Great Dane. And Clement knew of only one Dane in Canisbay.

'I see you found it?'

The voice came out of nowhere; calm, hypnotic. Clement's breathing stopped. Without moving, he lifted his gaze and faced his true enemy. He held the stare; cold, impassive.

'Little acts of kindness,' Aidan said, his eyes flicking to the fire that was now well alight. 'A good man's undoing.' From under the sling, Aidan raised a pistol then clenched it with both hands, the weapon motionless in his grasp, his finger slipping the safety catch.

Clement's heart pounded in his chest, his eye fixed on the muzzle of the weapon. Standing in front of the fire, Clement held Aidan Heath's gaze and slipped the note into his coat pocket. His fingers felt the cool metal of Reg's commando knife, forgotten, and lying in the greatcoat pocket. 'Did you kill the Frew sisters, or did Stratton?'

'Ah! Now I am insulted! Stratton had no finesse; no sense of the dramatic. Intimidation was much more his thing. And it was amusing watching you run around like a headless chicken. Now, put the note on the table.'

'Even if you kill me, you cannot escape. The submarine has gone. It didn't wait for you.'

'Please don't congratulate yourself just yet. You forget, Clement. I know where to find any number of boats that regularly make the crossing to Orkney or Shetland. So close to many of my friends in Norway. Now put the note on the table.'

Clement reached into his pocket again. While feeling for the note, he turned Reg's knife so that the blade was pointing downwards, ready for his hand to grasp the handle. Withdrawing the note, he placed it on the table then put his hand back into his pocket, the cool metal blade in his grasp. As Aidan reached forward to take the enciphered note, a coal burst in the grate, the sound like a discharged shot. Aidan spun around.

Clement lunged forward. With his hands together and his arms extended, he swung both arms down hard onto Aidan's pistol arm, deflecting the weapon. At the same time he punched his knee hard into Aidan's gut. He dropped the gun and staggered backwards, then fell to his knees in front of the hearth. Scrambling to stand, his eyes were wild, their gaze shifting between Clement and the fallen pistol that lay a yard away. But Clement knew he had the advantage. Once again he slipped his hand into his coat pocket. As Aidan lunged to his left and reached for the weapon, in one swift movement Clement withdrew Reg's knife and, aiming upwards, plunged it into the traitor's torso. With an agonized scream, Aidan arched backwards, then collapsed onto the floor. Clement bent over him, pulled the blade free then reached for the pistol, but Aidan, with unnerving strength, punched his hand into Clement's stomach. It felt to Clement as though all his internal organs would erupt through his back. Pain seared through his intestines; he fell sidewards, gasping for breath then endeavouring to stand, staggered forward, his head spinning.

Aidan still lay on the floor, blood flowing onto the carpet from the deep knife wound, but still he struggled. With one hand clutching the wound, his left arm stretched wide, his hand searching for the pistol. Bright red blood bubbled up through his lips. Yet even as unconsciousness descended, his desperate fingers still sought the gun. Clement picked it up and flung it through the kitchen door beyond reach.

Aidan's face twisted in pain, his breath coming in rattling gasps. Clement knew that death couldn't be far away. He stared at his enemy as Aidan emitted a deep, primordial groan. Despite his injuries, Clement saw with incredulity that the man was attempting to stand.

Still holding the knife, Clement backed away. 'It's over. You cannot win.'

'Killed by a piece of coal. Heil Hitler!'

The encrypted note sill lay on the table. Keeping an eye on the dying man, Clement grabbed it and pushing it into the coat's other pocket, felt the grenade. Withdrawing it, he held it in his left hand for Aidan to see. Clement saw the resignation in Aidan's expression.

Despite the agonizing pain in his gut, Clement forced himself to move. Doubled over in pain and with his eyes on his enemy, Clement backed through the kitchen towards the rear door, the grenade in his hand. Standing in the doorway, Clement stared for one second at a man he truly loathed. Using his teeth, he withdrew the pin. Counting aloud, he tossed it sideways into the kitchen, to where he knew Aidan, even if he could, wouldn't have the time to reach it.

With three seconds remaining, Clement turned and ran for the far side of the poultry shed. Throwing himself on the ground, he wrapped his arms over his head.

An explosion ripped the manse apart, blowing glass and debris of all kinds outwards in its deadly trajectory. The shock wave from the detonation thumped in his chest. He waited, his breathing suspended. Five seconds later, he smelt the dust of destruction as it wafted over the rear garden. Ten seconds later Clement stumbled to his feet. He was alive.

# 29

London, Thursday 8th May

Clement stepped from the bus as a wave of pigeons circled above him. More than two months had passed since his mission to Caithness and the farm where he had been sent to recuperate in the Peak District had been a much needed break. Now the sight of sand bags and bomb damage and Johnny's summoning letter reminded Clement that the war was not over.

He crossed Trafalgar Square and made his way to Whitehall Place. Regardless of his physical recovery, the haunting images of the Frew sisters and the grotesquely displayed body of Donald Crawford plagued him nightly. Ten weeks of rest surrounded by beautiful scenery and vibrant spring flowers somehow only seemed to make the memories all the more obscene and he feared the sordid visions may never leave him. Yet he didn't wish to forget them either. Not in any gruesome sense, but their deaths had been as much for king and country as any airman, soldier or sailor and the manner of their sacrifice was an ever-present reminder of the brutality of Nazism.

Turning the corner, his gaze fell on the elaborate stone entrance half way down the street. His experience had taught Clement one very important lesson about himself; if necessary, he could act alone. The final verse of St Matthew's Gospel rang in his ears. "I am with you alway, even unto the end of the world." He felt it. He believed the Divine Hand had been extended in Scotland and on more than one occasion. There was work for him to do on Earth. Death had been so close that he had felt the Dark Angel's breath, yet he had survived. Stepping through the door, Clement climbed the familiar steps.

'Miss Ballantyne,' he smiled, as he approached her desk.

'Major Wisdom. I trust you are sufficiently rested after your recent trip north?' Nora Ballantyne flashed a smile, her fingers never leaving the keys of her type-writer. 'You may go straight in.'

He thought for a second he may have glimpsed a genuine smile, but he wasn't certain. Leaving her, he tapped at Johnny's door before opening it.

'Clement! Wonderful to see you! Won't you sit down? Do help yourself,' Johnny said indicating the tea tray on his desk.

Clement poured some tea and sat in a studded leather chair.

'How are you, Clement? Quite rested, I hope? You've had quite a time of it, I know. I've read your notes. "C" is delighted. And, it appears, you have a bit of a reputation. You know they are all calling you *The Vicar*? The way they say it sounds almost macabre.'

'Perhaps, Johnny, but that is what I am.'

'Indeed you are.'

Clement sipped his tea. 'And what of Stratton?'

'Tried under the Treason Act and found guilty. He was hanged last week at Wandsworth.'

'Did we learn anything?'

Johnny shook his head. 'Not much from his lips. Miss Ballantyne attended the trial on our behalf, incognito of course. But she did unearth some interesting information for the Prosecution. In fact it sealed Stratton's fate. She discovered the grave of Reverend Aidan Heath.'

'What did you say?'

'Yes. It would appear that the real Reverend Aidan Heath is buried in Sighthill Cemetery, Glasgow and has been for over a hundred years.' Johnny placed his tea cup on the tray. 'The modern-day Aidan Heath was a complete fiction. It would appear that Stratton used his position as a police officer to access public records and was able to insert erroneous and misleading information whenever he wished. And as he lived at a boarding house in Sighthill when he was a young Constable at the Police Station there, he would have walked through the cemetery many times.'

'Then who?'

Johnny shrugged his shoulders. 'Stratton kept that secret to the end, despite our best efforts. While it would be safe to assume that the modern-day Aidan

Heath was a fanatical Nazi spy, it would appear that Stratton was equally zealous.'

Clement stared into his half-finished cup of tea feeling as though he had been punched.

Johnny went on. 'When Stratton was being prepared for burial, a tattoo was found under his upper right arm. It was a Hitler Youth emblem. Quite distinctive, with its diamond shape and central swastika. I asked Miss Ballantyne and her troupe of bloodhounds to do some investigating. It appears that as a young man, Stratton travelled to Germany quite often to spend time with his mother's family. It is possible that he and the man we knew as Heath met at Hitler Youth gatherings.'

Clement stared through Johnny's large windows, to the grey skies outside. Even though knowing both Heath and Stratton were dead, he felt that they were still laughing at him.

Johnny leaned forward in his seat. 'It doesn't matter what Heath's real name was, Clement. The fact is you located him and his accomplices. Names are immaterial and together with what we learned while on the raid in Norway, it has been a thoroughly excellent result.

'You were in Norway, Johnny?' he asked but his mind was still on Aidan Heath.

'Yes. On a raid on the fish oil factories in the Lofoten Islands to be precise. I saw a lone fishing trawler that I wouldn't have suspected without your information. Before the trawler sank, we managed to salvage the enigma rotor wheels and some code books. As I said, an excellent result. As indeed was yours.'

Clement leaned forward. 'And Stratton said nothing?'

'Tight-lipped to the end.'

'Why would he do that?' Clement paused, but his question was more to himself. He looked across at Johnny. 'Was he ever told that Aidan Heath is dead?'

'No.'

Clement nodded pondering such loyalty. 'Is it possible they were related?'

'We'll never have the answer to that.'

'Will you continue to investigate it?'

Johnny shook his head. 'Can't waste valuable time and resources on something that doesn't directly benefit the war effort. However, it may interest you to know that Miss Ballantyne learned something else interesting. She requisitioned Stratton's police records file. His request for transfer to Thurso had been submitted only a day after Stratton, himself, discovered the body of a murdered man in Sighthill Cemetery. Stratton, so his Chief Inspector at the time noted, had been unusually disturbed by the death. The murdered man was identified as a John William Nicholson by the man's wife, who the Chief Inspector subsequently believed may have had a hand in her husband's death. But before she could be questioned, she disappeared from Glasgow. And upon further investigation, no John William Nicholson was found in official records for the address given. Nor, in fact, were there any for the man's wife, one Mrs Jean Nicholson.'

Clement sat back, his mind reeling. 'So Stratton kept her out of prison and she was forced to do his bidding.'

'So it seems.'

'But it was Aidan Heath who did the killing.' Clement leaned forward and placed the cup back onto the tray. 'I've thought of little else, Johnny, while in the Peak District and I think I know how he did it. He must have been in the kirk and overheard Mrs Crawford tell me where her wireless was secreted. He was there to use his own radio transmitter which he must have kept in the vestry, connecting it to the long-range aerial in the rafters and using the brazier as a power source. That was why the German fighter bombed the bell tower. It was both the signal to escape and it destroyed the transmitter and antennae in the rafters. As soon as Aidan heard the aeroplane and saw that it was not one of ours, he left the kirk and ran into the graveyard where Jean would join him.' Clement paused. 'Everything that man said was a lie, including being afraid of heights. He killed those elderly ladies to make a telephone call to Stratton to arrange the logistics of his escape. Then he killed Donald Crawford because he knew to whom the call had been placed and, thanks to overhearing the conversation between Sarah and me, he knew exactly where to find Crawford. But what I find so despicable is that he took a cake the ladies had baked as proof that he was in their house, then sat calmly eating it.' Clement paused. 'He was seen, you know. It was something McAllister said when he came to the manse seeking help. "Aidan, you have to come back with me". Why wouldn't McAllister just say, "you have to come with me"? It only makes sense if McAllister had already seen Heath walking along the road. No wonder he went to such lengths to implicate McAllister.'

'Don't take it personally, Clement. Both Stratton and Heath are dead and you have done wonders, as I knew you would. In fact, I think I said that solo missions are for the young or those with a death wish. You proved me wrong and that doesn't happen all that often, I'm happy to say.'

'Thank you for the vote of confidence, Johnny. I'm not sure you are correct about that. However, I do know what I am capable of, if required.'

'If required? Now that does sound encouraging.'

'I would prefer it, though, if I wasn't completely alone next time.'

Johnny beamed. 'Anyone in mind?'

# Acknowledgements

My sincere thanks to Mr George Watson, of Thurso with whom I sat talking on several occasions discussing Caithness as it was during World War II. My thanks also to Angela Lewis for her kind assistance and to all the ladies at Dunnet and Canisbay Kirks.

My thanks also to my friend and editor, Janet Laurence and to Ian Hooper of Leschenault Press and Bronwyn Wood of Brand House.

My special thanks go to Peter for his unfailing support and enthusiasm as well as his company on my many missions to remote places no matter the weather or hour.

# Author's Note

The historical event that inspired *If Necessary Alone* was an attack on the 22nd February, 1941 by a German fighter on the lighthouse on Stroma Island in Pentland Firth, a body of water off the northern coast of Caithness. The attack caused no damage and no one was injured. It was one of two similar attacks on lighthouses in north Scotland that happened on the same day and for which there appears to be no obvious reason.

Lightning Source UK Ltd.
Milton Keynes UK
UKHW012244200919
350150UK00002B/663/P